Anna Jacobs is the author of many novels and is addicted to storytelling. She grew up in Lancashire, emigrated to Australia in the 1970s, and writes stories set in both countries. She loves to return to England regularly to visit her family and soak up the history. Anna has two grown daughters and a grandson, and lives with her husband in a spacious home near the Swan Valley, the oldest wine-growing area in Western Australia. Her house is crammed with thousands of books. In 2006 one of her novels, *Pride of Lancashire*, won the Australian Romantic Novel of the Year Award.

You can discover more about the author at www.annajacobs.com

SAFFRON LANE

Nell has come to feel at home in her beautiful corner of Wiltshire with her partner Angus. What she could do with, however, is a challenge — and the prospect of bringing life back to an abandoned row of houses, Saffron Lane, is just what she's looking for. Meanwhile, Stacy is trying her best to start a fresh chapter in her life. Elise, battling her nieces who would force her into residential care, longs for a home where she can get back to her painting. And Adam and his daughter Gemma are coming to terms with changes and discoveries that will set them on new paths. Could it be that in all of their cases, the solutions to their problems and the answers to their questions wait for them at Saffron Lane?

ANNA JACOBS

SAFFRON LANE

Complete and Unabridged

CHARNWOOD
Leicester

First published in Great Britain in 2017 by
Allison & Busby Limited
London

First Charnwood Edition
published 2019
by arrangement with
Allison & Busby Limited
London

A catalogue record for this book is available
from the British Library.

ISBN 978-1-4448-4335-4

Published by
F. A. Thorpe (Publishing)
Anstey, Leicestershire

Set by Words & Graphics Ltd.
Anstey, Leicestershire
Printed and bound in Great Britain by
T. J. International Ltd., Padstow, Cornwall

This book is printed on acid-free paper

This book is dedicated to the memory
of Harry Meageen (1937–2017),
a dear friend whom my husband
and I will miss greatly. I'll also miss
his astute comments as a reader.
We're both so glad to have known him.

Part One

1

Wiltshire, October

Just after midnight thunder boomed so loudly that Nell woke with a start. Lightning flashed and another clap of thunder seemed to shake the big old house.

She lay for a few moments listening to the storm then felt her husband jerk awake.

Angus didn't try to speak till another clap of thunder had rumbled away into the distance. 'Damn! The weather forecast didn't say it'd be such a heavy storm; they just predicted rain.'

She flung aside the covers and went to draw back a curtain and peer out across the formal gardens at the rear. 'It must have been raining for a while. There are puddles everywhere.'

As he joined her, a sudden squall pounded heavily against the windows, blurring the world outside. Once again conversation became difficult because of loud thunder.

'It couldn't have come at a worse time.' He thumped one clenched fist on the windowsill.

She knew why. The roof at the north end of this big house had been leaking and he was juggling his finances so that it could be fixed properly, not merely patched up. The last two owners, distant relatives of his, had done a lot of skimpy patching. You didn't always know where problems still lay until the weak spots

3

began to fall apart.

Angus sighed and dragged on his tatty winter dressing gown, thrusting his feet into equally shabby trainers. 'I'd better go and check the attics. The leak bucket will probably need emptying. You might as well stay in bed.'

'No way! I'm awake now so I'm coming with you. You may need my help.'

They heard it before they got to the open space at the north end of the attic: water splashing almost continuously, a lot more of it than the occasional drip there had been formerly.

He switched on the single light bulb that dangled forlornly from the middle of the ceiling at that end. 'Oh, hell!'

As thunder rumbled, lightning lit up the attic like a scene from an old horror film, the flickering black and white causing eerie shadows to jump around the walls. The sound of the rain beating down on the roof tiles in another heavy downpour drowned out the splashing for a few moments, then the rain eased off and they could hear the water coming down inside the attic again.

The bucket normally coped adequately with the small leak but the fault must have worsened because water was now trickling steadily over the top edge and spreading out across the floorboards.

He looked up. 'I bet the wind has dislodged some tiles.'

She bent to study the wooden floor around the bucket. It was dark with moisture and more was overflowing every minute. 'I know where there's an old baby bath. I'll go and fetch it.'

'Thanks.'

When she got back, he'd moved the bucket and put an old tin tray in its place. The tray was already covered by a shallow film of water. She put the baby bath down and he tipped the water from the tray into it at the same time as he used his foot to edge the bath into place under the leak. 'I'll go and empty the bucket in the bathroom up here.'

When he got back, he looked glumly at the baby bath. 'You might as well go back to bed, love. I'll have to stay up to keep emptying the water. I won't be able to do anything about fixing the leak till it's light.'

'I'll never get back to sleep. The storm sounds to be right overhead. How about I bring you up a cup of cocoa?'

'I'd murder for a hot drink. And could you bring my old sweater up with you as well? It's going to be a long, cold night.'

'We'll keep each other company, then.'

'Whatever did I do to deserve a helpmeet like you?' he said softly.

'Same goes for me. You make my ex seem like an alien from Planet Zog.'

★   ★   ★

It seemed ages till the storm passed and the rain eased. As soon as dawn lightened the sky, Angus went outside, squelching across the sodden lawn till he was far enough away from the house to

5

peer up at the roof through his binoculars.

When he came back, he said, 'A few tiles have been dislodged. They still look intact, though. I'll go up and see if I can push them back into place. Then I really will have to do something about the roof.'

'Can't you get someone else to sort out the tiles? It's three storeys above the ground.'

'I rather like climbing. I've been up on that roof several times.' He gave her one of his quick hugs. 'Don't worry. I won't take any risks. I always wear a safety harness and line. I fitted the necessary anchor points years ago when I had to go up and repoint the ridge tiles.'

She nodded, but she stayed outside to keep an eye on him as he worked, and she didn't stop worrying till he came down and put the ladder away.

'Done. For the moment.' He pretended to take a bow. 'Oh ye of little faith.'

'For a geek you're surprisingly good at the practical stuff.'

'Blame it on my dad's training and all the holiday jobs I did as a student.' He glanced at his watch. 'I'd better get back to my computer.'

'And I've got some grocery shopping to do. You will insist on eating every single day.'

For all their joking, she was concerned about their financial situation. They had to find some way of increasing their income. Since their marriage she had taken over the accounts and had been horrified at how expensive a two-hundred-year-old house was to maintain. It might be heritage-listed but it had been neglected for decades and restoring it properly wasn't for the faint-hearted.

Angus worked in IT and was capable of earning good money, but that wasn't nearly enough for the urgent major repairs the house still needed. He'd had a small app he'd designed take off recently, which was bringing in some useful money, but not a fortune, since it had a limited target group. He'd warned her that his app would probably be superseded within a couple of years, so they couldn't count on it long term.

What could they count on to keep this beloved monster of a house well tended, she wondered? There had to be some way of it bringing in a regular, steady income.

* * *

Two mornings later Angus came down late for breakfast then sat lost in thought, forgetting the piece of half-eaten toast in his hand.

'Not hungry today, darling?' Nell asked.

He jumped in shock and stared at her blankly for a few seconds, then cocked his head to one side and grinned. 'Sorry. I woke up thinking about our financial needs. You know that scrubby bit of land down at the rear of our grounds, the one with the dilapidated old buildings on it? I'm wondering if we can do something with that?'

That really caught her interest. 'I keep meaning to stroll down and have a closer look at it, but I haven't been in a hurry because you said it was in ruins.'

'You promised you'd not go there without me,' he reminded her sharply.

'I was planning to ask you, only you've been a bit busy lately on that project.'

'I finished it late last night, Nell, and good riddance. Whoever wrote the original program was an idiot and it was a tedious job unpicking it. Did I ever tell you that part of the grounds has actually got an official street name?'

'No. You just waved a hand in its direction and said it was rather dilapidated so to stay well away. What's its official name?'

'Saffron Lane.'

'That's pretty.'

'Yes. Unlike the street. I took a quick look at the outside when I first inherited Dennings, but I had enough on my plate making sure the main house was weatherproof to do anything about those cottages. I did check that they hadn't been damaged after one particularly bad storm and thank goodness they were all right. Actually, they look very sturdily built. But don't go into them on your own. I don't want you getting hurt.'

He gave her a loving smile as he said that, seeming unaware of the toast still in his hand. Her heart gave its usual happy little skip as she smiled back. Her second husband was so cute when he grew forgetful!

Before she could remind him to finish his toast, he said suddenly, 'I don't think my predecessor went inside them, either.'

She gaped at him. 'But they've been in your family for ever, and you've owned them for years!'

8

He shrugged. 'Well, no one expected me to inherit, even though I came here several times as a child. And after Dennings became mine, Joanna and I had enough on our plates bringing up the kids and dealing with the interior of the big house.'

He looked sad as he added quietly, 'We were discussing turning our attention to Saffron Lane when she was killed. I — didn't feel ready to follow through on that afterwards.'

Nell reached out to give his hand a squeeze. It was lovely to hear how he spoke about his first wife, who'd been killed by a drunken driver. He had a huge capacity for love, her Angus did. She'd never expected to marry again after an abusive first husband, but she'd tumbled headlong into love with this man.

She watched with a fond smile as he continued to think aloud, still waving the piece of uneaten toast to emphasise what he was saying.

'I don't even know who used to live in Saffron Lane or why it was abandoned. I'm still going through the various records but I haven't come across the ones dealing with it yet.'

'What made you think of it now?'

'I was wondering whether the buildings could be renovated and rented out. They aren't Grade I listed like this house, so we could even knock them down if we wanted without seeking permission and jumping through heritage hoops.'

'And put what in their place?'

'I don't know. Workshops to rent, perhaps, or

offices. Commercial properties are in short supply in Sexton Bassett.'

She frowned. 'It'd cost a lot to erect new buildings. It'd be better if we could convert the present ones, surely? But I don't think we have the money for that, either.'

He suddenly noticed the toast and put it in his mouth, but she doubted he'd tasted it, because he was still frowning in thought as he chomped.

She loved her new home and was planning to help him in every way she could, but he didn't want her to put her Australian house sale money into it, because he wanted her to have a nest egg to fall back on if anything happened to him.

Nell agreed that was wise because if anything happened to Angus she'd have to leave. The previous owner, Miss Henrietta Denning, had been obsessed by making sure the old house was kept in the hands of the family who'd built it, and the trust she'd set up stipulated that Dennings had to be passed to the next 'Denning by birth' in line. After Angus, this would be his son Oliver, currently working his way round the world.

'Um. I got an email yesterday. Another quarter's money has come in, not a fortune, though quite a nice amount. We could spend it on renovating the houses in Saffron Lane, as a sort of investment to bring in money steadily. What do you think?'

'I think maybe the roof of the big house has priority.'

'I think we can make the roof last a bit longer.'

'Are you sure?'

'Hmm.'

'How much did the app bring in?'

When he told her she was pleasantly surprised. 'I think you could be right. But let's go and explore Saffron Lane now. We can't make a final decision until we know exactly what we've got there.'

'I want to get someone in to make sure the buildings are safe first.'

'Oh, pooh to that! We're not stupid enough to go inside a building if there are holes in the floor and the walls are crumbling, but we can at least stand in doorways and look inside rooms. Actually, it's a wonder someone hasn't broken in, if they've been empty for half a century.'

'An old tramp did try to break into the end house two or three years ago, but he didn't even get any of the front doors open. He ran away down the street at the back screaming that the place was haunted. The police thought he was drunk and picked him up. When he told them what he'd been doing, they didn't bother to prosecute, he was still so freaked out. They just gave him a warning and sent him on his way. I didn't contradict his tale of the ghosts. Rumours like that are much cheaper than putting in a security system.'

She wasn't giving in. 'I'm not afraid of your family ghosts and I'm dying to look at Saffron Lane. Let's do it.'

She'd dreamt about his family ghosts even before she'd come to England, only she hadn't known who they were then. She'd heard their voices again soon after her arrival. They'd

11

seemed friendly to her, not threatening. She'd never been certain before this happened whether there were any such things as ghosts, but everything the women's voices had predicted had come true. They'd told her exactly when she'd sell her Australian house and that she'd find love here in England.

He put his arm round her shoulders. 'OK. You're on. I must admit I'd like to see inside the buildings now that I've got a bit of spare time, but we won't take any risks. We ought to wear our scruffiest clothes and safety helmets.'

'Most of your clothes are scruffy. You're as much in need of renovation as your house.'

He chuckled. 'My computer doesn't care what I wear and you fell in love with me in spite of my sartorial faults.'

'I didn't realise then that you were *allergic* to buying new clothes.'

'Shopping is a total bore.'

'Well, we're going out to buy you some new clothes tomorrow, so get used to it. I'm not having my new English relatives seeing me walk around with a scarecrow.'

'You're such a nag.' He plonked a big, sloppy kiss on her cheek.

For a moment she had difficulty breathing, then she realised from his poorly concealed smirk that he was distracting her, changing the subject. He always did when clothes were mentioned. She gave him a mock slap. 'Yes, and I intend to spend the next few decades nagging you. Get used to that as well, and gird up your loins, because you're definitely going to face the horrors of shopping for new clothes tomorrow.'

She looked round and smiled involuntarily. 'But today the storm has passed and we'll go exploring, eh? I fell in love with your house as well as you, Angus. Dennings is beautiful and living here is exciting, so very different from being an office manager in Australia, not to mention my difficulties as a divorced woman raising three lively sons on a pittance.'

'One of them has just produced a son himself, Grandma Nell.'

'I still can't believe I'm a grandma.'

'You're a step-grandma as well. I think it's great being a grandfather. I just wish Ashleigh lived closer, but her husband's farm is non-negotiable as a place to live. Now, hurry up and change into some old clothes. I'm starting to feel excited about what we might find in Saffron Lane.'

★   ★   ★

They strolled through the rear gardens hand in hand and down towards the left corner of the property. The buildings were behind some huge old trees and overgrown bushes, so hardly anything showed from the rear drive except an entrance that really did look like a lane, only just wide enough for two cars to pass.

She paused to stare round. 'It's as if this corner of the grounds has been asleep and is waiting to be woken up again.'

'Well, don't move forward till I've cleared a path. I'll get the gardener to clear the connection

13

between Saffron Lane and the street. It won't take him long with our small tractor. Good thing it's not a made-up road with asphalt, just a dirt track. The weeds grow quickly but are easy to clear and then the road can be levelled.'

Angus stopped to pick up a stick-sized piece of dead branch and whacked a few of the nettles out of their way on the path, trampling on them for good measure. 'I don't want you to get stung. Nettles are always happy to prove that a human being can itch and hurt at the same time.'

Nell followed him along the narrow path he'd cleared but they stopped again on the other side of the shrubbery to study the houses. 'It's hardly a street; it's only six houses long and one-sided.'

'Well, they gave it a name and the council approved it, so someone must have felt it mattered.'

She was still staring. 'They're not what I call cottages. They might not be big but they're detached houses, and three of them have dormer windows in the attics. The two houses at the end standing at right angles to the others are bigger with Number 6 the biggest of all. They're a charming group of buildings, aren't they? Let's go inside.'

He grabbed her hand. 'Put your safety helmet on first. We'll go slowly. No rushing into the buildings.'

'I'll be careful, I promise. We might as well start at Number 1 and work our way along.'

'Your wish is my command.'

'You know, the street is more attractive than modern housing in England, where every house

14

seems to be almost a carbon copy of the one next to it. When do you think these houses were built?'

He stopped again, head on one side. 'Early twentieth century, I should think. When I find the full records we'll see exactly when and, I hope, find out *why* they were deserted. I have a vague feeling they've been deserted since World War II. That's surprising when they had such a housing crisis in Britain after the war, but I don't think the War Office returned them to the family for a while after it ended.'

He took out his phone. 'Wait a minute! Let's take a photo of the whole row as it is now, before we even trample down the weeds.'

She continued to study the houses as she waited for him to finish. 'They've all got large front windows. I think they might have been shops.'

'Could be. There used to be lots of little local shops instead of these horrible, soulless shopping centres.'

'The shopping centres are highly convenient in bad weather and when you need to buy a big load of groceries.' She watched him take out a bundle of labelled keys and unlock the door of the first house, then hold up one hand to stop her going inside. She waited, dying to explore but knowing he was right to do this slowly and carefully.

'There's a dusty smell, but it doesn't smell damp, so maybe the floor will still be sound.' He put one foot on the floorboards in the entrance, then stamped hard, still holding on to the door frame. 'Feels sound.' He stepped inside and jumped up and down vigorously, still staying near the door. 'Not a sign of sponginess.'

She moved forward and joined him inside.

'Yes. Stay there till I've tested the rest.' He stamped his way across the middle of the floor, after which he stood still and turned round on the spot, studying the ceiling and walls. 'Doesn't seem to be anything wrong with it, apart from years of dust and cobwebs.'

'Good.' She went past him and opened the door at the rear of the room, looking to her right. 'I think this must be a storeroom. It's quite big. There's a small barred window at the far end of it.'

He joined her as she went into the back room. 'This would have been the kitchen and living area. And this door leads to . . . a bedroom and bathroom. Very modern plumbing for those days. Shouldn't be hard to upgrade.'

'So it's a house and workshop or shop, with living quarters for one person.' She stamped on the floor. 'It feels sound in here as well.'

'I'm still hiring an expert to check the houses out before we start renovating them. Let's take notes and photos and move on to the next one.'

'Just a minute! What's this?' She opened a door in one wall that looked like a cupboard and found some steep narrow stairs.

He grabbed her arm. 'I'll go first.'

With a shrug, she humoured his protectiveness and stepped back, waiting for him to get to the top.

'The stairs creak but they don't seem rotten in

any way,' he called. 'Come up and join me.'

She went up to find that there was an attic, after all, but it had its single dormer window in the rear side of the roof, so it hadn't been visible from the front. The space was completely empty.

'It's huge. You could easily put another bedroom up here.'

'Or a separate workroom.'

'OK. Let's move on.'

★　★　★

In the next house the shop area was a little smaller, the middle room bigger with a French window opening on to a side garden about three yards wide.

Before Angus could stop her, she had gone on ahead and disappeared into the back part of the house. 'Nell, wait!'

There was no answer. Suddenly afraid, he rushed after her and found her standing staring round her as if someone had hit her on the head. 'Are you all right?'

'Yes. I just — don't laugh, but I thought I heard voices. The same voices I heard before I ever came to England: your family ghosts.'

'Ah.'

'I'm not making it up. I did hear them!'

'Did they sound threatening? Something terrified the man who tried to break in, after all.'

She smiled. 'Not at all frightening. They never do. They sound like a group of motherly older women. Today . . . '

'What?'

'They told me this will be Stacy's house.'

'Who the hell's Stacy?'

'I haven't the faintest idea. I thought you might know.'

He shook his head. 'I don't know anyone called Stacy. Did they tell you anything else about her? Did she once live here?'

'I don't know. That's all I heard.'

'Maybe you were just imagining things.'

She pretended to beat him over the head while chanting the lines from *Hamlet* at him — and not for the first time: *'There are more things in heaven and earth, Horatio, Than are dreamt of in your philosophy.'* They'd had this discussion before and she refused to back down.

'Well, if you've finished communing with my ancestors, let's continue our explorations.'

They went upstairs to an area that seemed larger than that of the first house, with two decent-sized bedrooms and an old-fashioned bathroom with the sort of free-standing bath on curly feet that was fashionable all over again.

There was nothing in the rooms and the bare boards echoed beneath their feet as they walked to and fro.

★   ★   ★

The silence was suddenly broken by his phone playing the beginning of the 'Hallelujah Chorus'. 'Just a minute. I need to answer that ringtone quickly because it's the agency that gets me casual project work and it usually means a job.'

After a brief chat with someone called Jared,

he turned to her. 'I was right. They've offered me a small job. It's urgent and they'll pay a bonus for a speedy result.'

'And the houses?' But she knew the answer already. When someone from the IT industry called, Angus stopped what he was doing and paid attention. It was usually very lucrative, because he had some sought-after specialist skills, and a reputation for an uncanny instinct for diagnosing problems quickly and accurately.

They walked back together, once again holding hands. But his thoughts were already elsewhere, she could tell, and he hardly said a word.

She stopped at the door to his office and grabbed his sleeve, shaking him slightly. 'Pay attention for one minute more, Angus. Is it all right if I start looking through your family records?'

'What?' His eyes blinked briefly into focus.

'Your family records — shall I go through them and see if I can find out more about Saffron Lane?'

'Good idea.'

'And if you can't go shopping for your clothes tomorrow, my lad, we'll go as soon as you've finished this job. You're not wriggling out of it.'

'Slave driver.' He gave her a quick hug and was gone for the rest of the day and half the night, too.

She'd been looking forward to a day out in Swindon shopping and having lunch somewhere nice. However, they needed the money Angus made on these specialist jobs, so it was a good thing she had her own interests and had taken over the business side of the property.

He had been one of the trailblazers in his area of IT, but he said technology changed quickly, so he needed to make as much money as he could before things changed again and left him trailing behind. Of course, he might luck out and get into another developing area or his next app might take off. He had a few ideas he wanted to fiddle with. Who knew?

She felt sometimes as if the world had suddenly turned into a roller coaster and people no sooner adjusted to one change than they were whirled away in another direction entirely and had to scramble to keep up.

But perhaps that was her own view. Some people seemed to enjoy change.

Oh, who knew anything? She'd better make a start on those records. Saffron Lane seemed very interesting.

2

The day ended badly when Stacy spilt coffee all over herself and the tablecloth.

Her mother grabbed the dishcloth and began to mop up, scowling at her. 'You've got to snap out of this — this dopiness, Stacy Walsh, and join the real world again. You're still down in the dumps about your divorce, I know, and it was hard when it happened so suddenly, but it's been over a year now. More than time to move on.'

'I know. I'm getting there.'

'You always say that and you haven't got anywhere noticeable yet. Just look at you! When was the last time you had your hair trimmed? Or bought a new top? That one's too small for you now.'

'Leave me alone. Please, Mum. I've had a hard day at work.'

'So have I. So has your dad. Employers don't pay anyone to sit around sunbathing, you know. Anyway, I'm not going to leave you alone from now on. I've tried doing that and it doesn't work. I love you too much to stand by while you go on like this, hiding from the world except for going to work, treading water instead of doing something with yourself. You're only twenty-five. Your life isn't over yet.'

'Mum, I — '

'Apart from anything else, you're spoiling our lives too.'

That was the last thing Stacy had expected to hear, and the last thing she wanted to do. 'What do you mean? I don't intrude on your privacy. I'm quiet and I do my share of the housework.'

'Well, I wish you would intrude on our privacy more. You used to be so lively, but now I wish you weren't so quiet. We hardly know you're there.' She mopped her eyes. 'We worry about you, Stace. You spend most evenings moping in your bedroom, fiddling with your computer. It has to stop, and soon.'

'What's the urgency?'

'We're selling this house, so we need you to find a place of your own and move your things out of our garage.'

'Selling the house? But you've lived here ever since you got married. It's your *home*.' And it still felt like her home, too.

'Not any longer. It's more than time for us to try something else. And even if we weren't moving, when I said you could come and live with us for a while, I didn't mean for ever. I was going to give you another month or so to get your act together then tell you to move, but it's been taken out of our hands. Your father's just been made redundant.'

'Oh, no! What are you going to do? Can he find another job?'

Her mother smiled. 'He doesn't have to. We're not without savings and he's getting quite a generous payout which will top them up nicely. So I'm giving up my job and we're going to move to the country. You know we've always planned to retire early and run a B&B.'

'I thought that was just a dream.'

'There's no 'just' about dreams, unless you want to drift along dreaming. It takes hard work to make them come true. We've always planned for a B&B, we've even done courses about it, and this is our chance. You've still got a job, so you can afford the rent on a flat of your own, or you could even put down a deposit and buy a small flat with your share of your own house sale. That'd keep you on the housing ladder.'

She waited and when her daughter didn't reply, added in a firm tone of voice, 'We'll give you a fortnight to find somewhere for yourself, your furniture and your junk, then this house is going up for sale. It's Saturday tomorrow so you've time to go round the estate agents and talk to them about what's on offer. You could even look some places up online tonight. And, of course, your father will help you move your stuff when the time comes. He can borrow his friend's van as he did when you broke up with that horrible Darren Cooke.'

She waited and when she got no answer from her daughter, said sharply, 'I mean it, Stace!' and left the kitchen.

★　★　★

Stacy was so shocked by this ultimatum she didn't move for a moment or two. Then she made a fresh cup of coffee and took it up to her bedroom. No, not *her* bedroom, she mustn't think of it like that any more. This was her parents' spare bedroom.

She caught sight of her own face in the dressing-table mirror and that gave her a further jolt. Her mother was right. She did look a mess. She hadn't bothered to change out of her drab work clothes, her hair badly needed cutting and, admit it, she'd put on weight since the divorce — a lot of weight, a couple of dress sizes. Setting the cup of coffee down carefully on the table mat, she sat on the edge of her bed staring at her reflection, not liking what she saw.

Crossing her arms round herself she rocked to and fro, beyond tears, but feeling full of pain. Bad enough that Darren had started being a bit violent. She hadn't known what to do about that, had felt too ashamed to seek help.

Then last year he'd suddenly told her that he'd met someone else and was having an affair. He'd doubled the blow by saying that he'd have left her anyway because he didn't like being married and didn't want to settle down and have a family. And she wasn't much fun in bed. Ha! That was because he'd started hurting her. He always apologised and said it was because he got carried away, but she'd gradually come to realise that he enjoyed it.

She'd been so stupidly, blindly in love it had taken her months to understand she'd been more in love with being married, having her own home and planning to have children than she'd been with spending her whole life with Darren. She'd been such a fool, and that had added an extra layer of humiliation to the break-up.

Now her parents were throwing her out and it felt as if no one wanted her.

In the end she couldn't hold the tears back any longer and wept herself to sleep, crying quietly for a long time, not wanting her parents to hear.

She woke again just after midnight and couldn't get back to sleep, so she went online for a while and had a look at houses for rent. The costs had shot up since she'd last rented anywhere and she definitely couldn't afford to rent a whole house on her own. A small flat, not even one near the centre of Bristol, was the best she could hope for.

After a while she went back to bed, yet even though she felt exhausted, sleep still eluded her. As the darkness morphed slowly into the grey of early dawn, it began to feel as if the river of tears had cleared some blockage inside her. Her parents were changing their whole lives, and if they could move on, so could she.

She didn't need to look into the mirror to remember how awful she looked, but when she got up, she did face her reflection again, staring back at the puffy face and body. She'd fought so hard to lose the last of her plumpness for the wedding, because Darren liked girls who were sylph-like; now all the fat was back on again, plus a little extra.

The first decision about her new life was easy to take: the weight wasn't going to stay on. She'd lost it before, could do so again. It wouldn't be easy because her body seemed to be pro-grammed to be bigger than men liked. But she'd work on it.

The main decision kept eluding her, however.

Where should she go? Should she try to get a new job and move right away from here? She had enough computer and graphic design skills to find a job easily, even if it wasn't a particularly highly paid one. Yes, that might be a good idea. If she stayed in Bristol, everywhere would remind her not only of Darren but of her carefree years of working hard during the week and squeezing out time for her own art at weekends.

She still had a few friends around the place, good friends, too. She'd neglected them after she got married because Darren preferred them to go out mainly with his friends. Why had she let him do that to her? Why had she just given in? She'd hardly been out at all since they broke up, too ashamed of the failure of her marriage to face the success of her friends' relationships.

She'd go round some estate agent offices this morning. Surely there would be something available to rent in her price range?

She knew what she really wanted to do. Her parents weren't the only ones to have a dream. But she doubted that it'd be possible to make a living from her art, however hard she tried.

She wasn't going to *buy* a place of her own until she was sure where she wanted to live long term. She'd really loved the little house they'd bought when they married. So had other people. It had sold very quickly, bringing them a good profit to share.

The profit was mainly down to her and so she'd told Darren, but he'd shrugged and said the courts would share things out equally, so they might as well save themselves a pile of legal costs by halving everything themselves.

He'd been right but it wasn't fair because she'd been the one who'd had the ideas as well as the one doing most of the renovations. Her father had brought her up to use tools and build things. Darren was clueless about do-it-yourself and not at all interested in learning, so he'd worked as a barista three evenings a week to bring in the extra money they needed for the renovations.

That was how he'd met *the other woman*.

Stacy understood now that another thing he hadn't liked about his wife was her being more capable in practical matters than he was. Well, too bad. She wasn't going to pretend to be a helpless female unable to use a hammer, just to stoke his ego, or any other man's either.

She'd heard that Darren had recently split with the other woman and couldn't help being glad about that. The only thing she was certain about was that she was going to move forward on her own. She'd done with men.

Hurrying downstairs to grab some breakfast, she gave her mother a big hug. 'Thanks for putting up with me — and for telling me the truth last night.'

'Oh, darling! Welcome back.' Her mother returned her hug and they stood close together smiling mistily at one another, then Stacy picked up her dad's morning paper and a pen. 'Let's see what's available to rent.'

★   ★   ★

It took ten days of gruelling house hunting for Stacy to find a suitable flat. The one she settled on was larger than average but old-fashioned. It was part of an old, revamped building in an industrial area, not as smart as new-build flats.

It was quite a way out of the city and the flat was distinctly shabby, but it was cheap and there was generous storage available in some sheds in the backyard for a small extra weekly payment. That tipped the balance. She had too many art things to fit into a small flat, even when they were packed up in various containers, as they were now.

She'd preserved her boxes of 'stuff' even during the bad times, and Darren hadn't counted them among the household goods when they were dividing up their mutual possessions because he'd always considered them rubbish. Well, they were salvaged pieces of metal, all sorts of shapes, from which she built and welded little sculptures, many of them animals or 'creatures' out of her imagination.

Darren hadn't thought much of her finished pieces, either.

Even her parents hadn't offered more than faint praise for occasional pieces. Well, her mother liked china figurines of ladies in old-fashioned clothing, which were about as far away from Stacy's pieces as you could get.

She didn't care. One day she'd show them all. In the meantime, the first thing was to move into the flat, then sort everything out and start practising her welding skills again. She'd thought she could manage to clear a working space in the storage area she'd also hired, as long as she didn't work on large pieces, but she wasn't at all sure she could work in such a cramped space.

Well, she would try to sort something out once she got off these horrible antidepressant tablets that made her feel so sluggish.

Being depressed had to be better for an artist than being dopey like this, she told herself firmly on her first day of following the doctor's instructions for coming off the drug. He wasn't sure she should even do that, but she was determined not to rely on them any longer, so she insisted.

It took two more weeks for her head to feel truly clear and her artistic imagination to burst into life again. Tears of joy rolled down her cheeks when she realised that the bits and pieces of metal she'd been fiddling around with had turned into a little creature, a bit like an otter. It was so cute, she photographed it then taped the pieces it was made from together. She'd weld it properly when she'd cleared her storage area and had the space.

It didn't even matter when her parents sold their house almost immediately and went off house-hunting in the country, because eventually she was going to live somewhere else too. Anywhere except Bristol, she decided, the first time she bumped into Darren.

The second time she ran into him, he had the gall to suggest them spending a night together for old times' sake, because they'd always been good in bed.

As if!

Her only trouble was losing the weight. She couldn't seem to lose it as quickly as she had last time. She didn't even lose weight every week, however carefully she ate and exercised. Well, it wasn't a crime to be plump, she told herself. She'd stopped putting weight on at least, and her clothes were a little looser.

For the first time in over a year, hope seemed to be hovering on the horizon, sparkling and twirling there like an expensive ornament, waiting for her to catch up and reach out for it.

3

The following morning Nell tiptoed out of the bedroom and left Angus sleeping off his twenty hours of hard work. His concentration was so intense he barely noticed her coming into his office with the occasional cup of tea and some of them were left to go cold.

As she thought about what to do with her day, she ate a satisfying breakfast of fruit, and a boiled egg with narrow toast 'soldiers' to dip into the yolk. No use planning to go out clothes shopping for Angus, even locally, because he would probably sleep until mid-afternoon.

It'd be best to continue her efforts to find out more about Saffron Lane. She hadn't discovered anything at all about it yesterday, and was eager to continue hunting through the Denning family's mountains of records. She was intrigued by the small, abandoned street, amazed that it had sat there hidden for so many years and no one had bothered with it.

It could be so pretty and — an idea struck so forcibly that she sat perfectly still for a few moments while it sank in: if the other houses were also shops or workshops, as seemed highly likely from their exteriors, maybe they could start an artists' colony at Dennings and rent out the cottages to creative people.

She'd seen such colonies in one or two out-of-the-way places in Australia and they attracted tourists. She wasn't artistic herself, but she loved looking at paintings and sculptures. They wouldn't be able to get the highest possible rents from artists, but it'd be an attraction for the small town.

And maybe — she smiled as another idea struck her — maybe one of the houses could become a little café or kiosk. There was a small park close to the top end of the next street that ran parallel with Peppercorn Street, and lots of families went there at weekends. And there were allotments nearby too. People working on them might like to buy snacks from time to time.

They'd have to check the local regulations, but she was quite sure she could set up and manage a small café, even if she couldn't be the main person working there. She was a good organiser and a good cook, too. And they could have the back part of the ground floor as a small gallery, selling the pieces the artists made — and taking a commission on those sales, of course.

There was a faint sound of applause and she looked round in surprise, but there was no one nearby.

'It's just us,' a woman's deep, melodious voice seemed to echo around her. 'The family ghosts.'

There was laughter at that phrase and it sounded to come from several women.

Then another, lighter voice added, 'Your idea will work out very well for Dennings, Nell, but only if you persevere and don't let anyone get the better of you.'

As the voices faded, Nell took a deep breath. It wasn't her imagination, definitely not, but oh my, conversing with ghosts certainly took some getting used to. It made her feel spaced out, not exactly dizzy but drifting for a moment or two. That was the only way she could describe it.

What would Angus say to this latest encounter? And what would he think of her idea? He'd probably give one of his wry smiles and suspend judgement about the ghosts, but he might like her idea. Managed properly, it'd bring in regular money.

After clearing up, she went into the room they called the library. It was such a peaceful place, she loved spending time there. Yesterday she'd searched two large cupboards and labelled the different packages of documents she'd found with sticky notes. Today she intended to go through the big drawers full of family papers and account books, which formed the bottom layer of the row of bookcases that covered the whole of one wall. She'd done no more than peep into them until now.

Again she began noting down what was in each and sticking a list on the front of each drawer as she finished going through it. Then she found something useful and stopped to draw in a deep, happy breath. Eureka! She'd have to wait for Angus to resurface to check it out properly, but these papers and account books looked promising.

How many other secrets did this old house and its grounds hold? How fascinating it was to live here. Her parents had chosen to emigrate to Australia. She had returned to England after her sons grew up and felt equally at home in both countries. Though she missed her sons, two of them were married, one with a child, and she had Angus now. She already loved Dennings and somehow knew that she'd stay here from now onwards.

Choices could be difficult, bringing happiness but losses too. She'd heard it called the migrants' dilemma, having people and places you loved in both countries, and now she too was facing it.

★   ★   ★

Angus came downstairs in time to join Nell for a late lunch, only he wanted what hotels called 'a full English breakfast': bacon, sausages, eggs, fried tomatoes, hash browns and mushrooms.

'Can do, except for the mushrooms,' she said. 'Sit down and I'll make you a mug of tea, then you can listen to my nacky idea.'

'Nacky?' he queried. 'Is that a real word?'

'It is to me. My mother used to say it.' She put the mug in front of him and got out the food.

After he'd taken two or three mouthfuls of tea, he prompted, 'Go on. Tell me about your *nacky* idea.'

She explained about setting up an artists' colony in Saffron Lane and his face lit up.

'Brill!' He shovelled more food into his mouth, murmuring his approval of it.

'Is that all you can say: 'brill'?'

'It's all I need to say. I'm with you entirely and it's a brilliant idea.' He studied her face. 'There's something else, isn't there?'

'Yes. I've found some documents from World

War II. Apparently the War Office took over the whole of Saffron Lane early in the war and housed some obscure unit there. They simply turned the tenants out and took over the houses. They didn't even pay rent, nor did they ever reveal what had been going on there. And they didn't hand it back to your family for several decades.'

'Well, it was total war, you know, on the home front as well as on the fighting fronts. Everyone had to make sacrifices; everyone had to contribute.'

'I'm amazed when I think what people went through, how much of their personal life they had to give up.'

'We have some books about what went on locally if you want to find out more.' He eyed her again. 'Go on. From the look on your face, there's something else, isn't there?'

'Yes. The War Office had planned to take over the big house as well, but decided it was too dilapidated to be worth saving. That seems strange because you said the place hadn't been touched for decades when you and Joanna moved in. Was it really so dilapidated?'

'Not at all. Just horrendously old-fashioned. The most urgent needs were rewiring and extending or renewing the plumbing. Luckily, I have my electrician's ticket so I could do the rewiring once someone more experienced than me had helped to draw up an overall plan.'

There was tinkling laughter nearby and she looked at Angus but he didn't seem to notice anything.

'Why do you think the house seemed dilapidated?' a woman asked, sounding amused.

'You don't suppose the ghosts made the house seem worse than it was, do you? So that it'd be left alone.'

He gave her a puzzled glance. 'What made you think of that? *Could* they do it?'

Once again she seemed to be the only one hearing the women's voices. '*We can do what is needed to save Dennings. We all lived here at one time or another and care about our old home.*'

More laughter then gradually the sensation of someone else being nearby faded. 'I think they've gone,' she whispered.

He shook his head in bafflement. 'If you say so.' As he finished his meal slowly, he looked thoughtful.

When he brought his crockery across to the dishwasher, he said, 'Well, let's return to more tangible matters. We'd better get someone in to inspect the houses in Saffron Lane structurally, but first, would you like to have a look at the rest of the row? I'm feeling like a stroll in the fresh air to clear my brain.'

'I'd love to. I've had enough of sorting through dusty documents and it's a beautiful afternoon, though they're forecasting showers for tomorrow.'

* * *

Saffron Lane seemed to be waiting for them, the dilapidation of the houses softened by the

36

lengthening shadows cast by the nearby trees.

'I like the look of the bigger houses at the far end. Let's go and look at those two first. Number 6 is much bigger than the others, double frontage, three full storeys.'

'Your wish is my command.'

He stopped at the door and barred the way with one arm. 'Wait there! I need to check that it's safe.'

'Ooh, you're so masterful!'

He twirled an imaginary moustache. 'You wait till later, my lady, and I'll show you masterful.'

She pretended to be afraid of him, but she wasn't, couldn't ever be, she was sure. There had been a time when she'd been afraid of her first husband and his sudden outbursts of angry shouting, not to mention the hurtful things he said, but that had been long ago. Her Angus didn't have a nasty bone in his body.

She watched him jump around again, testing the floor, then he beckoned her to join him.

There were two rooms with big windows at the front, again looking as if they were meant to be used as a shop, though a much bigger one than the other houses. The wooden floors were scuffed and marked, the walls covered with dingy pale-green paint. A big noticeboard still hung on one wall.

'I don't think it's been touched since the MOD moved its people out in the fifties,' he said. 'Look at that old-fashioned plug socket.'

She sniffed and wrinkled her nose in distaste. 'If you ask me there are mice here.'

'We'll buy some traps.'

'If we catch any, you're disposing of the bodies. I can't bear to touch them.'

'OK.'

Once again there were storerooms between the front and rear of the house, and to their surprise a big wing to one side with a large kitchen and bathroom in it.

When they went outside, it was obvious that this wing was an add-on. 'Very utilitarian, isn't it?'

'Perhaps it was done during the war. I can't understand why it's just been left. It wouldn't take that much to bring it up to date and rent it.'

'The elderly relative I inherited from did everything as cheaply as possible. There was some really shoddy work done, a lot of which cost more to repair in the long run.'

She made a sympathetic murmuring noise. Angus couldn't abide shoddy work. She led the way outside and he followed.

His phone rang then and he answered it. 'Oh hell, I forgot. We'll be with you in five. We're at the other end of the garden.'

He turned to Nell. 'I forgot. I invited the lads and their wives over for a drink — you'd call it a sundowner in Australia, wouldn't you?'

'It's a good thing I always keep stocks of emergency snack food, isn't it?'

'Sorry.'

'Ah, your friends are nice. I'm sure they'll understand why we weren't ready for them. They must know you lose track of time, if they're such good friends.'

It was strange, though, how something always

stopped them from doing a thorough survey of the houses. It felt as if things were being gradually revealed. She still wondered who this Stacy was who was supposed to come and live in Number 2.

After all, everything else the family ghosts had told her had come true, so a woman called Stacy might turn up any day.

4

Elise Carlton stared at her face in the hand mirror and stuck her tongue out at her reflection. She often did that when she was feeling particularly old and it usually made her smile, it was such a silly, childish thing to do. Seventy-five today! She hadn't told anyone in the rehab hospital, didn't want strangers pretending they cared about an old woman's birthday.

How could she possibly be so ancient? Inside her head she felt young, as if she was still able to run and dance round her little corner of the world.

One of the nurses came into her room and started chatting, her eyes assessing Elise, her busy hands straightening and tidying automatically.

Then Elise's niece arrived and asked the nurse if she could take her aunt outside into the gardens to have a private chat.

That seemed strange because Mary was usually in and out of the place within a quarter of an hour at most, and as for privacy, this room was totally private if you shut the door. But Elise welcomed any excuse to leave this dreary little space whose window didn't open and they wouldn't let her move around the hospital grounds on her own. It had been fine all day and she would love some fresh air and sunshine on her skin.

Mary didn't bother to ask the usual perfunctory question about how Elise was, but said abruptly, 'They won't let you stay in this rehab centre for much longer now you're walking better, so Kerry and I have found you a place in a care home, Auntie, a really nice one.'

As her niece went on without waiting for an answer, her voice becoming soft, as if talking to a half-witted idiot, Elise struggled to hold back her anger, because she knew that Mary's mother-in-law had developed Alzheimer's, and Mary and her husband had borne the brunt of caring for the poor thing. Perhaps Mary now expected all older people to be a bit stupid. Who knew?

'Now I know you aren't keen to go into care, Auntie, but let's look on the bright side. You'll have lots of company of your own age in this lovely place we've found.'

'I've told you several times, Mary, that I'm *not* going into a care home, not under any circumstances. I'd rather jump off a cliff, far rather. Living in an institution, even a luxury one, is my idea of torture. This place has shown me only too well that I'd go mad surrounded by people and noise all the time. I can't wait to get out of here into my own quiet space again.'

'You'd have your own room at the care home and the staff are really kind.'

'I do not need people to be kind to me, as if I'm a pet dog, I need them to be interesting. And what about a studio to do my painting in?'

She was, if she said so herself, starting to make a name as an artist these days, though she hadn't liked to boast about it to her family, who weren't really interested. If it hadn't been for that dratted fall, she'd have been in her home studio at this very moment with her beloved paints.

Her art had been such a consolation after her husband died. All she could do at the moment was draw sketches in the lined notebook Mary had brought her, with an HB pencil and cheap child's rubber, for heaven's sake. Her niece never really listened to her requests with more than half an ear, probably didn't know 2B pencils existed.

'I know you love painting and I can't tell you how many people have admired the meadow of wildflowers you did for me — the colours go really well with my décor — but you can't look after yourself properly any longer, you know you can't. And there is an art room in this care home. I made sure of that. They run all sorts of painting classes there for residents. You'll be in your element.'

Elise's indignation began to burn higher but if there was one thing she'd learnt in life, and usually learnt it the hard way, it was not to jump in with both feet till she'd made sure of her landing ground. Honestly! *Painting classes!* After her recent success in selling her paintings she had started to run such classes, and people had paid her some nice chunks of money to do so.

Neither of her nieces was into art, or anything else that switched on the dull grey area between their ears. They were almost as unleavened as their sad sack of a father. What her sister had seen in him to make her rush into marriage, Elise had never worked out, and sadly the marriage hadn't been a happy one, unlike her own.

After her Tom died Elise had turned to painting full-time to fill the dreadful, aching gap he'd left in her life. And amazingly, in her old age she'd started to find the fame that had eluded her in her youth. Much more important than fame, she enjoyed giving pleasure to the people who bought her paintings. She realised her niece was still wittering on about something, so tried to pay attention.

'I'd worry all the time if you were on your own in that big old house, and with the best will in the world, *I* can't give up work to look after you.'

'I wouldn't ask you to do that!' Apart from the fact that Mary had a family of her own, if they had to live together she and her niece would drive each other mad in two days flat — two hours even!

Elise admitted, though only to herself, that she was indeed struggling to look after such a big house, even with hired help. She wasn't going to admit that to her nieces, though, because they were such a bossy pair. Now their own children were almost grown up, they had joined what she called 'The Me! Me! Me! Brigade', people who thought only of themselves, however much they pretended to care for others.

She was planning to sell the house herself and buy a smaller one, and to do it without telling them and having them interfering.

What worried her most was how she would manage the move. Clearing things out and packing took a lot of strength and energy, and

43

she wouldn't be able to lift and carry things for a good while to come. Still, she could no doubt pay someone to do all that under her own supervision. Life would be much easier once she was allowed to drive again. She realised her niece was still talking at her and tried once more to concentrate.

'We'll see to everything when you move out of that huge old place, Auntie. There are people who clear homes, actually, so we can easily find someone to do that for you. And you'll sell the house easily because they're crying out for old places to knock down. They can put up three modern houses on that piece of land, if not four.'

Elise spoke slowly and clearly as she repeated what she had said before, 'I am *not* going into a care home, Mary. And I'm *not* having some stranger throwing out my possessions. When it becomes necessary to clear the house, I'll do it myself.'

'The time has come for some plain speaking, Auntie. You'll have to resign yourself to being helped. And I must say you don't seem to have taken on board *my* side of things, let alone showing a bit of gratitude. I have a job as well as a family and I've just been offered a promotion. If I turn it down, the manager won't ask me again. They don't give women as many chances as men, you know. There's still a glass ceiling, however much they pretend there isn't.'

Elise bit back angry words. 'Congratulations on the promotion, Mary. And I am grateful for all you've done. Very. I can't thank you enough for stepping in when I had that fall. Just leave me to make my own arrangements from now on. I don't even need crutches any more. I'm doing really well with a walking stick, which shows how much better I am. I shan't need to ask anything else of you.'

If her one and only son hadn't emigrated to Australia she'd not have asked him to help her, either. Well, Connor wouldn't have done it. He was the most thoroughly selfish young man she'd ever met. She and Tom had failed somehow with their much-loved baby, who had come as a delightful surprise after years of trying to have children. Connor had been obnoxious as a teenager and had left home as soon as he could, to 'find himself'.

He was forty now and had never looked like marrying or settling down in any way. Last time he'd come to England she'd asked him straight out if he was gay and he'd been furious with her for even thinking that. He didn't want the responsibility of raising children, that was all, nor did he want a mortgage hanging round his neck like a millstone, thank you very much. It was easy enough to pull the chicks without committing to marriage, so he got the best of both worlds.

'Pull the chicks!' What a way to talk about women and relationships. He was another one who'd joined The Me! Me! Me! Brigade, just like his cousins.

'I really am grateful for your help, Mary,' she repeated, trying to soften her niece's steely determination.

'You're family. It's what family do for one

another. Anyway, today I want to take you to see the care home. Do that for me, at least. Come and see it.'

Elise had been intending to say no, but perhaps she'd better have a quick look round the place, because then she could say she didn't like the looks of it. End of story.

When they got out into the car park, Mary's car refused to start, giving off only a sickly cough and expiring with a dull thunk. *Thank you, car!* Elise told it. *You've saved me a lot of trouble.*

But to her dismay, Mary got out her phone and called a taxi, then phoned her husband and told him to come and sort out her car *at once*.

Goodness, her niece was certainly into ordering people around.

The taxi didn't arrive for fifteen minutes, by which time Mary had given up trying to make conversation and was fiddling with her phone.

When the taxi did come, a cheerful young man with a name tag saying 'Ali' helped Elise transfer to it. 'You getting better now, missus?' he asked with a strong accent.

'Yes, thank you.'

'Could you just help me with these, driver?' Mary called.

Elise looked out and to her horror saw two of her suitcases from home being lifted from Mary's car into the taxi, followed by the bag she'd brought with her to the rehab centre. There was no mistaking the cases and bag because she'd painted flowers on the tops for easy recognition when travelling.

'Take me back inside this minute,' she

demanded as Mary slid into the taxi beside her. 'And take my belongings home. How dare you pack cases for me without my permission?'

'You can't go back inside. I've signed you out for good. Just come and see the care home. I'm sure you'll change your mind.'

'*I do not — want to go — into a care home!*' she yelled at the top of her voice. '*I have a home of my own!*'

The taxi driver turned to stare at them in shock but she didn't care. She tried to open the car door and get out, but Mary prevented her, holding her hands away from it as easily as if she were a naughty child.

'Carry on, driver,' Mary called.

'Stay here, driver!' Elise shouted.

'The old lady don't want to go.'

'She's a bit under the weather, not thinking straight. Carry on.'

'I'm not under the weather, or under anything else,' Elise cried. 'She's tricked me into this taxi, but you'll have to drag me screaming into the place at the other end, I promise you, Ali.'

After another moment's hesitation, he set off, but she saw his eyes reflected in the extra-big rear-view mirror. He was watching her carefully and looking worried. Was there any chance of getting him on her side? She forced herself to speak slowly and calmly, pleading with Mary not to do this to her but take her home.

'I'll call the police,' she threatened in the end.

'And tell them what? That I'm looking after you? Anyhow, I've got your enduring power of attorney, so I have a right to make suitable

47

arrangements and they won't even try to stop me.'

'*What?* But we only set that up during the recent emergency.'

'It's not called a *lasting* power of attorney for nothing. 'Enduring' means lasting, Auntie. You gave that power to me and my sister for emergencies and I consider this to be one, so I'm afraid we'll have to override you, for your own good. You'll be glad we did this once you've settled in and made a few friends.'

'I'll never be glad and I'll find a way to escape from that horrible place, see if I don't.'

'And go where?' Mary smiled triumphantly. 'That big old house is simply not suitable for an elderly woman, as your fall down the stairs proved. We've already started sorting things out and called in an estate agent to value it. He thinks it'll sell quickly. Once you're in the care home, we'll go ahead and put it on the market. You won't have anywhere else to go.'

Elise heard the taxi driver's breath hiss into his mouth at this and a quick glance showed him to be shaking his head disapprovingly. She forced herself to start crying, something she normally despised.

Her niece ignored her, exuding triumph and righteousness.

But the driver continued to watch them.

Elise had never felt so helpless and afraid. The more she thought about it, the more real the sobbing became. What was she going to do? They were going to lock her away and would probably forget about her once she was inside.

48

And worst of all, they thought they were doing the best thing for her and many people would agree. But it wasn't what she wanted. She'd go mad in a communal place. She wasn't a joiner, never had been.

★   ★   ★

Shortly afterwards the taxi pulled up outside the care home. Elise refused point-blank to move out of it, batting away Mary's hand when she tried to drag her out of the vehicle and clinging to a convenient handhold with the strength of desperation.

'Can you help me with her?' Mary asked the driver.

'No, missus. Not my job to force old ladies to do something they don't want.'

'It's for her own good!'

'Not if she don't want it. I don't like to see old ladies crying like that. I'd never do it to my mother.'

'Then I'll have to fetch someone from the home to help me. Wait here.'

When she'd gone, the driver turned round. 'You want to go somewhere else, lady, you say so quickly. I been listening and you don't sound to me as if you've lost your marbles.'

Elise stared at him and for a few seconds her brain refused to work, then she said breathlessly, 'I definitely haven't lost my marbles, Ali. Please drive out of the car park straight away so that she can't get help to drag me out of the car. I need to see my lawyer. Will you take me to him?'

After another searching look at her, Ali nodded and said, 'A lawyer is a good idea.' He did as she'd asked and drove off.

He was only just in time. As they drove towards the exit, she heard someone yelling at them to stop.

'Drive faster!' Elise said. 'We need to go towards Swindon.' She gave him Victor's address, then slumped back in her seat, her heart pounding.

'You all right, lady?'

'Yes. Yes, I am. And thank you very much indeed, Ali. I definitely don't need to be put in a care home.'

'Those places aren't happy. I been in them. But the people I took there really had lost their marbles, poor things. You haven't.'

'Is that why you're doing this?'

'Partly. I got a mother about your age. You look a bit like her. She lives with us.' He chuckled. 'She drives me and my wife crazy sometimes, but we'd never put her in a home. Never. She looked after me when I was little, now I look after her. That's what we do in my family.'

'She's lucky to have you. My son is in Australia.'

'He don't come back to visit you?'

'No. He says he's never coming back to England again.'

'Bad son. Bad niece. You're an unlucky lady.'

'No. My luck turned today when I met you. Your mother would be very proud of how you're helping me, Ali.'

She could see his broad grin in the rear-view mirror, and for the first time that day she did indeed feel lucky.

5

Victor went out into the front garden to hoe the weeds from round his flowers. He was feeling sad because there was a particularly fine show of blooms this year, but his best friend wouldn't be here to see them. She wouldn't be able to share her birthday bottle of champagne with him tonight, as she usually did, either. From what he'd been told, she'd never be able to come here again.

Life could be so cruel!

He straightened up, clutching his aching back, surprised to see a taxi stop in front of his house. When he saw Elise get out of the car and wave to him with one hand while leaning on her walking stick with the other, he stared in shock. She looked normal, her old self. As she waved and moved towards him, joy filled him and he tossed his hoe aside.

He flung open the gate and hugged her. 'Elise? I can't believe it. I thought you still couldn't walk and here you are limping brilliantly. I thought — well, never mind what I thought. Happy birthday, my dear.'

She hugged him back and clung to him for a minute as if needing the reassurance. 'Thank you, Victor. It's been an interesting birthday so far.'

He studied her carefully. 'You don't look or sound any different from usual.'

'Why on earth should I?'

'I heard about your fall and was going to come and visit you in hospital, but when I rang your niece, she said you weren't fit to receive visitors. She told me the hip operation had affected your mind and you wouldn't recognise me. It does that sometimes with old people, I know. Well, we both saw it with poor Liz Burford. I was so sad about it happening to you as well and I didn't even try to go, because I couldn't face seeing you like that.'

Elise couldn't believe what she was hearing. 'Mary told you that? Oh, how wicked of her! Well, you can stop being sad, Victor. The heavy painkillers slowed me down for a few days, and affected me so badly that when I insisted on reducing them, the doctor let me. I'm not taking any of them at all now, just over-the-counter painkillers, and I'm feeling like my old self. I loathed feeling so dopey.'

She stole a quick sideways glance at Victor, shocked at how much older he was looking. 'I wondered why you'd abandoned me.'

'I'd never abandon you, my dear, not as long as you can recognise me, anyway.'

As he stood back to let her go through the gate she hesitated for a moment. 'I'd better confess: I've run away from Mary and I'm hoping you'll give me shelter till I can sort things out.'

He looked at her grimly and she could see his quick understanding of the situation. 'Is that why your niece tried to keep me away?'

'Yes. She's wants to put me in a care home.'

'*You?* You'd go mad. Or murder one of the

53

other inmates. Or both. I'll not only give you shelter, my dear, but help fight off any nieces who come after you. We and our spouses were friends for a good many years, and that hasn't changed now there are only us two left from the quartet.' He hugged her again.

She didn't immediately move away from his embrace because he'd started to let go of her, then grabbed her suddenly.

'What's wrong, Victor? Are you all right?'

'I'm a bit dizzy. Just let me hold on to you for a minute. It'll soon pass. The doctors have got me on some new heart medicine and I don't think it agrees with me.'

'I thought your blood pressure was under control?'

'It is. Mostly. Never mind that. Let's get you and your luggage inside.'

She turned to the taxi driver. 'Did you hear all that, Ali? My niece has been stopping my friends from visiting me.'

'She's a bad 'un all right, missus. Good thing we got you away from her.' He walked past them to set the biggest suitcase down near the front door, and went back to the car for the other bags.

'You're sure you don't mind if I stay with you for a while, Victor? If I go home, Mary will come after me and arrange to have me put away by the authorities, I know she will. She's already threatened it.'

'I'll make legally sure she can't and regrets even trying. This is elder abuse.'

Elise sighed. 'Unfortunately, I think she truly

believes she's doing this for my own good. She's always been bossy, thinking she knows better than anyone else.'

'She was very patronising to me on the phone, I must say. Talked to me slowly and loudly.'

'She would. You're even older than me, therefore you must be senile.' She patted his wrinkled cheek. 'My dear friend, there's nothing whatsoever wrong with my brain, I promise you. I broke my hip and had to have a new one fitted. It happens to some old lady every day. Easy enough to fix. I'll be as good as new soon — better, because my old hip had been hurting a lot recently and I was being a coward about having the operation.'

'I could tell. You limped sometimes or winced for no obvious reason. Come inside and tell me all about it over a cup of tea. Young man, could you please carry the cases and bag in for us?'

'Happy to.' Ali beamed at them both. 'This is another good thing, lady, having a good friend to help you.'

Victor flourished a bow and offered her his arm, then they walked slowly inside. She didn't know which one of them was leaning on the other. And did that matter?

Ali followed with the luggage, by which time Elise had described exactly how the taxi driver had saved her.

Victor let go of her to pump Ali's hand vigorously. 'Well done, lad. Well done indeed! How much do we owe you?'

She watched him press double that amount into Ali's hand.

'Have you got a card? If we want a taxi in future, we'll try you first.'

Ali beamed at him. 'Thank you. Where do you want your suitcases?'

'Put them in the bedroom at the back right, the blue room.'

Ali did that, then came down and said to Elise, 'Don't you give in to that niece of yours, missus. You do what you want with your life.' He left with a cheery wave.

'Fine young fellow, that. We could do with more migrants like him,' Victor said. 'Fancy a cup of tea?'

'Yes. I'm parched. The stuff they gave us in the rehab place was always stewed. Do you still have your special tea?'

'Yes, of course.' He settled Elise in a chair and brought in two pretty china mugs of it. When he'd given her one of them, he sank into the other armchair and pointed one hand at her. 'Now, let's hear the whole story, every single detail this time.'

She went through exactly what her niece had done, ending with, 'So I desperately need your help legally, Victor.'

'You certainly do. Why on earth didn't you give me the power of attorney, old girl?'

'I knew your heart was playing up and I thought you had enough on your plate. And we were in a hurry after my fall.'

'Ah.'

'And Mary — well, I must give the devil her due, she came as soon as I had the accident. She helped a lot, fetching my things from home.'

Elise began fiddling with her teaspoon. 'The worst of it is, she's right about one thing: I can't manage that big house on my own any longer. It's going downhill rapidly. I've been having difficulty with those stairs for quite a while.'

'You could fit a stairlift.'

'I don't have a lot of money to spare until I sell the house and buy something smaller.'

'Painting not paying a lot?'

'Starting to pay some, but it comes and goes. I'm not quite in the big league yet and I've had the council rates to pay and a huge electricity bill. Tom's stupid superannuation died with him, you see. He got a bigger amount by agreeing to a lifetime limit. He always seemed in far better health than me so I didn't protest but — Oh, my!' She looked across the room at one of her own paintings hanging on the wall.

'I bought that one because I love bluebells. I can't walk in a real wood full of them any longer, because I'm not risking uneven ground, but I mentally walk through that painting every day.'

'Oh, Victor, what a lovely thing to say. But you shouldn't have *bought* it. I'd have given it to you happily!'

He waggled one finger at her. 'You never were businesslike about your work.'

After a short silence, she raised her head to look him in the eye. 'What on earth am I going to do, Victor?'

'Well, you can change who has the power of attorney at any time, so we'll get that sorted out for a start, then your niece can't force you to do anything. After that we'll sell your house and find you a new home. Easy.'

She chuckled. 'Easy! It seems like a very high mountain to climb to me.'

'Well, you've got me to help you now, so we'll climb it together. I was getting bored. A new hobby is just what I need.'

She pretended to be indignant. 'Are you calling me a *hobby*?'

'Yes. Let me ring the old firm and tell my nephew to come here as a matter of urgency. He can sort out the power of attorney and we'll get my neighbours in to witness the new document, if necessary. They changed the rules, so I'm not up to date, but Gordon will know the specifics.'

'Will your nephew do that for me?'

He chuckled. 'What, upset the chap who still owns a quarter of the firm? He's not that stupid, even if we didn't get on, which we do. I've made him my heir, since I don't have any heirs of my body. And about your need for money, my dear, I can't spend a tenth of what my investments bring in, so please let me give you what you need till we sort the house sale out.'

She took his hand and held it to her cheek for a moment. 'Thank you.'

He leant forward to kiss her cheek then picked up the phone and had a brief conversation with someone. As he put it down, he looked at her smugly. 'My nephew is coming round straight away. He was promoted to partner last month because he's as sharp as a tack. He'll sort this out in no time. You'll see.'

He studied her face. 'Feeling better now?'

'Starting to.'

'You must definitely stay with me till we work out something permanent, Elise.'

'I can't manage the stairs yet. I'll have to sleep on your sofa.'

'No need. I had a lift installed immediately after your fall, just in case something similar happened to me. I'm like you, couldn't bear to go into a care home.'

'Where on earth did you put a lift?'

'It's at the back of the garage and I've used it a few times already for taking loads upstairs, but only for that, mind. I can still manage the stairs perfectly well if I want to. The lift is about to pay its way big time for you.'

He stabbed one finger at her. 'And you, my girl, can visit my physio and get an exercise programme set up. Best way to prevent a fall is to stay strong. I've been looking into it for myself.'

Her voice was thick with unshed tears. 'You're a wonderful man, Victor Pinkett.'

'You're my oldest surviving friend, Elise. Not many left now from our original group. Once we've got you fixed up, we'll have to see if we can both make some new friends.'

She yawned suddenly, feeling exhausted.

'Just hang on till my nephew's been to see you, then you can have a little nap.'

'How do you know I need one?'

'You look sleepy and you just yawned.' He grinned. 'Besides, I usually have one myself at this time of day. Once Gordon's gone, we'll both have a little snooze.'

59

'I don't know how to thank you, my dear, dear friend.'

'Nice to be of use to someone. I've been feeling a bit past my use-by date recently.'

He patted her hand again and she gave him a tremulous smile.

★   ★   ★

Victor's nephew arrived a short time later, accompanied by an older man.

'Gordon, this is my very dear friend, Elise Carlton.'

She shook hands with him. 'You look like your uncle did at your age.'

'He's not *that* good-looking,' Victor joked. 'And this is Peter, our highly respected head clerk.'

'I think I've met you before, Peter, haven't I?'

'Yes, and it's nice to see you again, Mrs Carlton. I'm sure you'll cheer Mr Pinkett up. He could do with some company.'

The nephew didn't waste much time on greetings, but demanded to know what the crisis was. After listening to their tale, he said crisply, 'Your niece wasn't telling you the truth. You can revoke that power of attorney quite easily. In fact, Peter can handle it for you.'

'Didn't I just say he was a sharp fellow?' Victor said to Elise.

Gordon asked her to write a letter cancelling the power of attorney and he witnessed her signature before handing the papers to Peter.

Someone drove up to the house just then and

Victor went to peer out of the window.

'Your nieces didn't waste much time pursuing you, did they?'

Elise hauled herself to her feet and limped across to join him. 'Good heavens, both of them! And who's that getting out of the other car?'

Gordon joined them at the window. 'She's a social worker. Nice enough woman. I've dealt with her before. They must have brought her in on this. I wonder what sort of tale they spun to get her here.' He grinned at his uncle. 'Good thing you didn't waste any time sending for me, eh?'

'No one's ever accused me of being stupid.'

He patted the old man affectionately on the back. 'And I shan't be the first to do so.'

Victor turned to Elise. 'I'll let them in. You need to sit down. You're looking wobbly.'

He was looking wobbly too but she didn't say that. He seemed so happy to be helping her.

He flung open the front door as the bell rang for the second time. 'Impatient, aren't you?'

Mary tried to push past him. 'We're worried about my aunt, Mr Pinkett. I know she's here. Where else could she go? Anyway, I saw her at the window.'

Victor put out his arm to prevent her entering. 'And who is this?' He looked at the older woman questioningly.

Gordon came into the hall. 'This is Jenny Williams, Uncle. Haven't seen you for a while, Jenny. This is my uncle Victor, who's been a friend of Mrs Carlton since before I was born. May they come in, Uncle?'

61

'As long as they don't badger poor Elise any more. She's very tired after having had to escape wrongful imprisonment.'

The social worker looked at him in surprise, then turned to Gordon. 'How is Mrs Carlton?'

'She's fine. In full possession of her faculties, if that's what you're delicately hinting at.'

'You don't know her like I do. My aunt's not at all herself,' Mary protested.

'I know her far better than you do and she's as intelligent and sane as she ever was,' Victor snapped. 'And actually, I see her far more often than you usually do, young woman, because she's my best friend and we've known one another since we were in our twenties. Until this happened I doubt you saw her more than two or three times a year.'

As Mary glared at his uncle and opened her mouth to reply, Gordon intervened again. 'Come and meet Mrs Carlton, Jenny. She's been revoking the enduring power of attorney her nieces held.'

Mary let out a growl of anger. 'You must have been exerting undue influence.'

'Mrs Carlton has a perfect right to choose whoever she wants to help her.' Gordon's quiet tone was in great contrast to Mary's sharp voice. He glanced quickly at the other sister, who had remained in the background and was looking worried, but didn't say anything to her.

Mary glared at him. 'I'm sure I read somewhere that until the change is registered, we still have the power to act. I'm *not* letting you coerce my aunt. She needs looking after and I know how much lawyers cost, even if she doesn't.'

He breathed deeply but didn't reply to that one.

★ ★ ★

As they came into the room Elise spoke up loudly and clearly, 'No one is trying to coerce me except you, Mary. How many times do I have to tell you that I do not wish to go into a care home?'

'You can't look after yourself, let alone that big house!'

'I agree about the house, not about myself. Anyway, I'm making other arrangements.' She turned to the social worker. 'Do we need to fetch a doctor to prove that I'm in my right mind?'

Jenny smiled. 'I don't think so. I wouldn't usually have interfered but your niece seemed so upset about your state of mind. Perhaps, since I'm here, you and I could just have a private chat for a moment or two to set my mind completely at rest about the situation.'

Gordon smiled.

Elise saw Victor slip something into his mouth, but didn't say anything.

She shouldn't have come to him. He didn't look at all well.

He caught her watching him and shrugged. 'Why don't you two ladies use the dining room for your chat?'

★ ★ ★

When she was alone with the social worker, Elise took the initiative. 'My niece always has been bossy. She thinks she knows what's best for me, but she doesn't.' She gestured to the wall where another of her paintings was hanging. 'I'm an artist, still working when I'm not breaking hips. That's one of mine, so were the bluebells in the other room. I sell my paintings and I'm preparing for an exhibition. The mere idea of me going into a care home is ridiculous.'

Jenny walked across to study the painting. 'It's beautiful. You must tell me where the exhibition is. I'd like to see more of your work.'

Elise felt tears well in her eyes and fumbled for a handkerchief. 'Sorry. I don't usually act like a watering can, but it's been a horrid day. Mary tricked me into her car and tried to take me forcibly to the care home.'

'*She did what?*'

Elise repeated it with more detail.

'Not a good way to do things. We'll try to do better from now on, but you are going to need some help, my dear. Where are you going to be staying tonight?'

'Here. With Victor. He has a lift so I won't have to negotiate the stairs. Well, I don't think I could.'

'Good. If I may, I'll come and see you again in a couple of days and we'll make some long-term plans.'

'Checking on me?'

'Yes. My job is to provide a service to help older people to live independently. I prefer *not* to put people into homes, if there are alternatives.

They don't always thrive there. You'll find dealing with your niece easier if I'm on your side. Though I don't think she's trying to be malicious.'

Elise sighed. 'Nor do I. It'd be easier if she was. Mary's rather ageist, I'm afraid. I think that's because she's had some bad experiences with older relatives. She's in for a shock when she turns seventy! I wish I could be there to see it.'

Jenny laughed and stood up. 'I think the mere act of turning seventy upsets a lot of people. I meet some wonderful oldies in my job as well as some sad cases.'

When they went back into the other room, Elise said, 'Can I have my house keys back, Mary and Kerry?'

Mary flushed. 'You *gave* them to us, Auntie. We didn't steal them from you.'

'Well, I'm taking them back now.'

'I think it'd be better if I kept them a bit longer. We made a start on packing up your household things. If you're determined to continue putting yourself in danger, we'll have to go back and unpack them again.'

'I'd rather you didn't come near me or my house for a good long time, thank you very much.' She held out her hand. 'My keys, please.'

Mary exchanged a long-suffering glance with her sister and they both fumbled in their handbags for them. She scowled at Victor as she added, 'You know where I am if my aunt needs help, Mr Pinkett. I think I'm in a better physical state to help her than you are.'

65

For a moment, her unkind words silenced the others, then Victor started to get up. 'Let me show you two out.'

'I'll do it,' Gordon said quickly. 'You stay there, Uncle.'

When Gordon came back, he said, 'My goodness, your niece doesn't give up easily, does she, Mrs Carlton? She gave me a mouthful before she'd step outside, about not letting my uncle take advantage of you.'

'Call me Elise, please.'

Victor snorted. 'Does that young woman think I'm short of money?'

'She's suspicious of the whole world,' Elise said. 'She lives her life adversarially, always on the defence because she expects people to try to take advantage of her.'

He shook his head sadly. 'She doesn't at all resemble her aunt. You aren't nearly suspicious enough, Elise. Now, Gordon, we oldies need our naps. I think we've finished all the paperwork. I'd be obliged if you'd register it for us. Let me see you out.'

★ ★ ★

After the others had left, Victor came back to find Elise still standing near the table. He put his arms round her and said gently, 'Go on, cry it out!'

She did shed a few tears of sheer relief, cradled against his shoulder. After she'd mopped her eyes, they went back into the sitting room, where they each took a sofa and lay down.

66

Victor smiled across at her. 'Aaah! This sofa is so comfortable. It often tempts me into an afternoon nap.'

'Thank you for rescuing me.'

'My pleasure.'

She could feel herself drifting off into sleep and snuggled down against a soft cushion, feeling safe for the first time in ages and feeling hope for the future.

6

Stacy saw Darren again at her local shopping centre and wondered what he was doing there when he lived on the other side of town. She tried to slip away without him seeing her, but as she was getting into her car she heard footsteps running towards her.

'Hey, wait! Stace, wait a minute!'

She spun round and leant against the car, arms folded, not hiding her annoyance. 'What the hell do you want, Darren?'

'Let me buy you a coffee and I'll tell you.'

'I don't want any coffee. I'm on my way home.'

'Then invite me round to your place for a cuppa and I'll tell you about it. It'll be just like old times.'

'No. It'll never be like old times. We broke up last year, Darren. You wanted your freedom. Well, now you have it, so go and find someone else to share it with. I'm busy.'

'You haven't got another guy in tow, you must be lonely.'

She could feel herself stiffening. 'How would you know about my social life?'

'I ran into Penny from your work and we got chatting.'

Just wait till she saw Penny! 'I don't need a guy to enjoy life.' She turned to open the car door.

He pulled her away from it. 'I was wrong, Stacy, wrong to break up. Please . . . give me another chance.'

'No.'

He looked puzzled. 'That's all. Just no? When I'm offering to take you back?'

'You heard correctly. I don't have to give reasons. Now, I've got things to do.' This time she got the car door open but he pushed her to one side and slammed it shut again, looking furious.

She was so surprised by this she did nothing for a moment but stare at him.

He took a deep breath and the anger vanished from his face as if it had been wiped clean. 'It's just a cup of coffee. Come on, Stace.'

'I said no and I meant no. I don't want anything more to do with you. *Not — ever.*'

'You ungrateful bitch!' This time as she turned away from him, he grabbed her and slammed her hard against the car.

'Get your hands off me!' she shouted.

'You'll damn well talk to me, give me a chance. Whatever it takes.' He snatched at her keys but she thrust them behind her back.

Seeing two older men coming towards them she yelled at the top of her voice, 'Help! Help me!'

Darren tried to put his hand across her mouth and she bit him.

As the men started running towards them, he said in a low voice, 'You'll regret this. No woman treats me like that.' He spun round and ran off.

The men didn't try to chase him.

'You all right?' the nearest one asked her.

'I am now. He wouldn't let me get into my car.'

'Do you know him?'

'He's my ex-husband.' She couldn't stop shaking and her words came out in jerky bursts. 'He's the one who — who broke up our marriage and now . . . now he's pestering me to get back together. He won't accept no for an answer.'

'Take your time. We'll stay with you till you feel all right to drive.' He fumbled in his pocket. 'Here. This is my card. If he keeps pestering you, I'll happily be a witness to him manhandling you today.'

'Thank you.'

'Good thing I happened to be looking in your direction, eh? I was close enough to see you were in trouble. I don't approve of men who treat women roughly.'

'I took a photo of him with my phone,' the other man said, also offering a business card. 'Same goes for me. I saw it too.'

'I'm grateful for your help.'

The first man beckoned to two older women who were standing watching. When they joined them, their husbands explained what had happened and one woman put her arm round Stacy.

It took her a few minutes to pull herself together. Nothing like this had ever happened to her before, and Darren hadn't been so violent during their marriage, just — well, a bit rough sometimes, but he hadn't beaten her.

One of the men looked at his watch. 'Have you

somewhere safe to go, Stacy?'

'Um. I'm not sure.' Where could she take refuge? Normally she'd have gone round to her parents' but they were away house-hunting, living in a hotel somewhere now they'd sold their house.

She'd do her grocery shopping tomorrow, and do it somewhere else.

There was nowhere to go but back to her flat. At least there were usually people within call there. Most of the time, anyway.

⋆　⋆　⋆

She didn't notice the red car following her till she turned into the street where she lived and it turned too.

That was Darren's car!

She drove past her block of flats and out at the other end of the street. She didn't hesitate to go straight to the local police station.

Darren followed her all the way, tailgating her till he saw where she was going, then braking suddenly. She stopped just inside the car park and saw him point to her and raise a clenched fist, then accelerate past the entrance and drive off down the street.

Feeling shaky all over again, she found a visitor's bay and went into the building.

When she reported what had happened, the officer at the desk looked a bit bored. 'He just followed you, right?'

Then he suddenly leant forward, indicated her right arm and asked, 'Where did you get that bruise? It's a big one.'

She hadn't even noticed. 'It wasn't there when I left home this morning. It must be where Darren grabbed me and thumped me against my car.'

She got a lot more attention then: an interview with the officer in charge of women's safety, photocopies taken of the two business cards, and a photo of her bruised arm.

One woman excused herself and left, rejoining them ten minutes later. 'Your witnesses bear out your story and are perfectly happy to testify about what happened. I'm afraid it'll only mean a warning for your ex this time, but maybe it'll make him think twice about attacking you again.'

'I can't believe he did it at all. He never seemed the sort to, well, *stalk* someone. And it was he who left me, for heaven's sake.'

'Something must have happened to him. You never can tell what will tip some guys over,' the female officer said. 'They don't have 'stalker' tattooed on their foreheads. Do you feel safe going home?'

'Not really.'

'Are there neighbours close by?'

'Yes. But they come and go.'

'We'll get one of our cars to drive past those flats every hour or so to keep an eye on you. Make sure your doors and windows are locked and put this number on quick dial.'

'Believe me, I will.'

Stacy didn't drive straight home, though. She wanted to be with people, so went to another shopping centre and finished buying her groceries. She kept an eye on the crowds and checked the car park for a red car before she went back to her own vehicle.

Then she got angry and told herself not to let him frighten her. It wasn't as if he was a murderer, and he probably hadn't meant to bruise her. Or had he?

There was no sign of Darren or his car when she got home, but though it was quite a warm day for this time of year, she didn't leave the door or windows open.

She'd planned to work on her latest sculpture, but couldn't get into the mood to create anything, however much of a talking-to she gave herself.

Damn you, Darren! she thought as she lay in bed that night, finding it hard to get to sleep.

That settled it, though. She was definitely going to look for a job in some other town and she wasn't going to tell anyone at work where she was going.

★   ★   ★

Angus didn't waste any time bringing in a structural engineer to check the houses in Saffron Lane. Hedley Preece came well recommended and they were both impatient for him to complete his investigations and tell them what he'd found, but he said it'd be days before he could get to their place.

When he arranged to see them one afternoon the following week to share his findings, he suggested meeting at Saffron Lane, so that he could point out one or two things they might have missed. That sounded ominous.

He was already waiting for them when they arrived, standing in the middle of the street, his face turned up to the sun.

'Ah, there you are. I was just enjoying the warmth and getting a free dose of Vitamin D.' He shook hands with both of them then gestured to the houses. 'This little street has a nice feel to it. They knew how to build solid dwellings in those days, my word they did.'

'Does that mean they're safe?' Angus asked.

'You can rest assured that these houses won't fall down on you or your tenants. Of course, they'll need rewiring and replumbing, but you don't need me to tell you that.'

Angus beamed at him. 'That's excellent news.'

'There are a couple of small faults that need dealing with if they're not to turn into larger faults: the roof of Number 4 has some damage to one corner, probably done by a storm, and there are gutters here and there that need replacing.'

'That's all?'

He chuckled. 'Do you *want* anything else to be wrong?'

Angus shrugged. 'I just want everyone who lives here to be safe.'

'There is something else I need to tell you, though. You said the War Office was the last occupier during and after World War II.'

'Yes. They requisitioned the whole street.'

'Well, they've left some stuff in the attic of Number 1. It's nothing dangerous, mostly papers and everyday office equipment, but if I were you, I'd contact them and ask what they want to do about it. You shouldn't just destroy any of it. I believe it has some significant historical value.'

Nell frowned. 'I don't remember there being anything in the attic of Number 1, just that it was smaller than next door's attic.'

'That's because there's a hidden door through to a deliberately concealed room. I hadn't realised you'd not noticed it. I can show you how to activate the door catch if you like.'

Angus and Nell exchanged surprised glances.

'How did you find it when we noticed nothing, Hedley?' he asked.

'I could tell that there had to be some other space under the roof and wondered why it hadn't been utilised as it had been in Number 2. Luckily, I'd seen a couple of other hidden rooms which opened like yours. I'm a bit of a World War II buff, you see. I didn't examine the contents in detail because I didn't feel it was right to touch or move them.'

'That's fascinating,' Angus exclaimed.

They followed Hedley into the house and up the stairs, where he showed them how to get into the inner attic.

'Goodness, this is a fully fledged operations room!' Angus exclaimed. 'You're right: it's World War II stuff.'

Mr Preece nodded. 'Yes. The government set up hidden places like this all over England in the early days of the war, just in case Hitler managed to invade and they needed to fight a guerrilla war. Some of them are still coming to light, they were so well hidden. A good percentage were unknown to the authorities because of bombings that destroyed records or the people who'd set them up being killed. Some were part of separate hush-hush plans, each of which was known only to a few key figures. With the Cold War in the fifties, I suppose they thought they should still keep something in reserve.'

'I've never heard even the faintest whisper about this one in the family.'

'They probably weren't told. When did you get the houses back?'

'The end of the sixties, I think.'

'That figures. I'll leave you to report this find to the Ministry of Defence. I'll send you my bill with the written report.' He turned away, taking his torch with him.

Angus followed. 'I'll see you out. Do you want to wait for me here, Nell?'

'Yes. I'm dying to look round this room properly.'

'I'd better nip back to the big house and fish out a couple of torches. You don't get a lot of light into the attic through this door, however wide you open it.'

* * *

When Angus rejoined Nell, he handed her a torch. 'Where do we start?'

'Does it matter? I suppose we'd better not move things, so we can only look.'

'We could open drawers and cupboard doors if we're careful.'

76

The papers they found were yellowed and nearly everything was thick with dust. After a while Nell sighed. 'I think we'd better leave this to the experts and lock the place up carefully. It could be an important piece of British history.'

Regretfully, they closed the door of the secret room again and made sure nothing indicated an opening there before going back downstairs.

'Dennings never ceases to amaze me,' he said. 'What other secrets do you think it's hiding?'

'I don't know, but if we spend our lives here, we're bound to find some of them, aren't we? Do you want to look round the other houses?'

He glanced at his watch. 'Not today. I've got work to do. Um, I'd better tell you more about my mother.'

'You haven't said much about her.'

'I hardly ever see her. She's in Spain and she hasn't forgiven me and my daughter for making her into a great-grandmother. She's very well preserved for her age, spends a lot of time and money on her appearance.'

'And her second husband?'

'He was American and suited her much more than my father did. Unfortunately Myron died suddenly last year so she was widowed for a second time. It sounds as if she's met someone else and apparently this guy is even richer than Myron, so I bet she'll marry him next. She comes to London every now and then to do some shopping and I usually go up to meet her.'

Nell made an encouraging noise, hoping Angus would tell her more because he didn't often speak about his parents.

'I did mention in my last email to Mum that I'd met someone special, preparing the ground for her to meet you, so to speak, though who knows when that'll be?'

Nell dared ask, 'Don't you get on with her?'

'We don't *not* get on because we hardly ever see one another. I'll take you to meet her next time she's over in the UK. Now, let's lock up here and go home.'

He didn't volunteer any more information about his family. Nell had met his daughter and Ashleigh had been perfectly polite but rather cool, not seeming to accept that her father could have formed a lasting relationship. His son hadn't returned from backpacking round the world and she knew Angus was worried about Oliver, who was still in South-East Asia somewhere. Well, it was a rare person who didn't worry about their offspring, however old they were and however long ago they'd flown the nest.

She worried about her children, too, and it was more than time she told them she was going to marry Angus.

He'd said a few times, 'When we're married, we'll do that properly,' or words to that effect but neither of them was in a hurry to tie the knot. They didn't need bits of paper to feel like a couple.

★ ★ ★

The Ministry of Defence sent instructions that Angus was not to touch anything in the attic nor

78

was he to let anyone else into the secret room. In fact, it would be best if he locked up the whole house until it could be thoroughly examined by experts from the Imperial War Museum because other valuable items might be concealed there.

'That's torn it!' he exclaimed. 'I was going to get all the houses replumbed.'

'Well, Number 1 will have to wait. What's the hassle? You can get the other five done and come back to that one later. What about the rewiring? It's a good thing you've got an electrician's ticket. Have you drawn up your new wiring plans yet?'

'I was going to do the work myself, but I think I'll find someone else to do it. I can sign up with an agency and earn more from IT work than I'd save doing the electrical work. Besides, it'd take ages on my own.'

'I think you're right.'

She knew he was worried about the roof and the winter weather, but one person could only do so much. The house had stood for over two hundred years. She was sure it'd last another few.

7

In Australia, Adam Torrington took a few days' emergency leave from his job as a university lecturer because his ex-wife Judith had died suddenly of an aneurism. Her death had shocked everyone because she'd always been so fit and healthy, and his daughter Gemma, who'd been living with her mother, was nearly hysterical with grief.

He'd rushed round to see her straight away when a friend of Judith's phoned to tell him the sad news.

'I can manage on my own,' Gemma shouted at him when he arrived at the house. She tried to bar his way in and he had to push her aside.

'No, you can't. You may be ahead a year at school, but you're still not even seventeen, and won't be an adult legally till you're eighteen. If you don't let me look after you, you could even be taken into care, because you have no other relatives in Perth.'

'You don't want to look after me!'

He stared at her in surprise. 'Where the hell did you get that idea? Of course I do. I want very much to take care of you now.'

'Then why did you hardly ever come to see me after you'd left?'

He sighed. 'You know why. Your mother wouldn't allow me to see you more often.'

'What? You're lying. She told me you didn't

want to see me more often.'

This accusation cropped up at regular intervals and for all her claims to be grown up, there were times when Gemma still acted like a small, sulking child about her parents' divorce.

'You should have treated Mum better then she wouldn't have divorced you,' she muttered.

'It wasn't anyone's fault. We just . . . grew apart. She was the one who suggested divorcing, actually. I wanted to try counselling.' Because he hadn't wanted to lose his daughter. He held up one hand as Gemma opened her mouth. 'I'm not arguing about that again. If you won't believe the truth, I can't do anything about it.'

'I've only got your word for what the truth is . . . *now*!'

He ignored that, reminding himself how badly she must be hurting. 'I'll go and pick up some of my clothes and move into the spare bedroom. Do we need to go food shopping?'

Silence, then she nodded. 'I don't have much money and we were due to go shopping. Mum used credit cards most of the time, not cash.'

'You'd better come with me, then. You'll know better than me what we need at the supermarket. After that,' he hesitated but it had to be done, 'we'll need to arrange the funeral.'

Which made her start weeping and slam off into her bedroom.

He gave her a few minutes then yelled from outside the door. 'I'm leaving in ten minutes. If you want to help sort out the arrangements you'll need to come with me.'

She joined him a couple of minutes later.

He went to his flat first to get some clothes and other stuff. Gemma stared round it as if she'd never seen it before, though she'd been here a few times. 'Pokey, isn't it? No wonder you want to come back to Mum's house.'

'That house is still half mine legally. I left it like that so that you could stay there till you grew up. Um, did your mother make a will, do you know?'

'I don't know. Could you ring her lawyer and ask?'

'I'd prefer to call in and do that face to face. It looks as if we've got a busy day ahead of us.'

It would probably be good to keep Gemma occupied, but he'd be up until after midnight catching up with some crucial assessments he had to do for work.

★ ★ ★

They got the shopping over and done with, then went to the lawyer's office, where the reception-ist was very helpful once Adam had explained the problem.

She nipped in to see her employer between clients and he took Adam and Gemma into a little side room to have a quick word and arrange for them to get a copy of the will.

'Two copies,' Gemma said. 'I want my own.'

He glanced quickly at Adam, who nodded.

'When you get the will, I suggest you go somewhere private to read it. Wills can be . . .

upsetting. Though this one is very straightforward.'

So they went to sit in the car, each with a copy.

Adam finished first and saw Gemma brushing away a tear. He didn't say anything, waited till she looked at him.

'So you own everything now except my half of the house, Gemma.'

'I'd rather have Mum back.'

'Of course you would. So would I.' He tried to hold her hand for comfort and she let him for a minute or two, then shook him off.

'What now?'

'We have to arrange the funeral. When your mother's friend rang me she said there has to be an autopsy, though they have a fair idea what happened.'

'Cut Mum up? That's horrid!'

'I agree.' He let a minute or two pass then said, 'Do you think your mother would have preferred a female undertaker?'

Gemma managed a nod but didn't seem able to speak.

'I know where there is one. A friend of mine used them when his mother died recently and he said they were very good.'

The undertakers were, but the interview was inevitably a harrowing ordeal and Gemma's anguish had tears welling in his eyes as well, more for her than for her mother.

His daughter even let him put an arm round her as they left.

She began sobbing loudly the minute they were in the car and throughout the journey, and bolted for her room as soon as they got into the house.

Damn. He'd forgotten to ask Gemma if there was a spare front door key. He might need to get a new one cut for himself because Judith had made a big show of changing the locks the very day he moved out.

★　★　★

After he'd put his things away in the spare bedroom, he went to knock on Gemma's door and heard her talking to someone. On the phone to a friend, he supposed. 'What do you want for tea?' he asked when she came to the door, eyes reddened, lashes damp.

'I'll get it for myself.'

'I'd prefer us to eat together from now on.'

'You're not a good cook.'

'Are you?'

She shrugged. 'Not bad. Mum taught me.'

'Then you can cook the evening meal and I'll clear up after it.' He could see her thinking this over and was hard put not to sigh in relief when she nodded.

It wasn't all bad living in his old home. He'd forgotten how quiet it was in a single dwelling compared to a large block of flats with mainly younger occupants and associated social events.

★　★　★

After breakfast, Gemma vanished and Adam found her in her mother's room, fiddling with

84

the things on the dressing table.

He cleared his throat to gain her attention. 'Do you want to start clearing out your mother's room?'

'Not yet. When I can face it.'

'It's better that we face it together. If you don't want to start till after the funeral, that's all right by me.'

She stared at him, then gave a reluctant nod.

'I'll lock her bedroom door until then so the cleaner won't go in there.' He definitely didn't want Gemma going through things on her own. He knew from friends that nasty surprises sometimes showed up when clearing out houses after a death.

'You have no right to lock me out of Mum's room! How did you find the key? She never used it.'

'I was looking for a front door key among the spares. Judith had labelled them all, luckily. She always was well organised about details. I can let you into her bedroom any time you need something.'

'As long as you stay out as well, I'd rather get the funeral and the exams over first, anyway,' she muttered.

'I wondered if you'd like to redo this year and take your final exams next year? After all, you're a year ahead of the other students.'

She shook her head. 'No. I'm ready now, really. I've been studying hard and I'm still getting As. I want to do Mum proud.'

'Good for you. Anything I can do to help, just let me know.'

'Don't your students have exams?'

'We assess during the year, mainly. My area of IT is a very practical, hands-on set of skills, more of that than theory. And I'm dealing with a postgraduate course mainly.'

★　★　★

Somehow the two of them rubbed along together in the house. Gemma alternated between being hostile and suspicious, and being extremely needy emotionally, trying his patience a dozen times a day, not to mention contradicting herself from one day to the next.

★　★　★

He waited till after the funeral and her exams were over to raise the subject of Judith's room again.

'We need to clear out your mother's things now.'

Tears welled in her eyes. 'My friend said you'd want to do that, get rid of every sign of Mum.'

'Well, she was wrong about why we're doing it, but I can't see the point of keeping some things, like Judith's clothes. You won't want to wear them, will you? No, I thought not. Though you can keep a few as mementoes if you like. Your choice.'

'I can clear her room out on my own.'

'As I said before, it's going to be a hard thing to do. Better we tackle it together.'

She looked at him doubtfully. 'And then?'

'Then we'll sit down and discuss the future together. And where we're going to live.'

* * *

After breakfast, he led the way upstairs, unlocking the bedroom door and hesitating to go in. It seemed longer than five years since he and his ex had shared this room and yet in some ways it was as familiar as his own hand. Even though she was no longer here, it felt as if he was invading *her* territory.

Gemma must have heard her parents quarrelling during those last few months and had given him dirty looks from time to time as if all the fault lay with him. The final straw had been when he'd done an exchange for one semester with an American lecturer, a very prestigious opportunity to gain, and had come back to ice woman and sleeping in the spare bedroom.

He didn't know what Judith had told their daughter about the divorce, but it must have been something that blackened his name because in spite of all his efforts, Gemma had joined her mother in keeping him at arm's length after he moved out. Even on his monthly meetings with her she was cool, talking mainly about school, her grades and her friends.

Gemma's voice brought him back to the present. 'Dad? Are you going to stand there all morning staring into space?'

He shrugged. Why the hell had he started reliving all that? It was long over and he'd never be able to set the record straight with his daughter without Judith to back him up.

Sighing, he ran one hand through his hair, still dark, though thinning and threaded with more silver than he liked these days, and said quietly, 'It's not easy to turn out someone's personal belongings, darling. Are you sure you don't want me to do it on my own?'

'No. I think Mum would want *me* to do it on my own.'

He wasn't risking that. 'Not a chance. But we'll do it together if you wish.' As she opened her mouth to protest he added quickly, 'Where do you suggest we start?'

For once, Gemma refrained from making a snarky comment and shook her head helplessly. When she brushed away a tear, he even dared put one arm round her, but that was going too far and she shook him off.

'Fat lot you cared about her.'

He looked at her in surprise. 'Of course I cared and I care deeply that she's dead so young. Whatever gave you that idea?'

'You were the one who was unfaithful while you were in America. So you can't have loved Mum.'

'Ah. So that's what she told you.'

'Yes.'

'Well, it isn't true.'

'Don't lie to me. She told me all about it. Someone wrote to her about it.'

Not possible because it had never happened. 'I was never unfaithful to her in the whole time we were together.' But he suspected that Judith had been unfaithful to him while he was in America.

Why else would she suddenly want a divorce?

'Easy to say when she's not here to contradict you.'

'I can only tell you the truth.'

When Gemma turned away from him, he tried to build a bridge without blackening his dead wife's name. 'It was Judith who asked for a divorce. I hadn't been unfaithful. I swear that by your best teddy bear.'

That familiar oath, which Gemma had created as a child because she didn't like anyone saying 'Cross my heart and hope to *die*', brought her up short and she frowned at him.

'Judith told *me* she'd fallen out of love with me.' He returned his daughter's gaze without flinching. 'By that, I assumed she'd met someone else.'

'Easy to say that when she isn't here to defend herself.'

'I'm not going to labour the point for that very reason: she isn't here to put her side. It's up to you whether you believe me or not.'

He hadn't wanted to lose touch with his only child as he'd seen happen with other divorced men. And yet, in spite of his efforts to keep the peace, it had happened to him, too.

He took a few rubbish bin liners off the roll and handed them to his daughter. 'All right. Let's get this job done. How about you go through her clothes? Keep anything you want as a memento. Put the good things in one bag, the throwaway clothes in another. Your decision. We'll take the good things to the charity shop and the rest to the rubbish tip. I'll go through

89

your mother's drawers.'

'I should do that.'

'You think I haven't seen her underwear before?' And he knew Judith had concealed things in her drawers, so he wasn't risking Gemma finding something that would destroy her illusions about her mother.

Without a word, she took the bin liners from him and went into the walk-in wardrobe. He heard her sniffle and blow her nose, and though her back was towards him, he saw her hand raise a tissue towards her face a couple of times, presumably to wipe her eyes. He didn't dare offer any comfort. Well, what comfort was there when you'd just lost your mother?

Sighing, he began to investigate the contents of the two matching chests of drawers: tallboys, Judith had called them when she inherited them from her grandmother. They didn't match the décor of this modern house but they were beautifully made pieces and she'd wanted to keep them, even though they made the room feel crowded.

He ran one hand across the polished wood of the nearest top, which had a neat inlaid border at the edges with black stringing, then forced himself to start on the job. He decided to work his way up the drawers from the biggest one at the bottom to the smallest at the top. He didn't know why he chose to work that way, it just seemed right, because you couldn't pile big empty ones on little ones as easily, could you?

Underwear, far sexier than she'd worn for him, went into the big plastic bag, followed by equally sexy nightdresses. They looked just about new so he asked Gemma which bag had the good things in and shoved them in as well.

To his relief there was nothing incriminating.

As he was pushing the last emptied drawer of the second chest back in, it stuck. It was the top one and jiggling it about made no difference. Pulling it out again, he bent his head to peer into the shoulder-height hole, thinking some piece of clothing must have been caught at the back.

To his surprise he could see a small piece of wood sticking out in one corner. When he reached in and tried to move it, it jerked and with a loud click the carved outer panel on that side opened. 'What on earth — ?'

Gemma peered out of the walk-in wardrobe. 'Something wrong? Oh. That must be the secret hiding place. Mum once told me there was one in one of the chests, but she wouldn't tell me where it was or how to open it. She said I had to wait till I was twenty-one.'

His heart sank. What were they going to find?

'I wonder if there's anything in it.' He touched the panel and found it opened wider, showing a tall, thin space with narrow shelves. The top two had big envelopes, presumably full of papers, standing upright on them, held in by strips of what was clearly modern elastic strung across from old brass hooks. The other shelves held small boxes, the sort which usually contained hatpins or sets of buttons.

He looked at his daughter. 'There are quite a few things hidden in it. Who'd have thought?'

As she reached out to pick up the nearest

packet, he blocked her hand. 'I'll deal with whatever it is.'

Gemma glared at him. 'I'm staying here. You're not hiding anything of Mum's things from me. She might have left me a letter, in case. People do, you know.'

He'd intended to send her away, just in case there was anything incriminating, but Gemma had that stubborn look on her face and if there was a letter for her she had a right to see it. 'Since you insist.'

If she didn't like what they found, she'd just have to accept it. 'I won't hide anything, but I'm going to take all these bits and pieces out first and put them on the bed. You can watch but I'll open them. If you try to interfere, I'll lock you out of the room again.'

With a disgusted look, she stepped back and folded her arms across her chest. 'All right. Go ahead, play Mr Dictator.'

'Sometimes you forget that you're still a child and I'm the parent.'

'You've never let me forget it. Mum was a lot kinder to me than you.' She sobbed suddenly and clapped one hand to her mouth. But she shoved his arm away as he would have put it round her for comfort and grabbed a tissue from the box to wipe her eyes.

He opened the first package, which proved to contain letters, all in the same handwriting, and using the same type of notepaper and envelope. They were addressed simply to 'Judith' and must have been given to her by hand. When he opened the top one, he quickly realised it was a love letter to his wife. He glanced at the date: a month after he'd gone to America. It was signed by a man she'd worked with for several years.

He stared at it in shock and disgust. It was a few moments before he realised that Gemma had come to stand next to him and had also read the letter. He spoke gently, 'Darling, this isn't for your eyes.'

'I've seen it now.' She looked at him with anguish on her face. 'I can't believe it. I've met Guy a few times and he's a horrible, smarmy creature. How could she?'

Adam hadn't liked Guy Fenton either.

'She said *you* had been unfaithful.'

'I told you I wasn't, Gemma.'

The silence that followed seemed fraught with their unvoiced thoughts and reactions, then he folded up the letter. 'I'll read a couple of the most recent ones and that's it: I'm going to burn the rest unread.'

'Send them to that man's wife!' Gemma said. 'I've met her, too. She seemed really nice. She deserves to know the truth.'

'No, darling. I won't do something as unkind as that.' He stared down at the envelopes, so many of them. It seemed ridiculously old-fashioned in a computer age to handwrite love letters instead of sending emails, but perhaps that had seemed romantic to the two people involved.

No need to check that Fenton knew Judith was dead, thank goodness. Only why hadn't the fellow been at her funeral? Others from her workplace had paid their respects.

Adam knew he ought to feel outraged, or something similar, but apart from disgust at having her cheating confirmed, he felt numb more than anything, had done since they rang and told him his forty-one-year-old ex-wife had dropped dead at work and suggested he might wish to tell his daughter.

He kept a surreptitious eye on Gemma, worried at how this might be affecting her. He saw her swallow hard, still looking shocked. She blinked her eyes to get rid of tears, but didn't make one of her spiky remarks aimed at him, thank goodness.

He wished now that he'd obeyed his first instinct and made her leave the room so that he could check the contents of the hiding place in private. Only if he'd done that, she'd still be blaming him for cheating on his wife, instead of realising it had been the other way round. And he wanted desperately to win her love again. She had been such an adorable little girl.

'Daddy's Princess' was an overused cliché, but nonetheless it described perfectly how he'd felt about his only child . . . still did.

Setting the love letters aside, he looked at the next bundle of letters, hesitating, absolutely dreading now what else he might find. Perhaps Fenton hadn't been her only lover.

To his surprise, Gemma moved closer and slid her hand into his. 'It's terrible when someone dies and all their secrets are revealed. I never understood that before.'

'I think the worst was that your mother died so suddenly and so young. Most people clear out

94

their stuff as they grow older. Gemma . . . this doesn't really matter now, so we won't tell anyone. Agreed? And it doesn't affect the fact that your mother loved you.'

She hesitated then nodded.

He waited to see if she'd say anything else but she didn't, just knuckled away another couple of fat, slippery tears. Taking a deep breath he opened the next packet of letters.

'These are older, from her family mostly. They seem to be in date order.' He fanned through them, then gasped as he saw one of the early ones. Even after all these years he recognised that elegant italic handwriting.

Before he could hide it, Gemma said, 'That one's addressed to you.'

'Yes. I wonder when it arrived?' He squinted at the date stamp and saw in shock that it had been posted the same year he came out to Australia. It must have arrived just before he and Judith got married after their whirlwind romance.

Gemma looked at him in puzzlement. 'Hadn't you seen it before?'

'No.'

'Who's it from? Do you recognise the handwriting?'

'Yes. A girl I used to go out with.'

'Why did Mum open it, do you think?'

'I don't know.' Relieved that his daughter seemed to believe him, he turned it round in his hands, staring at it through a blur of emotion. It brought back so many memories just to see that handwriting.

'Aren't you going to read it?'

'I think we should let the past go. Whatever's in that letter can't matter now.'

'I don't agree. It must be important if Mum kept it all these years.'

He was so relieved that his daughter was still talking to him civilly that he did as she suggested and held the letter so that they could both read it. She pressed closer to him and when he put his arm round her, she didn't pull away.

'Oh, no!' Gemma clapped one hand to her mouth, made a little mewling noise of pain and burrowed her head against his chest for a moment or two.

He didn't know what to say or do. His thoughts were spinning in a surge of fury and dismay. It was immediately obvious why Judith had kept the letter from him: she hadn't wanted anything to stop them marrying. But even though they'd been living together at the time, she'd had no right to open his mail. And it had been unconscionable to keep a letter as important as this from him.

He looked sideways at his tense, white-faced daughter. 'I don't know what to say.'

'Could it be true? Technically, I mean. Did you have an affair with this Dorothy Redman woman while you were courting my mother?'

'Not exactly. I've never played around with two women at once. I wouldn't do that. I knew Dorothy before I left England, but I hadn't met your mother then.'

She looked at him in puzzlement. 'But Mum always said you two met when she was on holiday in England. You met in Brighton, near the Pavilion, and kept in touch because you'd fallen in love.'

'Judith's aunt upset her by saying the two of us would never last and she accused me of using Judith to get permission to stay permanently in Australia. So Judith and I agreed to pretend that we'd known one another for longer, that we'd met when she visited England the year before.'

'You can't have loved that other woman if you left her behind.'

'I thought I loved her. I was going to send for her, but then I met your mother and I knew it hadn't been a lasting sort of love with Dorothy. I thought it'd be kinder just to vanish from her life, then she could blame me.'

'If you were so much in love with Mum in those days, what went wrong?'

'I don't know. Judith would never discuss it except to say she was bored by me and fed up of me going away. It started during that year where I had to work really long hours because a colleague was ill.' Was that really why Judith had gone astray? Because of his frequent absences? Or had she had other affairs? What did that matter now?

Gemma brought him back to the present. 'What would you have done if you'd known that this Dorothy person was pregnant before you married Mum?' She tapped the letter.

'Who knows? Gone back to England, I suppose. Accepted the responsibility, even if I did nothing else about it.'

'If you had gone back, you might not have returned to Australia. You might even have married her and then I wouldn't exist. That'd make your life easier now, wouldn't it?' She pulled away from him suddenly.

'Don't be silly. I'm glad you exist. I love you to pieces and always have done since you grasped one of my fingers in the hospital just after you were born. If we're being brutally frank, you're the main reason I stayed with your mother for so long. I didn't want her keeping me away from you.'

'How do I know that's true?'

'Teddy bear's honour.'

Again, the old phrase stopped her in her tracks. It was a silly oath, but she knew he'd never lied to her when he used it. They'd only used that phrase to make important statements to one another. Would it still convince her that what he was telling her was true? He prayed so.

Gemma moved away from him, shoving her hands in the pockets of her jeans and giving him that don't-touch-me look again. But behind it he could see pain and doubt.

Oh, his heart ached for her! She was too young to understand the tangles people got into with their relationships. Too young to know the truth of the French phrase: *tout passe, tout lasse, tout casse.* Everything did pass in the end, and you did grow weary of things, even of being angry at your ex-wife. He wasn't as sure that everything broke, but the journey to acceptance of change could still hurt.

There was silence, then he folded the letter, put it back into the envelope and slipped it into his inner pocket. 'I need time to think about this.

Please, Gemma, don't tell anyone else.'

'As if I would. I'm not *proud* of what Mum did.'

The question he couldn't possibly answer was: if he pursued this now, after all these years, would he make things worse for Dorothy? Would he even be able to find her again? A lot could have happened in eighteen years. She might not even be alive.

Had she had the baby — his baby — or had she lost it? There wasn't a second letter from her in the package.

'What are you going to do about it, Dad?'

'I'm not sure. Make enquiries, at least. Perhaps go to England. If Dorothy did have my child, I'd want to meet it.'

'Can I come too? The child would be my brother or sister.'

He took a sudden decision. 'We could go during the Christmas holidays, perhaps? Most schools and universities are closed for the whole of January.'

'I don't want to celebrate Christmas this year.'

'We won't decide anything yet. It's been a big shock — I can't see my way clearly. But I won't do anything without discussing it with you, working it out together. Will that be all right?' And it wouldn't hurt her to have a gap year.

She nodded, but she didn't meet his eyes and she'd hunched her shoulders again, as if trying to keep the whole world at a distance.

Well, both of them had had a bad shock today, hadn't they? It would take some getting used to.

And what the hell was he going to do about

99

this new problem? Hadn't he enough to deal with?

Only . . . what if he did have another daughter or a son? Adam had to find out. He couldn't live with uncertainty about something so important.

Part Two

8

After a few weeks of living with Victor and recovering some of her old energy, Elise confided in him, 'Mary and Kerry are my closest relatives now, Victor. I don't like to be estranged from them and I think they've learnt their lesson about interfering in my life.'

'You're more forgiving than I would be.'

She gave him a wry smile. 'I'm no saint and I do have an ulterior motive. If I cut all connections with them, I'll be cutting ties with Mary's daughter, Harriet, who has always been a favourite of mine. I used to look after her in the school holidays. I'd like to invite them to tea here, if you don't mind.'

'I don't mind, but will they come, do you think?'

'Who knows? Probably they will, if only out of sheer curiosity. I also want Mary and Kerry to learn that older people can still have a life. We don't all get dementia like Mary's poor mother-in-law did. They had a terrible time with her and I'm sure it coloured the way she dealt with me.' She waited a moment then added, 'Well? Would you mind?'

He took her hand and gave it a squeeze. 'I'll back you in anything you want, my dear, you know that. You're welcome to invite any of your friends or relatives here.'

★ ★ ★

When Elise phoned Mary there was a gasp and her niece asked, 'Is something wrong?'

'No, nothing's wrong except that I don't want to be estranged from my only remaining relatives. Life is too short to hold grudges, so I'd like to invite you and Harriet to tea on Saturday, Kerry too, if she wants to drive over here.'

'Oh. Well. Thank you. I was only trying to look after you. Truly I was.'

'I know. But I can look after myself.'

'I'm afraid of you having another fall in that house. You really ought not to live alone at your age.'

'I'm not alone. I'm living with Victor for the time being.'

'You're still there? Are you two together now?'

'Not in that way, no. I'm only here temporarily. There isn't room for a studio or we might have shared this house. We and our spouses knew one another for several decades. He's a very good friend, but only a friend.'

'But there was a studio in that home I found for you! I made sure of that.'

'Mary, I'll say it one last time: I couldn't bear to live in a group situation. I need peace and quiet to paint. I'm not an amateur; I'm *selling* my paintings regularly and I get two or three hundred pounds each.'

Another gasp. '*That much?*'

'Yes. And I have an agent interested in handling my work. I'm not only *not* retiring, I'm going to be working harder than ever before at my painting. But not in my old home. You're right about one thing. I can't manage that place.'

She waited, holding her breath, hoping this admission would soften Mary, and from her niece's softer tone of voice it did.

'Well, I'm glad to hear that.'

'So you'll come to tea? And bring Harriet?'

'Yes. I don't think Kerry will be able to make it, though. It's her best friend's birthday this weekend.'

'All right. Just you and Harriet — and Ian, of course, if he's not playing golf.'

Her voice sounded bitter. 'My dear husband always plays golf on Sundays, even in the rain. It takes snow or a thunderstorm to stop him.'

Elise knew better than to comment on Ian, who was a cold fish in her opinion. 'Right then, just the two of you. Four o'clock suit you?'

'Yes. We'll be there.'

*   *   *

On the Friday, Victor drove Elise to the shops because his housekeeper had called in sick a couple of days ago and they were running out of fresh food. She also wanted to buy something special for the tea party.

He seemed to be walking more slowly than usual but she knew he'd hate her to comment. She stopped a couple of times to look in shop windows and give him a break, wondering whether to suggest he go back to the car and wait while she grabbed a few groceries.

If she'd been at home, she'd have ordered

some groceries online and had them delivered, but Victor hated computers. Strange, that.

As they stood outside the cake shop she usually patronised, staring in the window, he suddenly grunted and pressed one hand to his chest. Then he fell before she could catch him, not making another sound or moving, just lying perfectly still on the floor.

Shock held her motionless for a moment, because she'd seen that look before and it hurt, it always hurt to lose someone you loved.

Bystanders rushed to help and she couldn't even get down to hold him, because she was still using her stick for walking and had to be careful how she moved. And in any case, what could she have done? Nothing except say goodbye.

A complete stranger began CPR and another put an arm round Elise's shoulders. 'Are you all right, dear?'

The woman meant to be kind, but the tone of voice was so much like someone speaking to a child that Elise stiffened her spine.

'Thank you. I'm as right as I can be when my dearest friend has just dropped dead.'

'They might be able to help him.'

'He's been ill for a while. I don't think he'd want to finish his life in a hospital.' She gestured to the figure on the floor. 'I've recently had a hip replacement, so I can't get down to him.'

'Come and sit on this bench. You're looking rather pale.'

She allowed herself to be guided to the bench and watched the stranger who was trying to resuscitate Victor. The man wasn't having any success and Victor's face looked so peaceful, she nearly told him not to bother.

It had been quick, at least Victor had had that mercy.

There was the sound of an ambulance siren outside the small shopping centre, coming closer and then stopping. Two paramedics appeared in the entrance and a man waved them across.

They got out a defibrillator. She wished they wouldn't do this to him.

Victor had said one evening, very quietly, 'When I go, don't let them make any heroic attempts to revive me. I don't want to live as a half-man.'

Younger people wouldn't understand that, but she did, because she felt the same. She didn't want to live a half-life, dependent on others for everything, tied to a bed or chair.

'Do you want to drive to the hospital with your husband?'

'Yes. Yes, please.' She didn't contradict their error because Victor would have wanted her to stay with him.

He didn't start breathing again and the paramedics looked at her, shaking their heads.

They were young enough to need reassurance, so she said quietly, 'You did your best.'

At the hospital they rushed his body away and a nurse took her to one side.

'Is there someone we can call to be with you?'

'Yes. His nephew.' She didn't have Gordon's number on her phone, so she gave them the name of the legal practice where he worked.

Then she sat and waited. Numb. Sad. Alone again.

Gordon arrived a short time later. 'Are you all right, Mrs Carlton?'

'Yes. I was half-expecting something like this. He tried to hide it but he wasn't at all well.'

'No. He knew he hadn't long to live. Heart condition. He wouldn't let them do anything else, said he'd had enough treatment.'

'Sometimes people know when it's their time. I'd better move my things out of the house and go home again.'

'There's no hurry. Look, if I put you in a taxi, can you go back and wait for me? Shall I ring your niece?'

'No. I'm perfectly capable of looking after myself. Victor's car is still at the shopping centre, though. Someone should fetch it. I can't take it back. I'm not allowed to drive yet.'

'I'll send Peter from the office. Do you have a key to my uncle's house?'

'Yes.'

He hesitated. 'My uncle asked me to keep an eye on you if anything happened to him. Are you OK with that?'

'He was always one to plan ahead.'

Gordon gave her a sad smile. 'Oh, yes. All his financial matters are in order, the funeral planned, everything. I've things to do here then I'll set it all going. Will you be all right staying there till tomorrow morning? I'll come round and speak to you then and help you make plans.'

'I'll be fine.' She didn't feel sure of that, was

daunted at the thought of clearing out her house and selling it on her own, but she wasn't going to admit it, not to anyone.

The house seemed very still without Victor smiling at her, chatting, making countless pots of tea. She was glad they'd had the time together before he died.

Now, she was the only one left of the four friends who'd met when they were so young.

How quickly life passed!

One thing she was certain about. She wasn't going to ask her niece for help this time. Somehow she'd manage.

If only she had more spare money, though! That lack was going to make the necessary changes more difficult.

★   ★   ★

That evening she rang her niece and told her that Victor had died and she was moving back home.

There was a silence, then Mary asked in a tight voice, 'Do you need any help?'

'No, thank you.'

'Let me know if you do.'

'I'll be fine.'

'I won't try to put you in a home again.'

But Mary would still try to organise things her way. 'I know. I'll bear you in mind if I do need help, but I'll be fine.'

Just as she was going to bed, Gordon rang. 'I'd like to come round tomorrow at about ten o'clock, if that's all right with you.'

'Yes. I'm always up at six, so come whenever you like after that.'

He'd want her out of the house. And that was one thing she could do on her own, pack, get ready to leave.

But she was dreading the next few steps because not only did she still tire easily but there were a lot of things she couldn't physically manage yet.

★   ★   ★

When the doorbell rang at eight o'clock the following morning, Elise went to peep out of the window before she opened it, to check that it wasn't her niece. She didn't feel she could face Mary yet. And if that was cowardly, well, there you were. She was about to go back to a comfortless house and manage on her own. That took all the bravery she had left.

But the caller was a pleasant surprise. She hurried to open the door. 'Harriet! How lovely to see you, dear!' Elise had seen quite a bit of her great-niece when she was younger. Mary had sometimes needed an after-school babysitter and in those days she hadn't had much money to pay for one.

But Elise hadn't seen much of Harriet in the last year or two. The scrawny child with braces on her teeth had grown up into a very nice-looking young woman, not pretty but surprisingly elegant in a casual way.

'I'm on my way into town to meet some friends and Dad dropped me off here. I didn't

110

think you'd mind me turning up unannounced.'

'I'm delighted. Come in quickly. It's really chilly this morning. Winter is almost upon us.'

Elise shut the door, then turned to find herself gathered into a big hug.

She clung to Harriet for a few moments, then pulled back and tried to smile. 'What brought that on?'

'You looked so desperately sad, as if you needed a hug. Mum told me about Mr Pinkett dying. I'm really sorry. I know you and he were close friends. Anyway, I haven't seen you for ages, so I wanted to hug you.'

'You can do that any time.'

Harriet grinned. 'I must say, you're looking better than I expected from what Mum said. You know what she's like, always expecting something to go wrong. Can I con you out of a cup of coffee?'

'Yes, of course.' She led the way into the kitchen and put the kettle on. Such a comforting ritual. 'I presume you're home on your Christmas break. What are you going to do with yourself?'

'Look for a holiday job.' She rubbed her forefinger and thumb together. 'Money is in short supply.'

'Tell me about it.'

Harriet looked at her in shock. 'But Uncle Tom had a good job and left you with that big house.'

'He was persuaded to convert his superannuation into one that only lasted for his lifetime, so when he died it did as well. He never thought he'd die before me, you see, because I was always the one falling ill.'

'I'm so sorry.'

'I'll be all right for money once I've sold the house. Well, I will as long as I buy something that costs less than I get for the present house.'

They had a coffee together and Elise listened to tales of the young man Harriet had been going out with lately, with a mention of the good results she'd got in the term's examinations thrown in with feigned casualness at the end.

Then Harriet glanced at the clock. 'Got to go. I'll come round to see you in a day or two. Let Mum and me know when you move back home.'

Her great-niece's visit had left Elise feeling much more cheerful. How a sourpuss like Mary and a dull man like Ian could produce such a lively, cheerful young daughter surprised her every time she saw the family together.

★   ★   ★

By the time Gordon arrived, Elise had packed her things, cleared up the kitchen and was ready to leave. He looked brisk and successful, was wearing a black tie and was accompanied by his chief clerk Peter.

Elise took the initiative the minute they came through the door. 'I'm ready to leave. I've only to call a taxi.'

'There's no need for you to rush away, Mrs Carlton. You could stay for a day or two longer if you wished, though my uncle did arrange to have the funeral from here, so if you can be out by Thursday . . . '

'I might as well go now. I've got a lot to do at home.'

'Could we sit down a few moments? I've something to tell you.'

She led the way into the sitting room. They waited for her to sit down. Gordon not only looked like his uncle had as a younger man, he had the same good manners.

'I have to be blunt, I'm afraid. How are you going to manage? Victor said you were short of money.'

'Short, yes, but not completely without.' She'd decided to pawn some of her jewellery but they didn't need to know that.

'You won't be able to drive yet, either.'

'No. But I will in a couple of weeks.'

'My uncle knew he was failing fast, so he changed his will and left you a little money.' He held up one hand to stop her protesting. 'Not a lot, just enough to tide you over till you can sell your house and find somewhere more suitable to live.'

She had to dab away the tears before she could reply. 'Oh, how kind of him! But I can't take Victor's money.'

'It's in the will; you can't avoid taking it. And I approve.'

'Oh.'

'He suggested I give you an advance on it if the worst happened, though he was hoping he'd live for another few months.'

'He never said how ill he was. He was as

cheerful as usual, just a little slower. I enjoyed his company greatly.'

'And he enjoyed yours. I want to thank you for making his last few weeks so happy. He was extremely fond of you.'

She had to blow her nose at that or she'd have wept, which wouldn't do. She had to be strong from now on. 'He saved me from being forced into a care home and gave me a respite here till this got better.' She indicated her hip. 'I'll be able to drive soon and then things will be a lot easier. In the meantime, thank goodness for online shopping. At least I'm online at home. Victor never really took to the Internet.'

'What do you really want to do? To stay till Thursday or go home today?'

'I'd rather go home today, if you don't mind. I'll call a taxi. There's a driver I use.' Ali would help her carry her things into the house, she was sure.

Gordon smiled. 'I thought you'd want to do that. My uncle said you always were very independent. That's why I brought Peter with me. He can drive you back and take you shopping on the way. Oh, and you might as well have all the food from here. I'm the main heir, you see, and I'm going to be selling this house, so you'll be helping me by clearing out the kitchen.'

He was trying to make her feel better about this gift, so she didn't protest.

He fumbled in his pocket and pulled out an envelope. 'Here's an advance on your little legacy.'

114

She took it without looking and shoved it in her handbag with a nod of thanks.

Gordon stood up. 'If that's all for the moment, I'll get on with my day. I'll let you know about the funeral arrangements and send a car to pick you up for the funeral, Mrs Carlton.'

When he'd gone, Peter looked at her shrewdly. 'You look tired. How about I pack up the stuff in the kitchen?'

'Thank you. I'm not a hundred per cent recovered yet, but they tell me I'm doing fine. It takes it out of you at my age, having a major operation.'

'It takes it out of you at any age.'

She sat down on the sofa and almost pulled out the envelope to look at how much money Victor had left her. But the cushions looked so soft and inviting, she leant back to have a little rest first . . .

★   ★   ★

When Elise woke up, she glanced automatically at her watch. Noon. Oh, no! She must have fallen asleep. She got up, stretching carefully and slowly, but as she moved, she bumped into a small table and the clatter brought Peter to the doorway.

'You're awake, sleepy-head.'

'I'm so sorry. You should have woken me.'

'Why? It's taken me until about ten minutes ago to sort out the kitchen. I had to go up and find a couple of suitcases in the end, there was so much food. Mr Pinkett always did like to keep a good stock in hand. I hope you've got a big freezer.'

'Um, yes.' Almost empty at the moment.

'Are you ready to go now?'

'I'll just use the bathroom first.'

As she was getting into the car she paused to look back at the house where she'd spent so many happy hours over the years. She'd miss this place as well as its owner.

* * *

'I'll carry everything in and unpack the food for you,' Peter said as they drove off.

'Don't you have work to do?'

'Mr Pinkett said my main job today was getting you settled in.'

'He's being very kind.'

'He'd hate anyone to know how soft-hearted he is. He's just as nice as his uncle.'

They stopped at the shops on the way home for some more food and she allowed herself one or two small treats. She could afford a bar of chocolate and she loved fresh fruit. Victor had mostly managed with tinned fruit, which seemed to taste more of sugar than fruit.

When she'd finished Peter took her home.

She got out of the car and sighed as she looked at her house. So depressing to see it looking shabby and unloved. She tried not to show her feelings and chatted as cheerfully as she could while Peter brought in more things than she'd have believed possible from Victor's house, as well as the fresh food she'd bought today. He unpacked them as she sat in the kitchen giving directions.

When he'd put everything away and taken her personal items up to her bedroom, Peter looked at his watch. 'If there's nothing else you need, I'll be off.'

'No. Nothing. Thank you so much for your help and please thank Mr Pinkett for me as well.'

She watched Peter leave, then she had a cry. Just a little one. Better to get your feelings out, her mother had always said. Well, she couldn't hold them in any longer, so she had no choice. She'd miss Victor dreadfully.

Taking a deep breath Elise went into the kitchen. She was alone now, had to manage, because if she didn't, Mary would try to take over her life again.

'Just get on with it, you silly old woman,' she muttered and squared her shoulders. She could manage. Of course she could.

9

Stacy applied for several jobs and had a couple of narrow misses, where she was in the final group selected and had to go for a second interview. She was desperate to get away because she kept seeing Darren at different shopping centres, and that couldn't have been a coincidence.

He couldn't be there to shop because he was never carrying any shopping bags or packages. He was simply ambling round the various centres, watching her from a distance.

She was waiting for the court order to be finalised, then he would have to stay over one hundred yards away from her at all times in public or near her place of residence.

Although he never came near her in the shopping centres, he smirked at her every time he saw her looking in his direction. Once he mimed holding a pistol to his head and pulling the trigger, doing it so quickly she doubted anyone else would have noticed the gesture.

After the second encounter, she didn't see him for a week and as the court order had come through now, she began to hope he'd given up tormenting her. Then he popped up again just as she was relaxing, staying the required distance away from her but making sure she saw him. That upset her so much she left the shopping centre without buying half the things she'd come for, too spooked to stay.

What had got into him? Whatever it was, it was upsetting her more than a little and she was afraid in a way she'd never experienced before. A couple of times she had been woken in the middle of the night by a clanking dustbin lid or a poor imitation of a cat yowling. When she looked out of her bedroom window, she was pretty sure the figure she saw in the car park of the flats, staring up at her flat and once even waving, was Darren.

Everywhere she went, whatever she did, fear seemed to hover beside her or creep up behind her. Sometimes she'd spin round thinking he was nearby, but see nothing untoward.

Her workmates kept asking why she was so jumpy and she was too ashamed to explain, so made an excuse about not sleeping properly.

Then she heard of a job through a friend who knew what was going on in her life. Lou had spoken to the guy, who was called Ellis, and told him about Stacy's problems and why she would prefer not to give references from the place where she was currently working. Ellis had offered to hold the job until he could speak to her about it.

Stacy hugged her friend.

'No time like the present.' Lou got out her iPad and contacted Ellis.

Ellis questioned Stacy in detail about her experience, and she thought she managed to show a sound understanding of the tasks involved. She must have done all right because he offered her the job on the spot.

'You clearly know your stuff, Stacy, and I trust

my cousin Lou's judgement about people.'

When they'd switched off, she hugged Lou again and shed a few tears of sheer relief. 'You won't tell anyone where I'm going, will you?'

'Of course not.'

The job was in Swindon and as it was on a contract that would last about four months, Stacy felt it would give her time to decide whether she wanted to settle in that part of the country permanently.

It would also be long enough to see if Darren managed to trace her. She'd heard it was a beautiful rural county and she'd never visited it before, so had no connections there. Surely that would make it safer?

When she gave in her notice, she told the HR people about her ex stalking her, so that they'd not give him any information. But she didn't tell them where she was going; instead she told them she was going overseas and asked them to forward any mail to her parents.

There was another bonus to this job. She didn't even have to look for somewhere to live. Her new employer happened to know a man who really was going overseas and wanted to rent out his flat for a few months only. He was looking for a trustworthy tenant through personal recommendation.

It all seemed meant to be.

★   ★   ★

The only major problem left was how to get to Swindon without Darren knowing where she'd gone. She lay awake worrying about that.

In the end, she went to a big, national removal firm and asked to speak to a woman manager. It might be sexist but she felt more comfortable telling another woman about her problems.

She was frank about her dilemma and was able to refer the woman to the police officer who had dealt with her for confirmation that she wasn't making this up.

'I'm sorry, but we have to be sure this isn't a burglary or one spouse cheating the other by taking all the household goods. You'd be amazed at some of the scams that have been tried. I'll just go and give the police a call.'

The woman returned a few minutes later. 'I was lucky. Your contact in the police was there and has corroborated your story.'

'Oh, thank goodness!'

'Don't worry, Ms Walsh. We've had other cases similar to yours. What we do is bring your possessions here, leave them in our storage area for a few days, then deliver them to you on an agreed date. We move them into another truck, and believe me, there are enough vehicles coming in and out of our depot to make sure your ex can't tell which one contains your goods — even if he could keep watch every working hour, which isn't likely.'

Stacy closed her eyes for a few seconds in sheer relief. 'You'll ask the removal men not to tell anyone where I go?'

'Of course. We'll put Stan and Bill in charge of your delivery. They're older men and Stan has a daughter about your age, so he gets angry at the thought of young women being stalked. They've done this before and know how to keep their mouths shut, I promise you.'

Stalked! she thought as she drove away. She kept avoiding the word, but there was no doubt that's what Darren was doing. Who could ever have believed that the charming guy she'd married could turn into this cunning monster?

Stacy saw her possessions taken away from her house and did a bit of checking, driving past Darren's workplace to make sure his car was in its usual parking place.

After that she drove north up the motorway to stay with her parents for a few days. Even now, she stopped in a services to check that he wasn't following her. She waited half an hour, sitting in a table by the window, from which she could see all the vehicles driving into the car park. No sign of Darren's car.

He wouldn't know their new address, though he could no doubt find out. But she'd have moved on by then.

It felt as if she'd left a heavy load behind her.

★　★　★

When she got there, she burst into tears and told her mum and dad what had been happening. They were horrified.

The next day her father had a long talk to her about security, and since he'd been in charge of that area in his old company, he knew a few things worth listening to.

'We'll not introduce you to our neighbours

here and we'll put your car in our garage straight away. I don't think the other people in the street are home from work yet. No, you stay there, Stacy. Your mother and I will swap the cars around. Give me your car keys.'

She fumbled in her handbag. 'Is this necessary? After all, he doesn't live near here.'

'You can't be too careful.'

★　★　★

That night the dog across the road suddenly started barking furiously and when Stacy peeped carefully out of the window, she saw the neighbour come out into his garden.

Her father spoke from the doorway and she jumped in shock.

'I thought that would've woken you,' he said. 'I won't let anything happen to you while you're here, love.'

'Thanks. Does the dog bark a lot?'

He hesitated. 'Mick was burgled last year. He's trained that dog to bark if there are prowlers. Don't go outside or even draw the curtains back! If it's Darren, he'll not know for certain that you're here.'

He went out to join the neighbour and they let the dog off the lead. It ran off up the street and there was more furious barking and a man's voice shouting, followed by a car starting up round the corner. The neighbour ran to try to see its number plate, but he was too late.

'Mick thinks it was a red car,' Stacy's father said when he came back a few moments later.

'Did the neighbour see this intruder well enough to describe him?'

'A man, he said, tall and thin. So it could have been Darren.'

'How did he find me so quickly?' Stacy whispered.

'It's probably our fault,' her mother said. 'We didn't think to keep our new address secret from our friends or our old neighbours, because we didn't know how bad things were for you. He could have got it from any of them.'

'You shouldn't have to keep things secret. You'll be needing to advertise your B&B soon and word of mouth from friends is important.'

'We won't need to advertise our B&B until the extensions are finished and Darren may have been caught harassing you by then. Or he may even have given up on you.'

She didn't think he would and from his next words, nor did her father.

'We can't be too careful.'

'Surely Darren won't come back tomorrow as well? Not after being chased away tonight.'

'Who knows? Just a precaution.' Her father looked at her solemnly. 'I've made friends with a guy near here who's an ex-policeman and I'm going to pick his brain.'

'He may think I'm exaggerating.'

'Not if I tell him you're a sensible lass.'

'Am I? I married Darren, after all, and let him boss me around and treat me like a doormat.'

'We all make mistakes and we thought he was a nice enough guy, even though he wasn't our sort of person.'

The following evening her father sat beside her on the sofa after tea. 'Look, I've been speaking to my friend. When he heard how tenacious Darren's been, he said we should take this very seriously indeed.'

'Believe me, I am.' She was uprooting her whole life, wasn't she?

'I don't think you ought go out of the house at all tomorrow. And we'll leave your car in the garage with the blinds drawn on the windows. There are a few other things we could do. My friend says you should change cars. We can leave yours round at his farm and I'll sell it once you've left. I'll take it round there after dark tonight and he'll run me back.'

She felt a chill shiver down her spine. Her father wasn't given to fanciful imagining.

'We'll buy another car for you from a newspaper advert and I'll pay for it by bank cheque. You should change banks, too, as well as buying yourself a new computer and scrapping the old one.' He looked at her grimly.

She was puzzled. 'Why?'

'He could have bugged it while you were married to keep track of what you were doing. Men like that try to control everything their wife does.'

She was beyond words.

Her father let that sink in, then added, 'Think about changing your service provider, too, if Darren is with the same company.'

'He is.'

'Then you'd better change.'

She lay awake for half the night worrying about what else Darren might do, worrying about her parents' safety too.

It was like living in a nightmare.

★   ★   ★

In spite of her anxiety and the need to keep out of sight, the few days spent with her parents had their pleasant side. But once she had chosen and insured a new car, which had also been taken straight to the farm, she steeled herself to leave. Living here would be taking advantage of their kindness and might even be putting them in danger.

She couldn't help being secretly envious of them, though. They were so happily busy, so much in love still.

They told her to come back and stay with them if the job didn't lead to anything more permanent, but she wasn't going to impose on them again if she could help it. They'd just moved into this lovely new home and were busy with the addition of a couple of en suite bathrooms and a small extension containing a conservatory and sitting room for their own use.

She tried to keep cheerful and not let her anxieties show, but saw how they watched her. As if people who knew her so well wouldn't guess how upset she was!

★   ★   ★

She left before dawn. Her father took her to the farm and she transferred her things to the new car, which filled it up, because there were not only clothes and necessities, but her computer and some basic art materials.

As she set off, she tried to look on the bright side. At least she had a job to go to, and with it the chance to start afresh.

She could only pray that Darren would meet another woman and get obsessed with her instead of stalking his ex-wife. Surely he'd come to his senses if she wasn't around? He wasn't a stupid man.

10

At last Angus received a phone call from someone called Dawn Harding, who introduced herself as dealing with heritage matters in the county and asked, 'Could my colleague and I come to see the hidden room you found?'

'Yes, of course. The sooner the better. I'm waiting to do up that house and rent it out.'

'I know and I'm sorry. Bureaucracies move slowly, but if the room's in as good a condition as Mr Budworth's notes say, we do need to protect it most carefully.'

'What do you mean by 'protect'?' He knew his voice had gone sharp but he couldn't help that. These delays were costing him time and money. The weather was going to get worse not better, it always did after Christmas, and while he believed in protecting historical artefacts, he needed to sort out this project to bring in money to run the big house. That was just as important as those artefacts, more important by far to him.

He intended to completely weatherproof the big house and deal with restorations to the rest of the interior later, because even a small problem could let in the weather and a lot of damage could be done to window frames before it was noticed.

'I can't say exactly what will be needed until I've seen the secret room for myself. I could come tomorrow morning if you're free?' She laughed gently. 'Is that quick enough for you, Mr Denning? And I'll bring a photographer with me, if I may.'

'My wife and I will meet you and your colleague at the house: Number 1 Saffron Lane.'

'Ten o'clock suit you?'

'Fine.' He put the phone down, muttering to himself as he went to find Nell. He couldn't share this Dawn person's humour about the situation. The repairs felt like a burden always weighing him down.

Thank goodness for Nell. She cheered him up, which helped a lot. He felt as if he'd known her much longer than a few months. Indeed, he didn't know how he'd kept sane without her.

He grinned as that thought sank in. Perhaps he hadn't been completely balanced in his outlook before. He was so lucky that she'd fallen in love with him in spite of his faults.

★ ★ ★

Dawn was an older woman, which Angus hadn't expected from her youthful-sounding voice. She looked at him somewhat warily and it wasn't till Nell dug him in the ribs and hissed, 'Smile!' that he realised he was scowling.

Fortunately Nell defused the situation by smiling and holding out her hand. 'I'm Angus's partner, Nell. I'm pleased to meet you, Miss Harding.'

'Do call me Dawn. And this is Mac. He's going to take some photographs if it's all right with you.'

129

Angus tried not to scowl and failed. 'Does it matter what we want?'

'Of course it does. Look, I'm sorry if the delays have upset you, but Mr Budworth died last week, so it was unavoidable. He isn't easy to replace. I'm standing in for him and I'll do my best, but I don't have anything like his breadth of knowledge.'

'Ah. I'm sorry.' He ran one hand through his hair and said, 'Perhaps we should start again. I'm not usually so grumpy.'

Nell threaded her arm through his. 'My husband was ready to make a start on renovating the whole row of houses, had his plans charted in detail and he gets very single-minded when he's working on a project.'

'It must be annoying to have to wait, but it's exciting too, don't you think? We will try to hurry things up, I promise you.'

'Let's go and look at the room,' Angus said. 'I'd love to know more about it, but we haven't liked to touch anything.'

'Very wise.'

When they went into it, Dawn sucked in her breath sharply. 'I hadn't realised it was still complete. My goodness, this is a treasure trove, Mr Denning, a *national* treasure trove. I don't think anyone can have touched it since they closed it up.'

Mac walked slowly round the central table, starting to take photographs.

'We'll bring in a team and work here on the premises, if you don't mind. That'll give us so much more authentic detail. I wonder . . . ' He

130

looked questioningly at Dawn. 'Are you thinking what I am?'

'The Kinnaird Trust?'

'Yes. This would be perfect.'

They turned as one to Angus. 'Jason Kinnaird's father, Stanley Kinnaird, worked in intelligence during World War II. Jason wants to set up a museum exhibit in honour of his father and those who worked behind the scenes. They didn't cop much recognition or gratitude, even after the war, and were still bound by the Official Secrets Act, so what they'd done wasn't revealed until well after Stanley Kinnaird's death.'

She looked round and nodded again. 'This place might suit his son's purpose nicely. He's not rolling in money, but he can spare some and is very determined to set up a memorial to his father.'

'Well, I'm not looking to sell the house, so he'll have to look elsewhere if he wants to buy it,' Angus said firmly. 'I don't want my inheritance frittering away, and anyway, I have plans for these houses.'

Nell stepped in again, explaining about the artists' colony they'd been hoping to set up. The two visitors looked disappointed.

'Well, whatever we decide to do with this find,' Dawn said regretfully, 'we need to document it carefully, not only the individual items, but exactly how they've been set up. Perhaps we can make a start by spending an hour or two here taking photographs, Mr Denning?'

'Yes, of course. I'm happy for you to do that

131

before you dismantle it. I'll wait with you, if you don't mind.'

He could see that they'd have preferred to be left alone, but he didn't care. It was *his* house and street, *his* plans they were disrupting, so he intended to keep an eye on every single thing that went on here.

Later, when they'd gone, he locked up and went back to the big house, where he found Nell preparing their lunch in the kitchen.

'How did it go?'

'All right, I suppose. They were very tight-mouthed.'

'You didn't exactly try to win them over, love.'

'I want to get on with things and who knows how long they'll be now the other chap has died.'

'So what are you going to do about the renovations?'

'I'll have to leave Number 1 out of the schedule, and that means it'll cost more. The plumbers are ready to come in and they were going to do the whole row.'

'If you need some extra money, I could — '

'I'm *not* taking your nest egg.'

The air was fraught for a moment or two, because she knew how this was stretching his finances.

Then he picked her up and swung her round in a circle. 'Never mind the money. It's you I care about, and we'll manage somehow.'

But she did worry about the money. She helped him in every way she could but the old house was a demanding mistress, regularly springing surprises on them.

She'd been shocked at how much it would cost to run a heritage house like this one, even in a frugal manner.

But it was still a lovely building, inside and out. She too had fallen under its spell. There had to be some way to make use of its undoubted charm, there just had to.

★ ★ ★

When they heard nothing for two weeks, Angus sent a registered letter marked 'Urgent' to ask what was going on.

He received a telephone call from a woman called Miss Peberdy at the Imperial War Museum.

'I'm so sorry, Mr Denning. Discussions are under way with Jason Kinnaird about how to deal with the house and — '

'You're talking about *my* property here, so any discussions ought to involve me.'

'It's the nation's history *we* are concerned about.'

'I know that and I'm concerned too. I could easily have destroyed that room and its contents and no one would have been any wiser, but I didn't. So at least grant me that I've acted responsibly so far and include me in any further discussions.'

There was dead silence at the other end, then she said, 'Noted. I'll be in touch as soon as there's news,' and ended the call.

He stormed into the kitchen, where Nell was preparing their evening meal.

'Put that aside, love. I need to go to the pub and have a beer or two.'

'Tell me why.'

He explained, sounding so sharp, so unlike himself that she immediately set aside the cooking and went to get her coat. 'Are we walking?'

'If you don't mind. Apart from the fact that I don't like drinking and driving, I'd really welcome a brisk walk.'

'All right. I'll just change into my trainers. They're much easier on the feet.'

*   *   *

After meeting a couple of friends in the pub, Angus began to cheer up and they combined forces for the meal. A couple of hours later he and Nell set off home, going the back way, which was more direct.

They didn't talk much because they were both pleasantly tired, so when they saw a figure slip across the drive heading towards Saffron Lane, they stopped dead and she sighed in annoyance.

'Shh!' He leant closer to whisper, 'I'm going to see what that person is doing on my land.'

'We're both going.'

'All right, but stay back if there's any fighting. I'm going to try to catch whoever it is. Get your phone out. We'll both stay back and call the police if there's more than one intruder.'

They walked along the soft edge of the path, staying out of sight.

He squeezed her arm suddenly and pointed,

but she'd seen it too. A faint light in Number 1. It bobbed about a bit on the ground floor, then vanished into the rear.

'I wonder if someone's after the stuff in that room, and if so, how they found out about it. This is what you get from such slow responses to a situation. People hear about the find and figure they can rob you.'

But before they got to the front door of the house, there was a strangled yell from inside at the rear and a man's voice yelled, 'Get away from me!'

Nell heard a woman's voice but couldn't make out the words.

The man shouted, 'You can stop that. I don't believe in ghosts. This is a trick. I've seen it done on the stage with mirrors.' Then he yelped suddenly and shouted, 'Keep away!'

They were close enough now to see a light shining from the rear of the house.

'What's that?' she whispered. 'It's too bright for a torch.'

'I don't know. Let's see what happens.' Angus put an arm round her and they stood just outside Number 1, able to see what was going on through the large shop window.

'It's *got* to be a trick,' the intruder repeated, as if trying to psych himself up but he backed out of the rear into the front room.

Nell saw a transparent figure follow him, stopping for a few moments in the doorway. It was a woman dressed in 1930s clothing. Light seemed to be flickering around her, sending shadows dancing along the walls.

'What's going on?' Angus asked.

'Can't you see the figure?'

'No.'

She watched as the woman began to drift slowly across the floor, hovering at least a foot above it and saying, 'Go away, Brendon Simcox, and never return.'

'How the hell did you know my name?' The man edged away, looking shaken.

A piece of wood lifted from the floor and whizzed through the air towards him. Another followed it almost immediately, taking him by surprise and hitting him on the side of the head.

'How the hell did that happen?' Angus asked.

'Ghostly magic.' Nell couldn't help smiling at how simple a thing it was to terrify the intruder.

With a strangled yelp, the man turned tail and pushed out of the front door, upon which Angus grabbed him.

He let out a screech of shock and terror, and after a desperate struggle, managed to get away and flee into the darkness, crashing through the bushes.

The ghost laughed softly. '*I worked in this house during the war. It was a very special place. I'm not letting him raid it.*'

She began to vanish, the light flickering softly as she faded, showing a very pretty face.

'I suppose you saw the ghost,' Angus said in a resigned tone.

'Yes, I did. I think it was Melinda Denning. There's a photo of her in the library.'

He sighed. 'I wish I could see her.' He raised his voice and called, 'Thank you.'

But there was no response and no further sound or flickering light.

Angus checked the rest of the house before locking the door again, then Nell linked her arm in his and they walked home.

11

For all his IT skills, Adam had difficulty tracing his one-time girlfriend. He found her marriage certificate to someone called Lionel Dobson, surprised at how quickly she'd married after contacting him. Had she lost the baby, or married to give it a name? When he tried to trace her and her husband, he drew a blank, which surprised him.

Were they deliberately keeping off the various local records or had they moved? There were enough Dobsons in the rest of Britain to put him right off contacting them as a method of finding her.

Frustrated, he hired a private detective in the UK and finalised arrangements to go there himself as soon as he'd finished up at university. He felt even more strongly that a gap year and some foreign travel might be a good thing for Gemma. It'd give her more experience of the world before she hit university.

He wouldn't mind taking a sabbatical, either. He'd been working unremittingly hard in the past couple of years and the money coming from the sale of his ex's house would make a nice financial comfort cushion as well as what he'd managed to save, and he'd had a few bits of luck with his investments. Not that he'd told Gemma about that yet.

He'd felt for a while that he'd like to revisit the

country where he'd been born, travel round it at leisure, not just fly in briefly for a conference, so it all fitted in.

His ex had always refused point-blank to go there for a holiday and hadn't had a good word to say for the UK. He could understand why now. She hadn't even come with him to help his father bury his mother, then a couple of years later to help his elderly uncle and cousins to bury his father.

Both his parents had been in their early seventies, which seemed like a short life to him, but there you were. Look at poor Judith, dead at forty-one.

He broached the idea to Gemma. 'How about we both take a gap year and explore Europe?'

She stared at him, a slight frown creasing her forehead. 'I don't have much money.'

'On the contrary, you'll have half of what this house brings when we sell it. Anyway, this trip would be on me, spending money for you included. I'm not short of money, love. I've earned well and had a bit of luck with one or two investments. I could even pick up a few short-term jobs while we're there, get some up-to-date experience in the field.'

'Can I think about it?'

'Of course.'

But he could see that she looked excited under that calm, unemotional reaction she often tried to assume.

He didn't push for an answer, just waited her out.

★   ★   ★

Two days later Gemma said abruptly, 'I think it'd be a good idea to go to England and then maybe we could see some of the rest of the world. My friend did a round-the-world tour and she said it was awesome.'

'Went round the world with her parents, you mean?'

She wriggled uncomfortably and avoided his eyes at first. 'Yes. I know why you're offering it and — and I'd like to get to know you better again because, well, I think Mum prejudiced me a bit.'

More than a bit, he thought, but managed not to say so. He tried not to let out his breath in a whoosh of relief, but failed miserably with that. 'All right. It's agreed. We'll go to England first and see what we can find out about Dorothy, then we'll decide what to do next. I'd rather leave my travel options open for the moment.'

But Gemma was looking so miserable, he found himself defending his ex. 'Remember your mother really did love you. It was me she fell out with.'

'But she shouldn't have told me such *lies*.'

Oh, the pain in the poor girl's voice. It hurt him to hear it.

Gemma gulped audibly and went to switch the kettle on to hide how close she was to tears.

Adam let her make the conversational pace after that, talking about where they might go in Britain and Europe. Which didn't mean she'd stopped being reasonable one day, unreasonable

140

the next. But he felt they were starting to mend the breach Judith had deliberately created between them, for which he'd never, ever forgive his ex.

Nor would he forgive her for keeping that letter from Dorothy from him, either. He kept wondering whether he had another child, and didn't know whether he hoped to find one or not.

The child might hate him. If he or she knew he existed, that was.

Maybe he or she loved another man as her father and wouldn't want to meet him even.

His world seemed full of maybes at the moment. Gemma wasn't the only one whose emotions were up one minute, down the next, but he thought he was handling it all right, as well as could be expected, anyway.

★　★　★

Adam was a little delayed in setting off by one of his postgraduate students running into major snags in an important project. Since he was seriously considering taking a year's sabbatical, he wanted to leave everything running smoothly. Besides, he'd guided Mark from a first-year student through to doing useful research for his master's degree. He cared about the guy's progress.

In the end he and Gemma had to take a last-minute cancellation and didn't arrive in the UK until two days before Christmas. Jet lag hit them both hard and they spent most of the first day sleeping. Well, twenty hours was a long flight and with an eight-hour time difference between the UK and Western Australia at this time of year, a big strain on the body.

It made him sad to think that his parents were dead, but he'd contacted his uncle who had spread the word that the wanderer was coming back for a visit. When their daughter, a cousin who'd been born after Adam left England and whom he'd never even met, invited them to spend Christmas Day at her house with the aunt and the rest of the family, he didn't feel he could refuse.

It was a pleasant gathering and luckily there were a couple of girls of his daughter's age for Gemma to talk to. Some of the younger relatives bombarded him with questions about Australia. It always amazed him how many Poms had considered or were considering emigrating.

He drove there and back in the small hired car. However, when the cousin offered them a bed, he pleaded another engagement the following day and took Gemma back to their comfortable London hotel.

'You don't look at all like them, do you?' Gemma commented as they drove back to London along the busy M4 motorway.

'No. Um, I'd better tell you now that I was adopted.'

'You never said!'

'I only found out after your mother and I split up at that time you and your mother weren't having much to do with me.'

'Did it upset you?'

'No. Actually, it didn't seem to matter at all. My parents did everything birth parents could have done and I loved them dearly. I'm not even sure any of the younger generation know about it, though my uncle and aunt do of course.'

'So those people today weren't our relatives at all, really.'

She sounded sad. 'No. But they're as near as I've got, except for you. And is there that much difference between a blood relative and the person who brought you up or the other people who welcomed you into their family?'

She shrugged. 'It feels different to me. I'd been looking forward to meeting my English relatives.'

'You've got your mother's family in Australia, if the lack of blood relatives worries you.'

'They aren't exactly a close family, though, are they? They hardly ever saw one another. I'm glad I've got you still.'

She gave him a sudden hug, then changed the subject quickly, as if embarrassed by her own emotions.

These occasional, spontaneous hugs meant a great deal to him.

⋆　⋆　⋆

They spent the afternoon of Boxing Day walking along the Thames, dodging showers and taking shelter in a café for a while.

They were both looking forward to the end of the holiday break, when places would be open again, including some of the tourist attractions they had on their list.

'It gets dark soon at this time of year, doesn't it?' Gemma complained as they went back to the hotel to sit in the bar area and read their books. Thank heavens they were both well supplied with e-books on their tablets.

At one point she said, 'I'm going to need a warmer coat than the one I've brought, Dad.'

'We'll go shopping and buy you one.'

'Just for a few weeks? We could look in a charity shop first. I've found some great clothes in them. Mum freaked out about that but I didn't care. I like to look a bit different.'

'I've never even been in a charity shop, so it'll be a new experience. You'll get more used to the weather after a few days anyway, I expect.'

'Even weather as cold as this?'

He grinned. 'Spoken like a true Aussie. Yes, even this cold. Make the most of the experience, and we only have to see some snow then you can really call yourself an experienced international traveller.'

She nodded, looking sad suddenly. 'Mum would never bring me to the UK. I know why now, but I was so jealous of my school friends. Most of them have spent holidays in Europe. We always went somewhere in Asia.'

'If you and I weren't on a specific mission, I'd take you on a tour of some of my favourite places near the Mediterranean, where it's warmer. The history here is fascinating, though, and they make a lot of it very accessible to visitors. I still marvel that I've actually walked on Hadrian's Wall.'

'Wow. I'd like to do that.'

'We'll see if we can fit it in, then. You'd better start making a list.'

As they parted company for the night, he said, 'The detective will be back at work tomorrow. Maybe he'll have news for us.'

He wasn't hopeful. It felt as if he was looking for a needle in a haystack. He wasn't even sure Dorothy had had the baby.

Anyway, he still hadn't worked out what to do if he did have a living child in England. He or she would be a year or so older than Gemma.

She'd said she'd love to have a brother or sister, but what if she and whoever it was didn't get on?

He punched the pillow into shape and tried once more to get to sleep, but it was a long time before he succeeded.

★ ★ ★

The following morning Adam rang the detective he'd hired from Australia to do some preliminary searching for Dorothy. He got a recorded message, which asked him to phone another number.

Wondering what the hell was going on, he did this and got an office called 'Secure Answering Services'.

'I was trying to contact Mr Topham, who's been doing some work for me.'

'And your name is?'

'Adam Torrington.'

'Just a moment.'

145

After a couple of minutes of canned music, the woman came back online. 'We have a message for you, Mr Torrington. Do you have a pen handy? Right. Mr Topham's wife is seriously ill and he isn't able to continue working for you. There is some paperwork about what he's discovered so far that I'm authorised to pass on to you if you can come into this office. We keep a skeleton staff on during the last week in December.' She gave him an address, adding, 'And, of course, there will be no charge from Mr Topham.'

'That's in Swindon, right? I'm in London at the moment.'

'We are in Swindon, I'm afraid. Can you get here? We don't use postal services for this sort of handover of confidential paperwork.'

'I was coming to Wiltshire anyway.'

'Good. We'll need to see some proper identification, a passport for preference.'

'I can provide that. What's your address and what hours are you open?'

'We're only open for handovers like yours from 10 a.m. to noon during the holiday period. My employer likes to verify people's identities himself. He takes the confidentiality aspect very seriously indeed.'

Adam grimaced as he looked at his watch. Not possible to get there in that time frame today. He reined in his irritation. It wasn't this woman's fault and if Topham's wife was ill, you couldn't blame him for putting her first. 'I'll be there at 10 a.m. tomorrow morning. Here's my mobile number if you need to change anything.'

Adam stood holding the phone till Gemma nudged him to switch it off. He explained the details she hadn't been able to guess from what she overheard.

'I wonder what he's found out. There must be something if he's making all this fuss about handing it over.'

'We'll have to wait and see. Probably nothing to get excited about.'

'So maybe we could go and look round the British Museum now, Dad? If Swindon is only a couple of hours' drive away we've plenty of time to get there if we set off mid-afternoon today.'

'Are you turning into a culture vulture or what?' he teased.

'I've always been fascinated by history — not the political stuff, but how ordinary people lived. Mum said you couldn't make a living from studying such dusty stuff and I should concentrate on the maths and science side, but I don't enjoy them half as much. She was just trying to do her best for me.'

She still defended her mother, still had reddened eyes some mornings.

He felt as if he was treading on eggs most of the time, but things were improving gradually and Gemma was confiding in him more, so he'd continue tip-toeing around the sensitive areas for as long as was needed.

Being a sole parent, he decided, was the hardest job he'd ever had. It was taking a long time for him to win Gemma's trust. But he wasn't giving up. He'd wanted several children but Judith had refused to have any more. He resented that about her, too.

'You'll have to share your knowledge of British history with me, Gemma. It's one of my weak spots.'

He got a glowing smile for that, at least.

'Let's see if someone at the hotel can book a room for us in a Swindon hotel for tonight before we go out. I don't want to be hunting around for accommodation in a strange town after dark.'

'I thought you grew up in that area.'

'I did. You don't stay in hotels in your hometown, though, and anyway things will have changed there, so what do I know about where to stay?'

'Oh yes, I see. Like I don't know which are the best hotels in Perth.'

Well, one thing about the delay in finding Dorothy was that it would give him time to think. He still hadn't worked out what exactly he'd say or do if — no, when! — they found her.

They booked rooms and paid a quick visit to the British Museum. He had to promise to come back another time to get her to leave it, she enjoyed it so much.

They came away with two fat books that he'd bought for Gemma. Not to win her affection, but because of the longing in her eyes. It was good to be able to afford things to feed her questing young mind.

If he found another child, perhaps he could help him or her as well. He'd like that.

★　★　★

The drive to Swindon was easily accomplished by taking the M4 motorway and once they were out of the capital, Adam began to enjoy the drive.

'Whatever happens, we'll make time to do some sightseeing,' he told his daughter. 'Why did we never go out sightseeing in Perth? There's history there too.'

'You used to go into college a lot during the summer holidays.'

'It was . . . um, peaceful there.'

'Away from Mum, you mean.'

'Yes. And she wasn't really into culture.'

'That kept you away from me, too.'

It was out before he could stop himself. 'She didn't give me a chance to look after you, had it all arranged for childcare near where she worked and told me not to muck the system around because it'd upset you.'

Adam didn't attempt to break the silence that followed. He was growing tired of playing peacemaker. He let the satnav guide them to the hotel. Swindon had changed so much he doubted he could have found the place unaided, even though he had recognised the name of the street it was on.

Gemma's silence lasted until they'd checked in and were in the lift on the way up to their rooms, then she said in a small, tight voice, 'I'm sorry for getting at you.'

'Thank you, love.' He gave her a hug and she hugged him back convulsively.

He had to remember that teenagers' emotions went up and down like yo-yos. So did his at the moment.

12

Harriet called in to see her aunt again, this time on behalf of her mother, who wanted to make sure Elise was all right.

'Mum does mean well,' Harriet said apologetically.

'I know, dear.'

'She's worried you'll have another fall, keeps saying you should have let her and Kerry find someone to clear your house for you.'

It was then that the idea struck Elise. 'I've been intending to find someone to help me do it, which is very different from giving away my possessions wholesale. I want to go through them and keep some that I'm particularly fond of. Um, did *you* find a job yet?'

'No. There don't seem to be as many going this year.'

'Well then, would you come and work for me?'

'If you need something doing, you don't have to pay me, Auntie Elise.'

'I need *a lot* doing.' She made a sweeping gesture with one arm. 'This whole house has to be cleared. That's far more than I can ask your help with as a favour. Besides, I'd rather pay you than a stranger. With your help, I might just get through most of the clearing out before you have to go back to university.'

Harriet stared at her intently, as if trying to

read her mind. 'You're not just making up a job to help me?'

'On the contrary, I'm quite desperate for help. I have to get this house ready to sell and I'm not even walking easily yet. You passed your driving test recently, didn't you, even if you don't own a car?'

'Yes. First time, actually. My instructor said I was a natural.'

'I have a car sitting idle because I'm not allowed to drive it yet. It's automatic, quite easy to drive.' She hesitated, then added, 'If it doesn't upset you, I'd be grateful if you could stay here while we're working, then you can drive me to the shops and help a bit with the housework and meals. I'm still rather limited in what I can do, and I don't really enjoy cooking, anyway.'

She found herself being ruthlessly hugged again and mentally thanked Victor for leaving her such a practical bequest. He hadn't left her enough money to upset her because he was respecting her pride. But she knew how wealthy he was, and his nephew didn't seem at all upset about the money, thank goodness. It was enough to make a huge difference to her. She'd be able to pay her niece for helping and tide herself over till she could sell the house.

In the meantime she could prepare for another exhibition of her paintings at the same art gallery which had suggested holding one before her accident and was still keen to do so. That'd bring in a little more money. And she had a small old age pension as well.

There was just one thing left to worry about.

151

'What will your mother say?'

'Don't worry, Auntie Elise. I'm used to managing Mum. I'll get Dad on my side first, then tell her I've got a job as a *general factotum*. She'll say how pleased she is about the job before I tell her I'm working for you. I don't think it'll really worry her even then, because she knows how badly I need the money. She fusses a lot but she's very practical and her advice is usually worth listening to.'

Harriet grinned and added, 'If she'd only wait till she was asked for advice it'd be a lot easier to accept it, though.'

They both chuckled at that.

★   ★   ★

They started work that very day and with Harriet's help and willing young body, Elise was able to make a start. She threw out a lot of 'stuff' ruthlessly but was rewarded by finding some old treasures she'd forgotten about, even her childhood doll's house, which had belonged to her grandmother and which she'd always loved.

The small house fascinated Harriet now, as it had fascinated a lot of children and even grown-ups over the years, with its dainty figures in period costume and its beautifully made miniature furniture. It was probably worth a lot of money but she didn't intend to sell it. 'I'll leave it to you when I die,' she offered.

'I'd love to have it, but I'd far rather you didn't die for a zillion years.'

'So would I, and I'll keep taking my vitamins,

but in the end you don't get much choice.'

She sat down to rest while Harriet was making lunch and started to put together a list of what she had to do: find an estate agent and put this place on the market, buy another house which had a room suitable for a studio, then arrange the move. There'd be plenty of time to search for the right place because houses like hers didn't sell quickly.

At the end of the busiest day since her accident, she rested again while her young helper made tea.

When the doorbell rang, Harriet called, 'I'll get it.'

She came back followed by her mother. 'Mum wants to see you. I said you were tired and she shouldn't stay long.'

'I won't upset my aunt, if that's what you're worrying about, Harriet,' Mary said sharply. 'I can see now that I was mistaken about her needing to go into a care home, but I meant it for the best.'

They were looking at one another like two dogs wondering whether to start a fight, Elise thought in sudden amusement. 'Why don't you carry on making our tea, dear?' she suggested.

'All right. But call me if you need me.'

When Harriet had gone Elise smiled at her niece. 'Why don't you sit down, Mary? I'm a bit tired and having a nice rest.'

'You shouldn't let Harriet tire you out.'

'Don't worry. She's tried to stop me doing too much, and sometimes I've heeded her, but I'm eager to sort out the house and get rid of all the

153

clutter. I'm told it's more attractive to buyers not to have a lot of things lying around.'

'That's why I came.' She hesitated. 'Look don't take this amiss, but I told you Kerry and I showed an estate agent round while you were in hospital. He brought a man to see the house the very next day.' She stopped, looking as if she was expecting her aunt to be angry.

'I'm too old to hold a grudge as long as you don't try to boss me around again.' She reached out to pat Mary's tense hand. 'You and I are still family, you know. Go on.'

'I gather the man wanted to buy it, but we didn't get round to discussing his offer because you got better and . . . well, you know what happened. So anyway, maybe you could get in touch with the estate agent and he could ask his client if he's still interested.'

Elise didn't hesitate. 'Oh, what a good idea! It'd be wonderful if I didn't have to keep the place ready for someone to be shown round at any time. I'm not good at keeping things immaculately tidy when I'm working.'

'There's just one thing: you might not like what he wants to do with it.'

'Go on.'

'He's a developer. He wants to knock this house down and build three modern houses in its place. People actually prefer smaller gardens these days.'

'It won't matter what he wants to do with it if I'm leaving anyway. What matters is how much he's willing to pay. I'll have to get some assessments made to find out what's reasonable.'

Mary took a deep breath. 'Um, we did some research into that before we brought him in. We weren't trying to cheat you, honestly. We were trying to get you the best price.'

Elise stared at her niece. 'You know what: I have an idea.'

'Oh?' Mary still sounded apprehensive.

'Why don't I pay you to sell the house for me? I'll give you one per cent of the price you get for me if you'll take all the hassle off my hands.'

Mary's jaw dropped and she made a little choking noise in her throat. 'You'd trust me to do that?'

'Yes. But Victor's nephew will be handling the legal side, so I shall have someone else involved and able to keep an eye on you. I don't think I really need to, though, do you?'

Mary shook her head, then burst into tears.

They were such great, gulping sobs that Elise didn't think selling her house was the cause. 'Tell me why you're upset. You had an anxious look to you when you arrived.'

'It's Ian. He's hopeless with money and he recently invested our savings without telling me in a stupid scheme which is *losing* money not making it. I'm furious with him! And upset about the money. We worked hard for it, saved carefully for years and now we've less to fall back on than we had five years ago. All that hard work down the drain. It'd be a godsend to earn a chunk of money to put away for our old age. And I wouldn't let him get his hands on it.'

Elise got up and gave Mary a hug, which made her niece stiffen for a moment, then hug her briefly back and murmur, 'Thank you, Auntie.'

Another thing she'd learnt in her long life was that people could always surprise you. She smiled at her niece. 'You'll be a godsend to me as well, actually. I'm not interested in business as long as I have enough to live on. What I really want is to get on with my painting, seize the moment, not have to haggle with men who're trying to get the better of me. The Blyne Gallery wants to put on an exhibition of my work, you see.'

Mary stared at her in shock. 'To sell them, you mean? The Blyne Gallery? That's not just a fond hope?'

'No. They've sold a few of my paintings already.'

'I didn't realise you were doing that well.'

'Well, now you do. So the sooner I can move, the better. Is it a deal?' She held out her hand and they shook solemnly.

★   ★   ★

Thanks to Mary's hard bargaining, the house was sold quickly and at an excellent price, and she pushed the buyer significantly higher than the amount first offered.

Elise felt good to see the load of financial worry lift a little from Mary's face at the prospect of being paid for her efforts.

With Harriet's energetic help, the house was cleared of everything Elise no longer wanted or needed. At the same time, she enjoyed working

156

with a much younger person and hearing a very different view of the world.

There was still one big problem, though. She'd been house-hunting, both online and in person, but couldn't find anything suitable. And it was even worse with rental properties. The ones available were either too small to have a room that was right for a studio or too expensive, given her limited funds. She was reluctant to waste her capital on rent anyway, because she needed to invest some of her money to bring in additional income. At her age, you couldn't rely on staying healthy enough to keep earning money.

What was she going to do? The contracts were being worked on, a provisional exchange date had been agreed and she had to get out of her house in three weeks' time.

★　★　★

Stacy settled into her new flat quickly, though it was rather small and felt horribly cluttered with her bits and pieces in it as well as the owner's furniture. She had to pile things up and weave around clumps of furniture, and the ugliness of it all depressed her.

Most of her art things and the furniture she'd taken from her marriage were still in storage. Desperate to find somewhere to house her art things so she could get to work on the ideas she'd had, she wondered whether it might be quite cheap to hire a small industrial unit.

She found her way to the main industrial area and drove round it slowly, but it was mostly single workshops or factories with few to-let signs showing and none on suitable smaller premises. When she came upon a group of smaller units, she parked and went to see if she could get chatting to someone. Perhaps a local might be able to point her in the right direction.

A guy in stained overalls was standing outside the second unit with a mug of tea in his hand. He was young enough to try to chat her up, but stopped when she told him bluntly that she had just come out of a messy divorce and wasn't interested in men at the moment.

He backed away, hands held out in a keep-away gesture. 'Been there, done that. Good luck to you. My damned ex took me to the cleaners, the lying bitch.'

'Sorry about that. Let's start again. My name's Stacy.'

'Luke.' He didn't bother to shake hands, just raised his mug in a salute.

'I'm looking to hire a small industrial unit for a few months. You wouldn't know where I could find one, would you?'

'What do you need, exactly?'

'I don't need anything fancy or any equipment. I'm an artist, a sort of sculptor. I make pieces from scrap metal, small stylised animals, whatever comes to mind, and I have my own tools. I need somewhere bigger than a room in a house, though.'

'Are you an amateur or a professional?'

She wasn't going to call herself an amateur. 'My work isn't paying its way at the moment, so I still need a day job to support myself, but I've sold some pieces here and there. One day I hope, no, *intend*, to do it full-time.'

'Good luck with it. Actually, Jim at the end isn't using all his space at the moment. If it's only for a few months he might be willing to come to some unofficial arrangement with you. Come on. I'll introduce you. It's worth a try.'

He led the way to the end of the short row, to what looked like the biggest unit. It was L-shaped, filling in the end part of the piece all the way across. Inside it an older man was working on some machinery she didn't recognise.

Luke held up one hand to stop her. 'Wait till he's finished. It's very skilled work.'

Even when Jim had finished he didn't notice them and Luke had to go inside and wave to attract his attention, because the machinery was still running and making a loud racket.

Luke got straight to the point. 'Stacy here is looking for somewhere to rent to work on her sculptures for a few months. She's just divorced and doesn't know where she'll wind up permanently, so this is only temporary. I thought about your side room.'

Stacy went across to join them.

'Jim, meet Stacy.'

They both gave a quick nod and eyed one another.

She decided to be assertive about her needs. 'Before I waste your time, is it always as noisy as this?'

'Nah. Just now and then.'

'How much is 'now and then'?'

'It'd add up to about an hour a day, two hours max.' Jim studied her, not in a sexual way but as if assessing whether she was serious, then pointed to a door at one side. 'Go and have a look in that room. It's empty at the moment. You'd have to share the toilet and kitchen with me, otherwise that space is all yours as long as you don't fall behind with the rent.'

The room was bigger than she'd expected, about twenty foot by thirty, with one workbench, plenty of electrical sockets and a scuffed stainless steel sink. She stood in the middle and turned round on the spot. It'd do. In fact it'd be great, because it was bigger than anywhere she'd had for working in before. She could even store her furniture here and save warehouse costs.

She went back to join the two men. 'How much?'

'Twenty quid a week, cash, plus five for the electricity, as long as my power bills don't go through the roof.'

'I'd want to store my furniture at one end till I find somewhere permanent to live. That all right too?'

'Fine by me.'

She got her purse out. 'Two weeks' rent in advance suit you?'

'Yep. Then weekly in advance.'

She paid him and put her purse away. Luke must have gone back to his work and Jim was looking at her thoughtfully.

'You all right, lass? You look as if you've been ill.'

'A bit stressed. I'll be fine once everything's settled. Um . . . my ex is violent so I don't want anyone to know I'm here.'

'Can't stand fellows who beat their wives. Nutcases, I reckon. Even if he finds you here, there are usually enough guys within earshot to keep you safe.'

She shuddered. 'I'm hoping I've covered my tracks. And I'm hoping that once I'm out of sight for a while, he'll turn his attention to something else.'

'I should think getting away is the best thing you could do.' He looked back at his job. 'Now that's settled, I'd just like to make it clear that I'm not a natterer when I'm working. So if you like to gossip, find someone else to talk to.'

'I don't natter when I've got work to do, either.'

'Good. And I don't want our arrangement talking about. It's unofficial.' He winked, by which she assumed he wasn't going to tell the landlord about subletting. 'If anyone asks, you're my niece, storing your furniture here.'

For some reason, she trusted him. 'Below the radar suits me best too . . . Uncle Jim.'

He grinned and pulled out a business card. 'Phone me when you've arranged delivery of your stuff. I can let the movers into your room if they want to deliver while you're working.'

'Thanks, Jim. I want to store the furniture at the far end and do my work at this end.'

'Makes sense. See you.' He nodded and turned back to his work.

She sat in her car for a few minutes, tears of

relief welling in her eyes. When someone tapped on the window, she nearly jumped out of her skin, then realised it was Luke.

He frowned down at her. 'Didn't you manage to come to an agreement with Jim?'

'Yes. I was just . . . relieved. Look, I'll tell you what I told him: I'm avoiding my ex, because he's violent, and I'd rather you didn't tell anyone about me or even what I'm doing here.'

'Understood.'

'Thanks.' She pulled herself together and drove back to the flat. She'd be starting work properly tomorrow. She'd popped in to say hello and Ellis had shown her round the offices. The suite was shabby but quite spacious, with a few rooms, two of them currently unoccupied. Only Ellis and another guy were working on the current project, with a part-time secretary and occasional part-time graphic designers like herself.

As she pushed away her half-eaten meal that evening, it occurred to her that no one round here knew about her, let alone cared what she was doing. Which was exactly how she wanted it to be.

But she had never been one to fool herself and as she sat staring into space, she admitted to herself that she didn't like being this isolated. The loneliness was biting already, even after only three days on her own. It'd be a relief to start work and have someone to talk to in the daytime.

She'd never felt so alone in her whole life.

It wasn't fair that Darren had chased her away

from everyone she knew, but there you were. Life wasn't always fair.

At least she and her father had made it hard for him to find her. Well, she hoped they had, couldn't think of anything else to do about it.

Surely he wasn't going to continue stalking her once she was out of sight? She had to hope for that. She didn't know what she'd do if he continued to pursue her unremittingly.

13

Angus looked up from his electrical work briefly, as someone knocked on the door of Number Three for the second time. He ignored it again, because he had freed up today for some solid work on this house. If whoever it was couldn't see that these houses weren't occupied, they could stand there and knock till kingdom come, for all he cared.

A short time later the knock was repeated for a third time and then someone had the cheek to open the front door and call, 'Hello! Anyone there?'

'Damn you!' Angus muttered and set his screwdriver down carefully. He strode out into the hall and found a man in a very smart overcoat standing just inside the front door.

'Ah, there you are.' The stranger was staring at him in a manner that was distinctly appraising.

'Who the hell asked you to come in?'

'Are you Angus Denning?' He sounded doubtful.

'What's that to you?'

The man stuck out one soft, manicured hand. 'Bryce Dorling. If you could just spare me a few minutes, Mr Denning?'

Angus made no attempt to shake the hand. 'You won't want to get your hand dirty by touching mine and anyway, I've no time to spare.

I've got a lot of work to do today. Close the door as you leave.'

Dorling's eyes narrowed for a moment. 'If this is an inconvenient time, I can come back later today or even tomorrow.'

'It's extremely inconvenient. I'll be working till the light fades and the same tomorrow, so tell me what you want in two minutes flat, then leave me to get on with my day.'

A card appeared in the man's hand and he held it out.

He'd have made a good conjuror, Angus thought sourly, making no attempt to take it off him. 'Your minutes are ticking away. *What — do you — want?*'

'I'm from Dorling and Cavendish. We're developers. We build groups of superior dwellings for people of comfortable means, and we'd like to make you a generous offer to purchase Saffron Lane.'

Angus cut him short. 'I'm not selling any of my land.'

'You haven't heard what our offer is yet. I'm sure we can tempt you.'

'I don't need to hear any offers because I do *not* wish to sell my land.'

The man made a graceful gesture, encompassing the whole row. 'Not even this scrubby bit of land at the far end of your grounds?'

'Not even one square metre of it.'

'We could offer to finish all the structural repairs to the outside of the big house as well as pay you a good price for this end bit.'

'*What?* It'd not be worth your while to repair

my family home. It'd eat all your profit.'

'If you let us survey it, we could make an informed decision on that. We'd put a ceiling amount in the contract, of course.'

'No, I said, and no was what I meant. It's spelt N-O in case the word is unknown to you. No, I do not want to sell and no, you're not surveying anything. Now, you've had your two minutes and I've given you my answer, so damned well go away and let me get on with my work.'

'At least think about it.'

Angus glared at him and stabbed one forefinger towards the door. 'Out! Or do I have to push you off my premises?'

His visitor held up one hand, palm outwards. 'All right. I'm going. But I'll just leave our offer here.' In another sleight of hand, an envelope appeared and was dropped on the windowsill before Angus could protest.

Dorling stepped away from it, inclining his head as he left.

Angus ignored the envelope and went back to work.

When the all-too-short winter daylight faded, he packed up and walked towards the front door. He hadn't got far enough to switch on the electricity at this stage of the rewiring, though he hoped to get finished with this house by tomorrow.

He stopped in the middle of the room, stared across at the envelope and shook his head. He should just throw the damned thing on the fire and be done with it.

But when he reached the front door, he

stopped again and with a growl of anger at his own stupidity, turned round, snatched up the envelope and stuffed it into his pocket. He didn't want any of the workmen who came in and out of the houses seeing this and he might as well find out what his land was assumed to be worth. Nell would want to see the figures, he was sure. A very savvy businesswoman, his Nell.

He smiled wryly as he locked the door and tramped across to the big house.

Who was he kidding? He wanted to know what they were offering, too. It'd save him having this bit of land valued, if nothing else.

★ ★ ★

Angus could hear Nell rustling some papers in the library, where she was still going through the records, but she must have done some preparatory cooking because a tempting smell greeted him as he entered the house. He stopped to sniff appreciatively and went into the kitchen to investigate.

Then he noticed that the table was set for four and the old child's high chair had been brought out.

He stuck his head out of the kitchen door and called across the hall, 'Did I know we were having visitors?'

She came to join him in the kitchen, plonking a kiss on his cheek. 'No. It was a spur of a moment thing. I met Janey and Winifred at the shops and realised we hadn't seen them for ages, even though they practically live next door. So I invited them and little Millie round for a scratch tea.'

Angus sniffed again. 'That doesn't smell like a scratch meal. Do you need a taster?'

'Well, it's a quickie recipe and no, I don't need a taster, thank you very much. I've made it hundreds of times. It's just a chicken casserole with a few bits and pieces added, and I'm using packets of pre-cooked rice and frozen peas with it. And Winifred is bringing one of her delicious cakes for afters. I told her I had some vanilla ice cream to go with it. Easy-peasy.'

'You are such a good cook. My mouth's watering already.'

'Well, you're learning quite a lot under my tuition. I'm never going to be the sole cook and bottle-washer again.'

'Pity. My food doesn't taste nearly as good as yours.'

'Practice makes perfect.'

'You're heartless.' When she shot him a stern glance, he suppressed a sigh. Her first husband must have been a lazy slob to leave her so determined about sharing duties. Not that Angus didn't agree with that in principle, it was just that he was flat out busy with renovating Saffron Lane. For the moment he judged it wiser to change the subject. 'It'll be nice to see them again. How was Winifred looking?'

'Really well. Since Janey went to live with her she seems to have grown younger. She doesn't look anywhere near her mid-eighties. And Millie is walking now, getting into all sorts of mischief. Janey might only be nineteen but she's a really good mother. You can see it from that child's rosy, happy face.'

She stopped and looked at him, eyes narrowed. 'You're only half-listening and if that isn't a half-hearted nod, I've never seen one. What happened today?'

'Are you a mind-reader?'

She chuckled and reached out to smooth the frown lines from the middle of his forehead. 'No, but I can read the signs on your face. What's happened now, love?'

'A chap turned up with an offer to buy Saffron Lane, one of those damned developers.' He paused. 'He didn't look like the other ones, though. He was much more stylishly dressed, more like a male model.'

'How much was he offering?'

'I don't know. I sent him away.'

'You might have found out how much. It's always nice to know where we stand.'

He fumbled in his pocket. 'He left an envelope. I think it contains specifics. Here. You open it.'

She grabbed it and tore it open, pulling out the piece of paper, reading it, then whistling softly.

He had been turning away, but now his interest was caught. 'How much?'

'I thought you weren't interested,' she teased.

He grabbed her and pulled her towards him, kissing her ruthlessly. When he let her go, they were both rather short of breath.

'Now will you tell me or do I have to punish you some more?'

She glanced at the clock. 'I'd not normally be able to resist your delightful punishments, Sir Jasper, but I'm afraid I need to get ready for our guests. Prepare to be astonished by what this developer is offering. I don't want you to have a heart attack.'

He gaped at her in shock after she told him. 'How can a scruffy little street be worth that much?'

'Don't forget they're also offering to finish repairing the outer structure of Dennings.'

'They know something we don't,' he decided. 'What's the council up to now? They wouldn't make an offer like this if they weren't sure of getting council approval for whatever they're planning.'

'Well, further discussion will just have to wait.' She gave him a push. 'Chop-chop! Our guests will be here in half an hour and I've still got a lot to do. Put the outside lights on for them, then grab a quick shower.'

⋆　⋆　⋆

Winifred and Janey walked up to the top of the street from Number 5 and down the drive to the big house, with little Millie bouncing about in her pushchair. Luckily, there was nearly a full moon to light their way as well as the street and house lights.

'Isn't it nice to be invited out?' Winifred said.

'Lovely. And Nell is a good cook, even when it's only what she calls a scratch meal. No one bakes cakes as good as yours, though. I can't wait to see her face when she tastes your new one. It's my favourite of all, Auntie Winnie.'

'I do love finding new recipes.'

'And I love testing them.'

The two women smiled at one another, one in her later years, the other not yet twenty. There was no actual relationship. Janey and her daughter rented rooms from Winifred, but she'd been told to consider her landlady an honorary aunt, and she hadn't got an aunt or Winifred a niece, so that suited them both perfectly.

'Did your solicitor sort out the paperwork you've been worrying about?' Janey asked.

'Yes, dear. All sorted.'

They arrived just then and Winifred hoped her blush hadn't shown in the light streaming from the doorway. She wasn't used to fudging the truth, especially with her dear girl.

'Come in! Come in!' Angus went to help Janey with the pushchair, and they all walked through the magnificent but chilly entrance hall into the kitchen. This was the warmest part of the house; it contained a big Aga cooker and was large enough to act as a sitting room too, most of the time.

Winifred gave her hostess the cake and when Nell peeped inside the tin and exclaimed in admiration at the way the top was decorated, that gave the older woman an excuse for any blush remaining. She wasn't used to keeping secrets, but this one was in a good cause.

In her whole life she'd never had so many compliments, let alone enjoyed herself so much. She'd been brought up strictly, had always done her duty and looked after her elderly mother when she grew too old to look after herself. But her ungrateful parent had treated her like a stupid child right until the end. It had been rather dreary at times, though Winifred had never complained.

Soon they were all sitting around the table with Millie in the old wooden high chair. After a brief chat, Nell began serving the main course.

'If this is a scratch meal, you can do one any time,' Angus said later as he put down his knife and fork. 'Any second helpings going?'

'Leave room for Winifred's cake.'

'Ah. Yes.' He collected the dinner plates and stacked them in the dishwasher while Nell brought out the dessert, which was eaten to the accompaniment of happy murmurs.

'If you don't allow me a second helping of that cake, I'm going to throw a tantrum,' he declared. 'Winifred, it's wonderful. I don't know how you do it, time after time.'

'I love baking cakes.'

'And I love eating them.'

★   ★   ★

Afterwards, as the two younger women were clearing the table, Nell asked in a low voice, 'How's your mother getting on, Janey? Or shouldn't I ask?'

'She's doing quite well, actually. She's moved out of the women's refuge and into a group of sheltered flats with a warden on-site. She's learning to stand on her own feet again. And since *he* won't be out of prison for years, she's stopped jumping when anyone knocks on the door.'

'Are things going any better between you and her?'

'As well as can be expected. I just wish she'd stood up to *him* occasionally, then I might not have had such an unhappy childhood.'

'I'm sure she wishes it too.'

'Yes, well, I'm seeing her occasionally and letting her get to know her granddaughter, but I don't expect we'll ever be close.' Janey blinked her eyes, trying to clear away the tears. Other people had close relationships with their parents and she envied them that.

Nell gave her a hug. 'I didn't mean to upset you. I'm sorry I brought this up.'

'I'm not. I have to learn to talk about it, don't I? My mother's part of my life now, one way or another, and at least she adores Millie. I do want my daughter to grow up with one grandparent, at least. And Mum babysits occasionally, which is a big help. She gets on well with Winifred and the two of them spoil Millie to death once I'm out of the house.'

'I'm amazed at how quickly that child of yours is growing. And tell me about your studies at tech . . . '

An hour later, Angus escorted the two women home and waited till they'd locked the front door before strolling back to the big house.

★   ★   ★

173

Winifred looked at Janey as they hung up their outdoor clothes. 'I heard you talking to Nell about your mother. You haven't really forgiven her for not standing up for you when *he* used to hit you, have you?'

'I've tried.'

'She must have had a hard life with him too. It doesn't do to hold on to a grievance, dear. I think the current generation dwells on their grievances far too much. Better to move on and focus on making the future better than live unhappily in the past.'

Janey flung her arms round Winifred. 'My future is already better. I'm so glad I met you and came to live here.'

Winifred hugged her back, thinking that sometimes Janey acted like the child she hadn't been for a long time, which was good to see. The dear girl had such heavy responsibilities as the sole parent of that lively little darling. 'We both benefit from sharing the house, dear. And from each other's company.'

'Yes, very much. Now, I must get this young lady to bed. How she can sleep in that pushchair, I don't know.'

'Children can sleep anywhere. I envy them that.'

Later, when she went to bed herself, Janey lay for a while staring into the darkness. Her mother was desperate for the two of them to grow closer but although she did her best, she hadn't yet been able to forgive her for letting her father bully her for years.

She was the one who'd kept her distance. She

said it was to stop her father from being jealous and treating her even more unkindly, but Janey wasn't sure she bought that.

And if she and her mother had been closer, maybe her father's best friend wouldn't have dared rape Janey and expect to get away with it.

She didn't think she'd ever be able to let go of this grievance, whatever Winifred said, even though it had brought her a darling little daughter.

She intended to be in a very safe place when the man who'd raped her came out of prison.

He'd once threatened to claim his daughter if she didn't do as he told her, but then he'd been caught and put into jail for another crime. He was never getting near Millie, no way!

14

The following morning Adam and his daughter took a taxi from the hotel to the office of the security company that was holding the information Topham had garnered.

Adam was shown into a small interview room to one side of the reception area and Gemma was asked to wait for him. She rolled her eyes at this but didn't protest, thank goodness, just pulled out her smartphone and started fiddling around with it.

An elderly man joined him in the small inner room, carrying a large envelope. 'Mr Torrington?'

'Yes.'

'I'm the manager of this document transfer business and I take the security aspects very seriously, so I'll need to see some reliable identification before I can hand over the papers that have been left here for you.'

Adam produced his passport and was amused by how closely his companion studied it, and then compared him and his highly unflattering photo.

With a nod, the manager eventually pushed the passport back across the table. 'If you'll just read this release form before you sign it?'

Adam didn't allow himself to sigh aloud at the sight of two pages of small print, but did as he was asked and started to work his way through the ifs and buts. No way was he stupid enough to sign something without checking what was in it first.

Only after the manager had witnessed his signature was the large envelope pushed across to him. Scrawled across the front of it was his name.

'Can you now verify that it contains the material you wanted, please?'

Adam had had enough. 'I have no idea what material it contains until I study the contents. I asked Mr Topham to find something out for me and have no idea what he discovered.'

'Ah. I see. Perhaps you could just glance at the contents, then, to check whether they *seem* to be what you were expecting?'

Adam tipped the contents of the envelope out on the table any old how, amused to see his companion wince at this cavalier treatment.

He scanned some of the papers and could see that they concerned Dorothy Dobson nee Redman. There was the old photo of her that he'd sent to Topham, but no photo of what she looked like now, so presumably the detective hadn't found her.

'They look about right.' He shoved the papers back into the envelope, causing his companion to wince again. 'Is that it?'

'Yes, Mr Torrington. I hope you find what you're looking for.'

Adam hoped so too. He went outside to rejoin Gemma.

'Did the detective discover anything, Dad?' she asked loudly.

'We'll go back to the hotel and discuss it in private.'

She sighed as if he was treating her badly, but didn't say anything else till they reached the hotel.

★ ★ ★

Once back in his room Adam prevented Gemma from grabbing the envelope. 'Let's treat these papers gently, eh?'

They spread them out on his bed and he immediately found a copy of the marriage certificate itself: Dorothy Redman had married Lionel Dobson a couple of months after she'd written to Adam in Australia. Dobson had a Frank Dobson listed on the certificate as his father and the marriage was witnessed by Edward Redman, father of the bride.

'Dorothy's father was called Ted,' Adam said. 'So that fits. I didn't take to the fellow at all.'

'She married quickly for someone who was supposed to love you,' Gemma said.

'Yes. I wonder why.'

'The baby. And he must have known it wasn't his.'

'Yes.'

'Do you think she loved him?'

'How do I know? I've never met him.'

'Well, I'd not have done that if I'd been in love with someone else.'

He ruffled her hair. 'No. And no one would dare try to make you, either.'

She grinned at him for a moment, then the

178

smile faded and she looked back at the papers. 'How will we find out whether the baby's yours?'

'This may be a start.' He'd set the marriage certificate aside almost absent-mindedly, but now jerked to full attention as he realised he was looking at a copy of a birth certificate. The date would fit his brief involvement with Dorothy. Was it . . . could this be his child?

Gemma read it, then turned to him. 'She had a girl, then: Catherine Jane. If she's alive, she's my half-sister. She's only a bit older than me.'

'Dorothy always said how much she loved the name Catherine.'

'What are we going to do now?'

'Start looking for a woman called Dorothy Dobson in the latest electoral rolls. We have her husband's and daughter's names. We ought to be able to find out something about her.'

'Is it that easy to find someone?'

'It can be.'

'Do you want this Catherine Jane to be yours?'

'I don't know. But if she is my daughter, I want to meet her.'

Gemma scowled down at the papers. 'Well, I don't want a big sister trying to boss me around, thank you very much, so don't expect me to cheer if you are her father.' She flounced off into her hotel room, which was next to his, slamming the door hard.

For a moment she'd looked frightened. Maybe of losing him as well as her mother. As if he'd not be there for her! How long would it take her to trust him?

He stared down at the mess of papers, then

sighed and began trying to sort them out. Some of them were paper-clipped together, others had little sticky labels on marked 'Miscellaneous' or 'Discarded'. Topham seemed to have been a careful researcher.

But somehow Adam couldn't bear any more discoveries today, so he didn't read any further. You could only face so much at a time.

Of course, they might not find Dorothy or her daughter. They could have died or gone into hiding. If people wanted to stay hidden, there were usually ways. Or they could even have emigrated.

What worried him most was that this search might come between him and Gemma. Perhaps he ought not to have started it. But he couldn't abandon it now. Oh, his thoughts were all in tangles.

After a while, he went next door and tapped on the door. There was no answer.

He tapped again. 'Gemma! Let me in.'

It seemed a long time till she opened the door and there were tears on her eyelashes. 'Oh, darling, I'm so sorry you're hurting.' He gathered her into his arms and kicked the door shut behind him as she sobbed against him.

When she'd calmed down, he asked, 'Is it the search that's upsetting you? Do you want me to abandon it? Your happiness and welfare are very important to me, you know.'

She looked at him, so sadly, so solemnly that he could see for a moment what she'd look like when she grew older, then she shook her head. 'No, Dad. We've come halfway round the world to find her. We may as well carry on with our quest.'

'Is something else upsetting you, then? Maybe I can help.'

'I'm missing Mum. You can't bring her back, can you? I know she wasn't fair to you, but she and I got on really well, so this has left a big black hole in my life.'

He could only hold her. There was no way he could fill that hole. No way she'd let him start to do so yet.

Perhaps one day, if he was very patient, they'd grow close in their own, different way. He had to cling to that hope.

★　★　★

With the help of various records, Adam and Gemma began to follow a trail long gone cold.

After a few days' search they found a house where Lionel and Dorothy Dobson had lived with their daughter for a good many years and went to see it. The whole place seemed to be sagging and long neglected. They knocked, but only on principle, because clearly it was unoccupied.

An old lady next door looked over the fence as they started back to the car.

'There's no one living there now, hasn't been for a year or so.'

Adam stopped. 'Have you any idea where they went?'

'I know where *he* is, but she's gone to ground.'

'Where is he?'

'In prison and serve him right too, the brute.'

'*In prison!* What for?'

'I don't know exactly. All sorts of things. Beating his poor wife up, for one.'

'Would that be Dorothy?'

'Yes. Do you know her?'

'I used to when we were both teenagers.'

She didn't answer because she'd stopped looking at him and was staring at Gemma. 'I thought at first you were Janey. But you're not, are you? You must be related, though. A cousin, maybe?'

Gemma shot a startled glance in her father's direction.

He stepped into the breach. 'That's what we're trying to find out. Do you know where Janey is?'

'If I did know, I'd not tell a stranger, not after what she's been through.'

Now she was studying him more carefully. 'Are you a relative too? You have a look of Janey as well.'

'I don't know. I may be.' What she said next surprised him.

'Do you have identification, something that proves who you are?'

'Yes. Why?'

'I may be able to get a message to Dorothy. But I won't even try unless I'm sure who you are, and I'll report you to the police if I think you're a bad 'un. She and Janey have been through enough.'

He fished out his passport and held it out to her.

'Can you wait till I fetch something to write

on? The social worker said I need to take down the number of any identification someone produces.'

'I can write the number and details in my notebook, then you can check them before you take the piece of paper.'

She thought about it for a moment or two, studied Gemma again, then nodded. 'All right. You do that. And put how to contact you. Where do you live?'

'Australia. But we're staying in Swindon at the moment.'

When he handed over the sheet of paper, she tucked it into her cardigan pocket and turned to leave.

'You haven't told us your name.'

She stared at him thoughtfully, then said, 'Linda'.

He didn't press for a surname. If she'd wanted them to know, she'd have given it to them. 'When can I expect to hear from you?'

She shrugged. 'I don't know. They're always busy at the centre after Christmas. Might take a few days.'

When they were in the car, he blew out his tension in a long, slow breath. 'What do you make of that?'

Gemma was scowling down at her lap. 'I don't know, and I don't want to talk about it till we find something out.' Almost as if talking to herself, she added, 'I don't really know what I want any more, Dad.'

Neither did he. So he shut up and drove back to the hotel.

But he couldn't get to sleep that night, because he kept going over everything the old lady had said, trying to work out what lay behind it, what 'the centre' was and who 'they' were. And how had a social worker got involved?

She'd said Gemma looked like Janey. That wasn't something she could have made up. And said that he had a look of this Janey too.

Then it occurred to him. Stupid not to have thought of it before. The baby had been christened Catherine Jane.

Oh, hell. Suddenly he knew for certain that he really did have another daughter. And after a few long, quiet breaths, he accepted it in a way he hadn't quite managed to before.

But what had happened to Dorothy? Had she really had such an unhappy life? And why was her husband in jail? He didn't think they put men in jail simply for beating their wives, though maybe they should.

What else had the man done?

15

No jobs were offered to Angus over the Christmas holiday period, so he and Nell didn't bother much with seasonal activities. They continued to work hard on the houses, both eager to get them finished. Already the insides looked brighter and more welcoming, as if they knew they were about to be occupied and loved again.

Which was a rather fanciful thing, Nell thought with a wry smile at herself. But then, if she could believe she was talking to family ghosts, why shouldn't she have fanciful thoughts about other things?

The plumbers started work as soon as the Christmas festivities were over, doing the preliminary setting up even before New Year, as long as Angus guaranteed that the new bathroom suites would not be stolen or if they were he'd pay to replace them.

They both enjoyed seeing men bustling in and out of the houses with purposeful expressions on their faces. They seemed a nice bunch of guys.

Angus agreed to Nell's suggestion of not fitting out the houses with any workshop changes the tenants might need till they were occupied, and she joined him in painting the rooms that wouldn't need plumbing or wiring work.

'I don't like to see you so tired,' he told her

after days of unremitting toil. 'Let's take New Year's Eve off, grab some takeaway and a bottle of fizz.'

'You're on.' She linked her arm in his. 'I don't like to see you looking tired either, my lad, but isn't it worthwhile? Things seem to be going well and no other problems have shown up.'

He made a sign of warding off evil. 'Don't tempt providence.'

★   ★   ★

When they went back to work after their little celebration, they stopped to study the street. 'It's good that they built such solid houses in those days, isn't it?' she said. 'Numbers 2 and 3 are just about ready to show to people, even if Number 1 still has to remain untouched.'

'I try not to think of Number 1. The wheels of bureaucracy grind exceedingly slowly, unlike our wheels of toil. Fancy the heritage people postponing a decision yet again!'

She grinned. He'd just about danced round the kitchen in annoyance when he opened the letter. 'You weren't going to dwell on that.'

'It's the comparison with how hard we're working and how quickly we're getting things done. I'd not have believed it possible that we could make so much progress in such a short time. I've never had such a capable assistant before.'

Her smile was grim. 'You should have seen how hard I worked when I had three lads at

186

home, a full-time job and an absentee husband. At least I'm only responsible for you and me now, and we can grab takeaways when I've no time to cook.'

'Who's dwelling on things now?'

She shrugged. 'I don't think I'll ever forgive Craig, but I do mostly manage to push him to the back of my mind.'

★   ★   ★

As they were walking home at the end of a hard day's work, Angus studied her face. 'I think the word that suits you best is 'indomitable'. As well as feminine, attractive and loving.'

'*Merci du compliment.* A phrase that suits you is 'highly focused'. Though at a personal level, I could add 'sexy' as well.' She mimed burning her fingers on a match.

He chuckled. 'You're a trifle biased, don't you think? I'm rather old to be considered sexy. I've got a lot of grey in my hair.'

'I still find you attractive.' She giggled suddenly. 'I read the phrase 'stud muffin' in a romance novel. That's what I'm going to call you from now on!'

'*Stud muffin?* Good heavens! Whatever will they think of next?'

He stopped and gave her a hug, then they stood close together for a few moments, as they often did.

When they started moving again she asked, 'How are we going to find artists to live in Saffron Lane? And what sort of artists are we

187

looking for? We've discussed it once or twice but we haven't come to any definite conclusions about how we should proceed.'

'I've been so busy I've not really got my head into that side of things. I don't think we'll have any trouble renting out the houses, though. I suppose we'll advertise. We'll plan what we want to say in detail tomorrow, have a real think-tank session. But I've had it for today so let's open a bottle of wine and make some toasted cheese sandwiches. I can't even be bothered to walk to the pub for a meal.'

'Good idea. I'm feeling really tired. If we eat an apple each for dessert, it's just about a healthy meal.'

She fell asleep afterwards on the sofa with half her second glass of wine still unfinished on the low table beside her.

He sat watching her for a while. Sometimes he couldn't believe they'd found one another, given that she'd spent most of her life in Australia. Sometimes he couldn't believe his luck about inheriting the house, either. But he valued her far more than bricks and mortar, even his beloved Dennings.

Life took things and people you loved away from you, sometimes with brutal abruptness. But it could give you other things and people as well, almost as if offering compensation.

One person couldn't replace another, but he'd been incredibly lucky to have two very special women to love.

★   ★   ★

When Angus woke in the morning it was nearly ten o'clock and he was alone in the big, rumpled bed. Amazed at how long he'd slept, he dragged on some clothes and went down to the kitchen, where Nell was sitting at the table, sipping a cup of coffee and staring into space.

'You should have woken me.'

'Why? You must have needed the extra sleep. Anyway, I haven't been up long myself.'

He yawned and stretched, then twisted his head to look at the pad on the table beside her tablet. 'What's that?'

'I'm making a list of galleries to ask about artists. Or else we can simply place an advert, both online and in newspapers, and see who contacts us.'

'Talk about mixing technologies. Why didn't you do that on your tablet?'

'I find it easier to scribble ideas down in between doing other things.'

He considered the list for a moment, head to one side. 'I'd prefer to place an advert than consult galleries. There'd be more chance of variety of artistic medium that way and we could maybe find a couple of artists who're just starting up.'

'They won't be able to afford to pay rent.'

'I was wondering if we should offer six-month rent-free residencies to give them a start. It might garner us some useful PR as well.'

She pursed her lips, then nodded. 'Good idea.'

After pinching a piece of her toast and crunching it happily, he added, 'I don't want to offer our houses only to people who do oil paintings, or even watercolours. And I don't want locals coming to live here, either, but an eclectic mix of people from all over the country. In fact, let's agree to have only one of each type of artist in our row of shop-houses.'

'Good idea. We'll draft an advert as soon as you've finished eating.'

But after two weeks without any calls for help, that was the moment his phone let out the sound of the 'Hallelujah Chorus', which signalled someone needing his services. As usual, he answered that particular sound at once.

Nell watched him, seeing the brisk business-man take over from the rather absent-minded man she found so endearing. He started firing questions, then grabbed her pad, turned to the next page and began taking notes.

She knew he was always concerned about finance so she didn't try to stop him accepting the job, but she wished whoever it was had left them alone for another week. They could have made so much more progress together.

When he'd finished talking, she barred the doorway. 'You're going nowhere till you've had a proper breakfast.'

He looked at her face and his intent look was slowly replaced by a wry smile. 'You're a terrible bully, Nell Chaytor.' Then he frowned. 'You know, we really ought to get married. We keep agreeing that we will, so I don't know why we haven't done the deed. Nell Denning sounds a much nicer name to me.'

'I might not take your name. Why couldn't you take mine?'

'Because of the house.'

'Ah yes. There is your dear little cottage to think about.'

'We'll get married as soon as we have a spare moment,' he said.

She plonked a kiss on his cheek. 'Whatever. But I don't need an official public agreement to tell me I love you and want to be with you, my darling. In the meantime, sit down and I'll make you some scrambled eggs. Won't take long.'

He stayed but he started working on his phone as he waited for her to make his breakfast and within a couple of minutes was lost to what was going on around him. She doubted he'd have noticed if she'd dropped a plate and smashed it right next to him.

He ate the food quickly after she'd waved the plate under his nose a couple of times to draw it to his attention.

When he'd finished she again stopped him leaving. 'One more thing, then you can vanish into your office: do you want me to place an advert for the houses or wait till you've finished this job and work one out together?'

'What? Oh, yes. Please do it now. We've discussed the criteria enough for you to put something together, haven't we?'

He went off to his office without waiting for an answer but she said it anyway, 'Well, we haven't really discussed it in detail, but if I attract the wrong people with my ad, we can always say no. I'm not giving a rent-free house to anyone I don't like the looks of, that's for sure.'

She was well aware that you couldn't always

tell what a person was like from just one meeting, so on the principle that two heads were better than one, she intended to get Angus involved in choosing which applicants to accept, if she had to tie him down to do that. She was quite sure they'd have a lot of responses to their advert, because she intended to place it in one of the big national newspapers and maybe see if the arts editor would like to do an article about what they were planning.

★   ★   ★

Two days later a man who said he was from the council rang to ask if he could speak to Mr Denning.

'He's busy. I'm his partner, so I'm taking all calls,' Nell said crisply. 'Who am I speaking to?'

'Um . . . Dillon Hobkins.'

Why had he hesitated before giving his name? She waited but he didn't clarify further so she asked, 'And which department are you from?'

'Town planning. Look, could you ask Mr Denning to ring me back, please? It's quite urgent.'

'Angus won't be available for a day or two, I'm afraid. He's working on a special project.' She didn't tell this man that Angus was working at home — though she sometimes thought of it as working in cyberland, because mentally he was more absent than present when a project was urgent. And they usually were critical, since he specialised in troubleshooting and apparently had a knack for seeing something that didn't fit

192

properly or had unforeseen consequences when a program was applied to a situation.

She waited and when there was still only silence from the other end, she prompted, 'Surely I could help? I am his business partner, after all.'

'Oh. Er, well, I'm afraid not. You don't own the land.'

Own the land? Why should this caller be so heavily focused on that aspect? She couldn't help thinking that developer might be behind this. A phrase from a passage in the Bible she'd had to learn by heart at school as a punishment leapt suddenly into her mind: *Exodus 20:17* 'Thou shalt not covet thy neighbour's house . . . ' She sometimes thought they were living in an age of greed where people always wanted more, more, more, sometimes even when things clearly belonged to other people.

She didn't probe further and tried to keep her tone indifferent. 'Then I'm afraid you'll have to wait to speak to him. His current project is extremely urgent and could last for several days.' And it was highly lucrative, too.

'I'll write to him. Please bring my letter to his attention and ask him to contact me at the earliest possible moment.'

'I'll do that.'

She felt uneasy as she put down the phone. Very uneasy. She didn't like the thought of the council getting involved in this because they had powers to purchase land compulsorily.

★   ★   ★

193

To Nell's surprise a letter was delivered by hand two hours later. She heard the sound of a small motorcycle then the door knocker was banged several times.

When she answered it, she found a youth holding a large envelope.

'It has to be signed for.'

'What is it?'

He shrugged. 'Dunno. I just deliver them for the council.'

She duly signed and studied the letter as he drove off. The envelope had the council logo on it and Angus's name with 'For personal attention only' on the outside.

She peered into Angus's office but he didn't even notice her, so she went back to the kitchen and stared at the envelope. He'd given her carte blanche to open his mail when he was deep in a project, insisting it was a relief to have her there in case something needed an urgent reply.

Should she or shouldn't she? Then she remembered what Hobkins had let slip and decided this was no time to hang back. Picking up the letter, she slit it open with a kitchen knife and spread it out.

Beneath several rows of headings and contact details, the letter said merely:

Dear Mr Denning,
It has come to our attention that you are making alterations to property on your land at Saffron Lane without the appropriate Council authorisation.
This is against municipal rules.

Please contact us at your earliest convenience to make an appointment so that we can rectify this matter.
Dillon Hobkins
Manager, Building Variations and Extensions, Planning Department

It seemed an unlikely coincidence that two people would be enquiring about that piece of land within a few days after nothing had happened about it for years except for paying the necessary council rates.

She couldn't see exactly how Hobkins would be helping Bryce Dorling, but people wanting to acquire some financially rewarding item could be very cunning in enlisting allies and trying to trick you. Bribery could take many forms and council employees were as susceptible as anyone else.

Even so, it'd take much bigger changes to municipal rules to force Angus to sell that piece of land, because for a start the matter would have to be made available for public discussion before Saffron Lane could be reclassified. And it wasn't in the way of a new highway or anything like that.

Besides, they were only making internal changes. She felt quite sure people didn't need official permission to put in new bathroom suites or rewire their houses, provided they used qualified tradespeople and got the work signed off. No, there was definitely something suspicious about this letter, she just knew it.

And the heritage question about Number 1 needed to be resolved as well. Did these people at the council know about the WWII operations unit? She doubted it. She'd keep that information in reserve till she found out more.

If this Hobkins fellow needed a rapid response, he couldn't have chosen a worse time to make his request. Even if she dragged Angus to a meeting, either her partner would only be half aware of what was going on because he was lost in solving some complex computing problem, or he'd be so furiously angry at being dragged away from his task that he'd be crushingly blunt and offend the official, which was no way to sort out a problem.

Either way, she had to protect him if possible. And protect Dennings, of course. She'd grown to love the big old house and its grounds too. It was . . . a very special place.

What was the best way to deal with this officious man, though? Nothing immediately came to mind.

As she sat tapping her fingers on the table, she noticed the pad on which she'd been drafting an advert. She'd promised herself to get this advert finished and placed in a national newspaper by the end of the day and she might as well get that job out of the way at least. Yes, and she must send an email about it to the arts editor.

Pushing the problem with the council to the back of her mind, she picked up her pencil to draft the advert. They were both keen to put tenants into the second and third houses as soon as possible, not only for the money but for security reasons.

After that she might get Angus to sign a form

196

authorising her to represent him at this projected meeting with the council. Yes, that would probably be the way to go. She was far less likely to lose her temper than he was.

If this was legitimate, there would no doubt be some fiddling little rule that they'd infringed and it'd mean filling in a few acres of official forms.

People were getting snowed under with paperwork these days. So much for the 'paperless office' predicted at the beginning of the computer age. Well, at least she could spare Angus one tedious chore.

But what if what Hobkins was doing wasn't legitimate? How would they even know that?

She still had a very uneasy feeling about this.

Part Three

16

Stacy was having a lazy start to her Sunday, having worked hard at her unit the evening before. She'd been pleased by what she'd done, but creativity could drain you, especially after a full day's work. The guy she was working for temporarily seemed to think that everyone loved working 24/7 on his project, as he did, and it was the last thing she wanted.

Yawning, she leafed through the Sunday paper, then shoved it aside and glanced out of the window. It was sunny, even if cold. She'd go for a walk.

The supplements and advertising material that came with the newspaper were numerous and slippery, and of course they fell off the side table and scattered across the floor when she stood up. Clicking her tongue in annoyance, she bent to pick up the various bits of paper. One fell open at an article which caught her eye: *Art and Crafts Village Opening in Wiltshire*.

She spread it out and read it carefully, sighing wistfully. It sounded like her dream, to live in a place where art of all types was valued, where there were like-minded people to chat to. It sounded as if the housing in this one was deliberately being kept at an affordable price and the occupants would be able to sell their work directly to the public.

Where was this Sexton Bassett anyway? She

looked it up online and found that it was about half an hour's drive away. There was no website or address given for the place, merely a suggestion that artists interested in applying for a residency, which offered a rent-free, six-month tenancy of a cottage, could email a certain address. They should give a brief description of their work and say what their goals were in no more than 250 words, and should attach no more than two photos of their work.

She read it again. This time she noticed a note in smaller print at the bottom which said 'Artists at all levels of their career are invited to apply'.

She probably hadn't achieved enough to get chosen for such an opportunity, but oh, how she'd love to be part of that. Why shouldn't she have a try?

She hesitated, wondering whether she was wasting her time even considering it. Then she got angry at herself for thinking like that. Darren had really eroded her self-confidence. The people who'd bought her pieces had been very complimentary about their whimsical or quirky quality, especially her little metal animals.

She studied the advert again, looking at every word, trying to work out exactly what they wanted. Then she switched on her desktop computer. The old clichés her grandma had often used bounced around her mind.

Nothing ventured, nothing gained.

No time like the present.

Where there's a will, there's a way.

After all, it'd only cost her an hour or so to

draw up a short piece about herself and select a couple of photos.

In fact, it cost her three hours, because she agonised over every word, and after that she had a hard time choosing the pieces whose photos she'd send.

In the end she chose the little animal made from scraps of metal, the idea for which had marked a turning point in her rehabilitation. Because it was so important to her, she'd not sold that one. And with it, she sent a bas-relief abstract made in the days before her marriage. It consisted mainly of cog wheels of all sizes, looking almost as if they were moving in groups across the canvas. Someone had told her it made your eyes follow the swirls.

It was bigger than her usual pieces and designed to hang on a wall. She'd stored it in the industrial unit with the rest of her furniture, and hadn't attempted to unpack it.

Darren had hated it and said it was a childish mishmash and she should be spending her time on more useful things, like decorating their house. After one of their rows, he'd thrown it away without telling her. But she'd seen it lying on the street verge and retrieved it secretly, leaving it with her parents for safety until recently.

And even after that unkindness, she'd stayed with him, desperately trying anything she could think of to hold their marriage together. Oh, what a coward she'd been! But she'd never expected her marriage to fail, never, because she wanted so much to have a relationship as happy as that of her parents!

She reread her application one final time, closed her eyes for a moment to make a fervent wish, then sent off the email.

Even if the people starting up this Arts and Crafts Village never replied, she'd had the courage to apply, and that soothed some raw place inside her. Just a little.

She was, she felt, getting there, wherever 'there' was, moving forward one slow step at a time into a new and more fulfilling life.

★ ★ ★

Elise studied the houses for sale online, then looked at the newspaper, which she didn't usually buy, but this time she'd had a fancy to read one in the old-fashioned way instead of online.

She didn't know why she bothered. She'd investigated all the places in her price range and just after Christmas wasn't the best time for selling or buying houses, so there weren't any new ones being offered. What was she going to do? Somehow she had to find a place to live, even if it was only temporary.

Sighing, she put the paper down and glanced out of the window. But there was no sign of Harriet. She was going to miss that girl when she went back to university in another couple of days' time, miss her dreadfully.

As if her thoughts had summoned her great-niece, Harriet drove up to the house just then in Elise's car and bounced into the house with some bags of shopping.

'It's only me!' she yelled. 'I got everything you wanted.'

She went to dump the purchases in the kitchen and came to the door of the sitting room with a disapproving look on her face. 'You didn't eat much breakfast, did you?'

'I wasn't hungry.' Elise found herself being ruthlessly hugged and clung to the loving young woman for a moment or two. As she pulled away she wished she had a firm young body again, or even a saggy middle-aged one, not an old wreck of a life vehicle that needed a lot of effort to keep it running.

'Cheer up, Auntie. You'll find somewhere to live soon, I just know it. And it won't be long before you're able to drive and go shopping yourself. No more hair-raising adventures with an inexperienced driver like me. I'm going to miss having a car, though.'

'I think you drive very well, considering. But you're right, it will be a relief to be independent again. And you'll be free from the mammoth clean-up chore.'

'I've enjoyed it. It's the nicest way I've ever earned money. It sure beats stacking shelves in a supermarket or working at a fast-food outlet.' She gave Elise another hug and dumped the colour magazine from the newspaper into her lap. 'Have you seen that?'

The magazine was open at a page with the heading: *Artists' Village Opening in Sexton Bassett.*

'What has that to do with me?'

'Read it.'

So Elise studied the article, then read it through a second time more slowly.

'If you could get taken on in this place, it'd be an ideal place for you to live, don't you think?'

'They're hardly likely to accept an old woman like me.'

'Now who's being ageist?' Harriet wagged her forefinger at Elise in mock reprimand. 'Is your computer switched on? Good. Go and write an application now.'

'I'd be wasting my time.'

'You have plenty of time to waste. Anyway, you aren't usually a coward. You could at least have a go at it. Go on. Do it for me.'

Grumbling, Elise sat down at the computer and started a new document. As she worked to sum herself up in one page flat, her confidence rose. She hadn't done badly, actually, when you looked at what she'd achieved. And if it wasn't for this stupid hip, she'd have had her second exhibition by now. Even without it, the gallery had just reported another sale of one of her paintings.

'Cup of coffee and a sticky bun,' a voice said beside her.

'Mmm. Thanks.'

When Elise looked up again the coffee cup was three-quarters full of cold liquid and the bun had had two bites taken out of it.

'How's it going?'

She turned to Harriet, who was hovering in the doorway. 'Have you time to read it and tell me what you think?'

She almost held her breath as Harriet bent over the computer.

'It's good but you don't do yourself justice. Give me a few minutes to work on it.' She made a shooing motion with one hand. 'Go on, finish eating that bun and then move your body about a bit. You're walking stiffly.'

When Elise returned after a stroll round the garden, Harriet was leaning back reading the piece and nodding.

'Here you are. See what you think.'

Elise read it in astonishment. Was this what her niece thought of her? She'd never have dared say such things about herself. 'Isn't it a bit . . . boastful?'

'No. Everything I've said is true.'

She could feel herself blushing. 'Oh. Well, thank you.'

'Which pictures are you going to send photos of, Auntie?'

'I don't know.'

'Which is your favourite? Oh yes, I like the lake at sunset too. Let me choose the other one. It has to show a different type of subject.'

When everything was ready, Harriet flourished one hand towards the computer. 'Go on. Send it. I'm not letting you alter a word.'

So Elise took a deep breath and clicked on send, then found herself being danced round the room.

'You'll get one of those houses, Auntie, I just know you will. Oh, I wish I could be here to see your face when you find out.'

'Don't be too disappointed if I don't get chosen.'

'Don't drop dead of shock when you *do* get chosen.'

17

Hobkins hummed and hawed when Nell phoned him but she used the 'broken record' trick and refused to be sidetracked, just kept quietly insisting that Angus was too busy to deal with this at present and that she had full authority to act on his behalf.

After she had refused to budge on the matter for several iterations, he made an irritated sound and agreed to deal with her 'in the first instance'. But not for a couple of days as something urgent had come up at his end.

He'd said his business with Angus was urgent, so what was going on here to make him delay, she wondered? She didn't trust him, not in the slightest.

In the meantime, she carried on, getting the walls of another couple of rooms painted and making sure Angus remembered to eat, since this job was proving to be what he called 'delightfully tricky'. Most people would have found that irritating, but her man loved puzzles of any sort.

★ ★ ★

When the day of her appointment with Hobkins came, she dressed in the one and only business outfit she'd brought with her to England the previous year. How long ago that seemed! How her life had changed since meeting Angus.

'Let's see what this stupid man wants,' she muttered as she went off to meet Hobkins.

She was puzzled to find another man sitting to one side of the office and waited to be introduced to him. But Hobkins only waved one hand and murmured something about his colleague sitting in.

'And does your colleague have a name — and the right to be involved in this?'

Hobkins had been fiddling with some papers and her words seemed to startle him, because he dropped his pen. 'Um, we work as a team here at the council.'

'Even team members usually have names. I like to know who I'm dealing with, and why.' She got out a notebook and wrote down the date. 'I'll just take the names of the people present for my records.'

Hobkins looked distinctly rattled by that. A few seconds ticked slowly past before he said, 'This is, um, Mr Dorling.'

Bullseye! she thought. That proved there was something fishy about this whole set-up. 'Of Dorling and Cavendish?'

The men exchanged quick glances, as if surprised that she recognised the name. Did the idiots think Angus wouldn't talk to her?

'As I told you before, Mr Hobkins, I'm Angus's business partner, so naturally he showed me the written offer from Mr Dorling's company, to buy Saffron Lane. What I don't understand is how a private contractor would be involved in minor council business like this — and for the same set of buildings.'

210

Dorling looked towards Hobkins and when the official made no explanation, he said in a soothing tone, as if she was a halfwit, 'I'm here in an advisory capacity, that's all, Ms Chaytor.'

'Well, *I* don't need advice and I'd prefer to deal only with a council officer if this is official business.'

'It, um, never hurts to consult an expert,' Hobkins offered.

'Then if you'll tell me what sort of expertise I need, I'll find an appropriate expert to represent my partner and myself, then we'll reconvene this meeting on a more equal footing.'

She waited, thinking what a poor conspirator Hobkins made and how clear it was from his uneasy expression that this was not all above board.

After the silence had dragged on for a minute or two, Dorling stood up. 'No worries, Ms Chaytor. If that's your wish, I'll leave you to discuss it without an adviser.' He paused at the door to stare at Nell and add, 'After all, Hobkins and I can always talk about the matter later.'

If that wasn't a threat, she'd never heard one. And how did he know her name? She'd never been introduced to him. Everything official at Dennings was in Angus's name, as was only right, and she certainly wasn't on the electoral roll yet.

When the door had closed behind Dorling, she looked at the council official and waited. Again it took him some time to speak.

'This is a matter of planning permissions,' he said.

'For what?'

'Alterations to property.'

'We weren't aware that the owner needed planning permission to renovate a house internally. There are no structural or external changes being made, beyond replacing roof tiles as necessary.'

He gave a mirthless laugh. 'After those houses have stood empty all this time? For several decades, in fact! I find it hard to believe that no structural changes are needed, whether internal or external.'

'The exteriors of the houses were properly maintained during that period and stayed watertight.'

'Nonetheless, I'd like to see for myself what's going on.'

'Are you calling me a liar? Because if so, I'll consult our lawyer and you'll definitely have to go through him before you try to push your way into our houses for a reason I would consider sheer nosiness. Are you just prying . . .' she paused, letting the final words follow slowly and emphatically, 'or are you looking for faults?'

His mouth fell open and a slight flush coloured his thin cheeks. 'I need to be sure nothing is being done that ought not to be, which is a major part of my role here. Those are old houses and might not be safe. I might even consider it in the public interest to demolish them.'

She looked at him in shock. Was that what they were intending to do? Just let them try!

'We've already had a structural engineer check the houses.'

'We didn't approve anyone.'

'You didn't need to.'

'Look, the matter can, um, be settled quite easily by me bringing one of our building inspectors to look at the houses.'

'You do employ your own inspectors?'

'Yes, of course.'

'Then why did we need Mr Dorling's expertise and advice today? Are you and your inspectors not fully qualified?' She could see that he was still sweating slightly.

'Of course I'm qualified to do my job. And we have some, um, very experienced staff, but sometimes they're busy.' He turned to his computer terminal. 'Now, about a time for this inspection.'

'I can't arrange that now. Mr Denning will want to be present to answer any technical queries. I'll present your request to him and he'll get back to you when he's finished this project, which is at a critical stage. He'll want to show you the structural engineer's report first, no doubt.'

'As I said, that wasn't an engineer approved by us.'

She was feeling more suspicious by the minute. If she had any say in the matter, Angus would consult a lawyer, whatever it cost, and have one with him at any future meetings with this man who was, she reckoned, on the fiddle and already planning to find a way to demolish Saffron Lane. He didn't make a very good conspirator, though.

She stood up and without giving Hobkins time to argue, walked quickly out of the room, not bothering to say goodbye or close the door behind her.

At the end of the corridor, she stopped to shake a bit of grit out of her left shoe and because she had excellent hearing and the office area was quiet, she heard him speaking on the phone. 'Dorling? She's gone. You can come back now.'

There was definitely something underhand going on.

Well, she intended to make sure those two didn't get away with whatever they were planning.

⋆ ⋆ ⋆

As she'd expected, Angus was furious when she told him what had been said at her meeting with Hobkins.

'Give me three or four more hours working on this thing and I'll be finished. Then I can give you — and Hobkins — my fullest attention.'

'No need to rush. I don't think we should do anything else or arrange any more meetings without having a lawyer present. Who's your lawyer for property matters?'

He gave a smile that was more shark-like than a sign of amusement. 'I've been using an old guy who knows the local regulations better than anyone, but I'm not sure he's up to an outright court battle these days. I'll contact him tomorrow and ask his advice about who would be useful to have on our side, as well as asking him about the legal situation.'

'Let me contact his office today, while you're working, and arrange a meeting early tomorrow, if possible. What's his name?'

'Clifford Olliphant. His phone number's in the book. He's got rooms just behind High Street. I wonder — ' He broke off in the middle of a sentence and walked out of the room, bumping into the doorpost and moving on again as if he hadn't noticed. She shook her head fondly. His mind was clearly back on his job.

When she phoned Mr Olliphant's office, his secretary said he was preparing to retire and would they like to speak to Mr Alexander instead, because he was taking over the practice? So they agreed on an appointment for the following morning at ten o'clock.

Angus had better be ready by then, Nell thought, because this wasn't something she felt qualified to deal with on her own.

Another of her grandmother's sayings popped into her mind. *Two heads are better than one.*

Especially if one head belonged to her super-clever partner and husband-to-be.

Angus managed to finish his project by midnight, letting out his usual wild yell of triumph and waking Nell, who had fallen asleep on the sofa.

She insisted on making him a substantial snack, because he was always hungry after a long stint in front of his computers. After that they went to bed and she listened to him fall instantly asleep.

She wasn't slow to follow his example.

⋆ ⋆ ⋆

The following morning they went to see Russell Alexander as arranged.

The lawyer, who looked to be about the same age as them, listened to their story and frowned. 'Would you mind if we brought Mr Olliphant in to hear this? It does sound dodgy and Cliff is still working here part-time. I reckon he knows the local building regulations better than anyone in town.'

Mr Olliphant listened to their tale and looked at Nell in surprise. 'Are you sure you've got it right, my dear?'

'Certain,' Nell said.

'Well, in my opinion, the only reason they can have for coming to inspect the property that would hold up in court is that someone has lodged a complaint against you, alleging that the houses are in a dangerous condition. Why would anyone make such a complaint? Who's been looking at your row of houses?'

'No one that I know of except the tradespeople working on them,' Angus said. 'Oh, there was also that Dorling chap, but he only got as far as the front room of Number 2.'

'*Dorling!*' Mr Olliphant's voice was sharper. 'Would that be Bryce Dorling?'

'Yes.'

'Have nothing to do with the fellow and don't

trust him as far as you can throw him, however plausible he sounds.'

He hesitated, then added, 'Strictly between these four walls, he's a con merchant. Unfortunately, I was never able to pin him down and prove it because he's not only cunning, but has influential friends in Sexton Bassett, including on the council. I'm fairly sure one particular councillor warned one or two of its members that it'd be personally dangerous to go against Dorling's projects.'

He shook his head regretfully. 'One chap told me about the warning, said they'd threatened his wife — not in so many words but that's what it amounted to: a threat to her safety. He refused to elaborate on that, let alone do anything about it. So Dorling was able to push through permission to erect a group of rather nasty modern buildings in a nearby village. Those buildings didn't at all fit in with the vernacular style of the other nearby dwellings and I'd consider them 'all show and no go' if I were thinking of buying one. They looked pretty from outside but were much smaller than you'd think inside.'

He sighed. 'Dorling threatened me too recently, though again very obliquely. But there was no mistaking his meaning. Please don't quote me about that because I don't have any witnesses. I'd have found a way to challenge him when I was younger, but I'm afraid I'm not in the best of health and I just want to retire without any hassles, so I've worked round him.'

'Oh dear!' Nell exchanged glances with Angus.

Mr Olliphant rubbed his chin, looking

217

thoughtful. 'Please tread carefully. We have some capable and socially conscious developers in this part of England, but his sort pop up here and there, and they give the industry a bad name.'

'He's got Hobkins doing his bidding, that's obvious,' Nell said.

'I'm surprised Dillon is going along with him. I've known him for years and always thought him an honest plodder. I wonder what hold they've got over the poor chap.'

'He kept turning to Dorling for help when they were talking to me,' Nell said. 'I wasn't imagining that.'

'Hmm. You'd better watch out for intruders on your property, Mr Denning. One house that was being disputed about being scheduled for demolition suddenly burnt down a couple of years ago. They said it was caused by an electrical fault, but the owner didn't believe that and nor did I. Only, once again, we couldn't prove anything. There always has to be proof for the law to take action — fortunately or unfortunately, depending on your standpoint in the dispute.'

He sat frowning for a moment or two longer, then snapped his fingers. 'I'll see if I can find out who complained about you, at least. I can't guarantee anything and it may take a few days, but I do have a contact who may know. I'd like to help you. My swansong, as you might say. It'll make up a bit for my being rather, um, careful whom I upset in the past year.'

As Angus and Nell were driving home, they discussed the situation, but it was hard to fight a battle with an enemy whose weapons were so nebulous.

'I'm disappointed in Olliphant, though,' he said. 'He used to be known as a fighter for the underdog.'

'He's getting old and probably feels less able to protect himself. From what I've been told by other older people, that can hit hard. There used to be some lovely oldies living in our street, and I don't think Australia is that different from England. One of them grew rather frail and was treated shamefully by her relatives, who shoved her in the cheapest care home they could find and waited to collect their inheritance. She obliged them by pining away quickly. Another had the most wonderful daughter who came to live with her when her memory began to fail and cared for her devotedly till the end. People can be amazingly kind as well as horrible.'

'Well, we both know which type Dorling is.' Angus smiled as he added, 'And I know which type you are, darling, the absolute opposite to him. I love being in a relationship with you.'

She treasured those words as she started work on another house in Saffron Lane. Her first husband had never said anything half as nice, not even in the early days when she'd been blind to his faults.

★   ★   ★

That afternoon, Nell was doing paperwork in the library when the old-fashioned phone rang. She debated not answering it, but in the end she

219

picked it up. If it was that idiot from the council, she'd put the phone down again without speaking. She hadn't the patience to deal with him today.

It wasn't Hobkins, though. Without waiting for her to speak, a husky disguised voice warned her not to block business initiatives in the town if she valued her own safety.

Her Aussie bluntness surged up in a tide of anger. 'And I'm warning you in return, you stupid galah, that I took an excellent self-defence course and can guarantee to give anyone trying to attack me a nasty surprise. So sod off and be careful who you threaten next time. I always fight back tooth and nail against bullying.'

The phone was disconnected, but not before she'd heard a gasp of what sounded like surprise at the other end. The voice had sounded very tinny, perhaps a cheap pay-as-you-go mobile phone. Who knew? She'd tell Angus about it later.

'Tell him now,' a voice seemed to say in her ear. 'He's in danger too.'

Was that one of the family ghosts?

She hesitated, then did as the ancestor suggested. She needed to stretch her legs anyway and could take Angus a snack while she was at it.

*   *   *

She called out as she entered Number 4 and Angus yelled, 'In the front bedroom.'

She dumped her food on the kitchen windowsill for lack of anywhere else. The new kitchen units weren't being fitted until the next few days.

When she went upstairs she found him kneeling on the floor just inside the door, finishing sealing the floorboards. He beamed at her. 'One minute and I'm done. To what do I owe the pleasure of this visit? I hope you haven't come empty-handed. I think I forgot to have my lunch.'

'You didn't come back to the house for it, that's for sure, so it's a good thing I brought you something to eat and drink. Do you have time for a break now? It's cold but we could sit on that old bench outside the kitchen. It looks to be a sunny, sheltered spot.'

He stood up, dusting down his overalls. 'I'm ravenous, so lay on, Macduff.'

She finished the quotation, 'And damned be him who first cries 'Hold! Enough!''

'You're one of the few people I've met who says that correctly, Nell, my love. Most say 'Lead on, Macduff!' and that makes me wince.'

'I used to read a lot when the boys were little. I didn't think you were an avid reader, though, Angus.'

'Not usually of fiction or poetry, but I do have an excellent memory for whatever I've read.'

⋆ ⋆ ⋆

When they were sitting on the bench she dipped into her bag of food and passed him a thermal mug of coffee, waiting till he'd had a big swig to hand him a sandwich.

'You're a lifesaver, my love.'

'I did leave you some coffee-making equipment in Number 2.'

He shrugged. 'I keep forgetting.'

She tried to work out how to tell him about the caller and his expression instantly turned serious. 'What's happened now? Just tell me straight out.'

'I had an anonymous phone call warning me not to block business initiatives in the town if I valued my safety.'

'What did you do?'

'Told him to sod off and said I'd taken self-defence courses.'

'And have you?'

'Oh, yes. And used the moves a couple of times, too, the first one against my husband when he hit me.'

'Did you hurt him?'

'Gave him a nasty twinge where it hurts a man most.'

He chuckled, then turned serious. 'Go on.'

'I wasn't going to say anything about the call till this evening, but one of our friendly ghosts warned me that you were in danger too and I should tell you straight away.'

They had both stopped eating.

He sighed. 'I'd better set up a security system for Saffron Lane after I've done the floors in here. In the meantime I'll make sure that anyone opening a door after dark in any of the houses sets off a very loud siren. I have some bits and pieces I can put together temporarily.'

'Good. On a happier note, the applications are

coming in for the residencies. We'll go through those this evening. The sooner we get tenants living here, the safer the properties will be. Numbers 2 and 3 are just about ready, aren't they?'

'Yes.' He finished his sandwich and stood up. 'You go back to the house now. I'll be up in a couple of hours.'

She was very thoughtful as she walked back, wondering if the anonymous caller would indeed attack her. Just let anyone try!

18

Tired of hotel life and catering, Adam and Gemma found temporary serviced accommodation to rent, of the sort sometimes used by businessmen working short-term in an area. It was utilitarian but with all the necessary facilities to communicate with the world.

The small block of flats was on the outskirts of Sexton Bassett, which looked to be a lovely little town. He didn't remember having much to do with that side of Swindon because he'd lived north of the city.

The owner of the flats had provided access to the Internet so Adam bought a second-hand desktop computer and printer, which were so much better on the body when working for long hours than peering down at a laptop or tablet and getting a crick in the neck.

With Gemma sitting by his side, he again went through the trail of clues that the private investigator had followed up on. Some had seemed promising at first but had led nowhere, and all were minutely documented, which was helpful.

In the early years of their marriage Dorothy and Lionel Dobson had lived near Swindon. But for the next few years it was as if the Dobsons had been deliberately avoiding notice.

Why would they have done that?

When they reappeared in the records, they

were living in the house Adam and his daughter had already visited. Which brought him back to relying on the old lady next door.

'I don't want to go off playing the tourist for more than an hour or two at a time yet,' he said a few mornings after they'd moved in. 'I haven't given up on the neighbour getting in touch with us.'

'I'll be surprised if she does.'

'She seemed genuine about her offer.'

'What shall we do if she doesn't get back to us, Dad?'

'Go and visit her again. I'll beg her help on my knees if I have to.'

She didn't say anything, but she patted his arm, as if she knew his emotions and thoughts were in turmoil.

★   ★   ★

But they had no need to go back to the old lady. Two days later Adam's phone rang before they'd even had breakfast. He pulled it out of his pocket. 'I don't know this number.'

He recognised the voice before the caller gave her name, though.

'Linda here. I promised to see if I could find Dorothy for you.'

'I remember. I was thinking of coming back to see you if you didn't phone us. You're the only real clue we have.'

She gave a rusty chuckle. 'No need, Mr Torrington. I spoke to Dorothy and she wanted time to think about it. Could you tell me exactly

225

why you came to England, do you think?'

'To find her. I only recently discovered an important letter she sent to me in Australia nineteen years ago.' He explained about going through his late wife's possessions.

'All right. You've convinced me. You can tell Dorothy about that yourself. She's going to ring you tomorrow evening at seven-thirty if I'm satisfied with your answers today. You didn't seem like a liar to me when I met you, and I'm pretty good at reading faces. If I hadn't trusted you, I'd not even have contacted her.'

'Thank you very much for your help. I'm really grateful.'

'It's for Dorothy's sake I'm doing it. She needs closure on certain things that have been upsetting her for the past nineteen years. And that daughter of yours might have an interest in the affair too, don't you think?'

He was struggling to find a satisfactory answer when she said, 'No need to go further into that, eh? It's between you and Dorothy to settle it now.'

The line went dead.

He had to sit down. How strange! He didn't usually feel wobbly about things. But this quest was starting to turn up some very important answers.

He realised Gemma had come to sit on the sofa next to him and was looking at him anxiously. He took her hand while he explained exactly what Linda had told him.

She was silent for a few moments but she didn't push him away as she said abruptly, 'You look upset and nervous as well.'

'I am. This could be so very important.'

'To us both,' she said quietly. 'She's my half-sister, isn't she? Though I still don't know whether to hope we make contact with her or to hope we don't.'

'I've been giving it a lot of thought and — '

'Is that why you're sleeping so badly?'

'How did you know?' He'd tried not to make a noise.

'I can hear you tossing and turning in this horrid little flat. And you look deep-down tired with dark circles round your eyes.'

'Oh. Well anyway, I've decided that if I do have another daughter, I don't just want to meet her; I want to get to know her. Do you mind?'

Her silence had him worried, then she said in a voice that shook, 'I think I'll want to get to know her too, unless she's horrible.'

'That isn't surprising, is it?'

Gemma gave one of those offhand shrugs she used to hide her emotions. 'Anyway, we came all this way, didn't we? If we have a chance of finding this Dorothy and her daughter, it'd be stupid to back out now.'

'Yes. It would.'

They sat in more of that heavy silence for a few minutes, each wrapped in thought, then he said abruptly, 'Let's go out for the rest of today. We've earned a break. Anywhere you like that's not more than a two-hour drive away.'

'Oxford. It's one of the places on my list.'

'Oxford it is.'

They met the manager of the flats on their way

227

out and she suggested they leave their car at a park-and-ride station on the outskirts of the city and ride in by bus. 'Can't find parking in Oxford for love nor money most days.'

So that was what they did.

★   ★   ★

As they strolled round the streets, Adam watched Gemma stare and marvel, not surprised at her oohs and aahs. It was a truly beautiful city, in spite of the traffic.

'Those students are so lucky to come here to university,' she said wistfully, watching a lively group at another table when they stopped for a coffee. 'There's something about these old colleges, an atmosphere you don't get with modern buildings.'

'Well, if you achieve the high marks expected in your final results, you might be able to study here too, if you wanted.'

She stared at him in amazement. 'You can't mean that! Even if I got a place, wouldn't it be too expensive?'

He took a deep breath. 'No, Gemma. You keep refusing to discuss your mother's will, but you've inherited her life insurance money, because she named you as the beneficiary, and that alone is going to be more than enough to cover your expenses. And once we sell the house, you'll have more money. In fact, you'll be extremely comfortably off.'

'But half the house belongs to you, so we'll be sharing it.'

'Yes. But Judith and I bought well and there isn't any mortgage to pay off. In our suburb house prices have zoomed up in the past ten years. Perth has grown rapidly as a city but it's a rather expensive place to live. I'd like to put the house on the market as soon as you're ready to move on, start afresh with you somewhere new.'

Her voice was sharp. 'I'll think about it.'

'No hurry.' He tried not to show that he'd noticed the tears in her eyes. 'We could make enquiries about places for you in one of the Oxford colleges once you've decided what you really want to study. I don't think it's business, is it?'

She shook her head.

'But it might be a good idea to go to a technical college or some other preparatory place of study for a term or two first to add to your attractiveness as a potential student.'

Gemma shivered. 'I'd be on my own in England if I did my degree here.'

'No, you wouldn't. That's the other decision which has been keeping me awake. I'm going to contact my head of department to confirm that I do want a whole year's leave without pay. I did warn him that it was possible and he said he understood. He's a family man too.'

'How will you live?'

'I've got some money saved and I can rent out my present flat to a guy I know. My skills are very portable and I can pick up odd jobs here and there in England.'

'It'd help at first to have you around. It all feels so weird. And if this half-sister and I get on well, I'll have her here too. If she wants to know me, that is.'

'I'm sure she will want to know you, darling.'

'I feel as if someone has given my life a good hard shake and jumbled up all the different parts of it.'

'Join the club. That's exactly how I feel. It'll be like a jigsaw puzzle putting the whole new picture together piece by piece, won't it?'

By the time they got home they were tired and went to bed early with the books they'd bought in Oxford.

They'd agreed to spend the next day quietly, perhaps with a drive out into the countryside and lunch at one of the beautiful rural pubs.

Who knew what the next evening would bring?

⋆　⋆　⋆

At precisely seven-thirty the following evening the phone rang. Adam took a deep breath and picked it up. There was silence at the other end but he was sure he could hear someone breathing, so he said quietly, 'Adam Torrington here. Is that you, Dorothy?'

'Yes. Only I've changed my name to Hope.'

'Nice name.'

Silence fell again. He couldn't think what to say. How awkward this was! 'Er, how are you?' Very original, that!

'I'm getting better all the time.'

'Have you been ill?'

'Sort of. I had to take shelter in a women's refuge. Lionel was . . . violent.'

'No! Is that why he's in prison?'

'Partly. The main reason is he was growing and dealing in marijuana with his stupid cousin.'

'Then he deserves to be behind bars.'

'You don't sound to have changed, Adam. You always seemed so vigorous and enthusiastic about life. Tell me about yourself.'

So he told her about meeting Judith, offering the information as frankly as she'd spoken to him about the sort of problem abused women usually hid. Then he spoke about Judith's recent death and his daughter Gemma. Strange that he still found it easy to talk to Dorothy. No, she was Hope now, he reminded himself.

'You have a daughter, Adam? That's nice.'

'Yes. And so do you, I gather.' He stopped speaking, giving her the chance to tell him about that.

'You know about my Janey, don't you? That she's yours, I mean.'

'I'd guessed. I didn't receive your letter all those years ago, or I'd have come back to England to help you. Judith intercepted it. Gemma and I found it among her things when we were clearing out her room.'

'Linda told me you'd said that.' She began sobbing suddenly.

'What have I said? I didn't mean to hurt you. Doro — Hope, I mean. What is it?'

'You've no idea how much it means to know you didn't deliberately abandon me back then because I was pregnant. Sorry. I still cry rather easily. Tell me about your daughter. Linda says she looks very like Janey.'

'She told us that, too. Hope, can we meet? It's not the same talking on the phone.'

'I'll have to think about it.'

'Can I have your phone number, then? I could ring you next time.'

'I'd rather not give it you. Not till I've seen my counsellor and worked through my feelings. I can't — I just *can't* do any more tonight, Adam. I will ring you again, though. If you need to get a message to me, call Linda.' She gave him her former neighbour's number, unnecessarily as he'd already taken note of it when Linda rang him, but he didn't say that.

'Promise you'll phone me again, Hope.'

'I promise.'

The line went dead.

He filled in the gaps for Gemma, who had heard only his side of the conversation because he'd felt putting the phone on speaker mode would have given the voices an echo and he hadn't wanted Hope to be put off by anything.

Gemma stared down at the rug, then looked across at him. 'It sounds as if she's had a tough life.'

'Yes. It does.'

'I wonder what her daughter's like, this Janey.'

'I'm praying we'll get the chance to find out.'

'She must have had a tough life, too, if her mother has. I'm glad Hope promised to ring again, Dad.'

'She wouldn't give me her phone number, though, would she? And it's a hidden number. The poor woman is clearly still in a delicate state of mind and cries easily. Damn this Lionel fellow

232

to high hell! I'd like to give him a good thumping.'

And damn Judith for keeping the original situation from him. But he managed not to say that to Judith's grieving daughter.

'We'll have to wait and find out if Hope will keep her word,' he said at last.

Gemma nodded and picked up her book, but he noticed she didn't turn many pages and did a lot of staring into space.

He couldn't concentrate on anything, either.

19

Elise used the picker-up gadget to get the letters that had fallen through the front door mail flap. She still used it rather than risk bending right down without anything to hold on to. That fall had certainly weakened her confidence in her ability to navigate the world.

She took the post through into the kitchen and spread it out on the table. More offers to sell her house: 'Buyers waiting'. Ha! She'd insisted on having the 'For sale' sign taken down but they could have rung her estate agent and found that the house had already been sold and not wasted their paper and her time. Fools! Heaven help anyone who put their most valuable possession into such hands. She tossed the junk into the rubbish bin.

That left one letter. It looked official and when she turned it over, she gasped at the sender's name: Sexton Bassett Arts and Crafts Village. She hadn't expected to get a reply so quickly.

She stood holding it, not in a hurry to see the rejection it no doubt contained, because she'd been allowing herself a tiny strand of hope. Then she got angry with herself and tore the envelope open so roughly she ripped a corner off the letter and had to hold it in place to read the final phrases.

Dear Ms Carlton,

Thank you for your application for a tenancy at our Arts and Crafts Village.

Without committing ourselves to anything, we'd like to move to the next stage with you.

We'd be very interested to meet you and I'm sure you'll want to see the village — though it's really only a street. Would it be possible for you to come to Sexton Bassett so that we can get to know one another a little better?

You'll want to look round the houses, but we'll warn you in advance that we haven't finished them off completely inside because we don't know what types of artists will be occupying them.

Perhaps you could phone or email us? Any day next week will be fine for a visit. Whatever suits you.

A map is enclosed to show you how to get to Saffron Lane if you're driving.

Yours sincerely
Nell Chaytor, Project Manager

Elise was so stunned by this response she collapsed on the nearest chair, still clutching the letter so tightly she had to smooth it out before she could read it again.

Positive, was all she could think of. It was a positive reaction. She'd got through to the second round. She smiled, then cried a little out of both pleasure and relief.

She made herself a pot of tea and while it was

brewing she got her road atlas out of her car. Sexton Bassett was two hours' drive away at least.

Oh dear! She was a bit worried about driving there and back at this stage in her recovery, even though she was now driving quite comfortably around town.

If only Harriet was here to take her.

She couldn't let this opportunity pass, so perhaps she could hire a car and driver? Yes, of course, that would do just fine. This was no time to worry about the cost.

She lost herself in dreams for a while. There was nothing she'd like more than to live in such a community. Her long-time home had become a very lonely place after her husband's death and she'd be glad to be away from the area now that dear Victor was no longer alive, either.

She finished her tea then went to her computer and researched hired cars with drivers. One caught her eye because it showed a photo of the driver, a middle-aged woman with a delightful smile.

She picked up the phone. 'Amy's Luxury Cars? I'd like to book a car and driver for the day next Monday.'

Only after she'd put down the phone did she realise she hadn't checked with Ms Chaytor as to whether Monday morning would be suitable. How silly of her! They'd said any day would do but she'd better check.

She picked up the phone again.

★   ★   ★

The post arrived early, just one letter. When Stacy turned it over and saw on the envelope who it was from, her heart started to thump. She decided she had time to open it before setting off for work if she was quick.

Without thinking she used the butter knife to open it and got grease all over the envelope.

'Idiot!' she muttered to herself.

The letter was from someone called Nell Chaytor, telling her she'd got through to the second round of applications for the Arts and Crafts Village.

She stopped reading to clap one hand to her mouth, she was so astounded by this, then took a deep, shaky breath and read the rest of the letter.

It didn't take more than a minute for her to decide she'd better ring straight away and book a visit for Monday morning, because that was her day off this coming week. She didn't want to tell anyone at work what she was doing. The two guys were nice enough but too busy working to chat much.

Her lack of social life meant she'd managed to do quite a bit of artwork in her spare time.

It also meant that she was feeling rather lonely.

But at least Darren hadn't found her. She prayed he'd let the stalking go now he'd spooked her into running away. Surely that would be enough to satisfy his ego?

She got out her phone and rang the number on the letterhead.

'Stacy Walsh here. I was, um, delighted to receive your letter, Ms Chaytor. Monday is my day off so I wonder if you still have a free spot then?'

'Morning or afternoon?'

'Either but I'd prefer morning.' Get it over with, she thought, then she'd not be hanging around worrying.

'Great. About ten suit you? Good. We'll look forward to meeting you. And perhaps we could see another of your creations?'

When she ended the call Stacy sat in utter numbness for a few minutes. She couldn't believe she'd got this far.

What if she actually gained one of the residencies? How good would that be? She could live on her savings for that long if she didn't have to pay rent and hope to pad them out with a few sales here and there.

She probably wouldn't get it, though. They must have had loads of applications. But until they told her no, she could allow herself to dream a little, couldn't she?

Then she saw the time and let out a squeak of dismay. She was going to be late for work.

★   ★   ★

Nell was delighted when she received a phone call the Monday after she posted the letters out to the two applicants they had liked best of all. Strange that out of so many applicants they'd only picked four, and then decided to start off with two, because it would be enough trouble getting two houses ready for occupation.

238

Strange how these two applicants had jumped out as exactly the sort of people they were looking for. They'd written such nice personal letters as well as sending photos of beautiful samples of their work.

But strangest of all that one of the most suitable applicants was called Stacy. The ghosts she seemed to hear might just have been right about whose house Number 2 was.

As she put the phone down, she smiled. She'd liked the sound of Stacy Walsh, who didn't come over as brash and overconfident.

The phone rang again. 'Nell Chaytor.'

'Elise Carlton here.'

'How nice to hear from you so quickly, Ms Carlton.'

'I was so thrilled to receive your letter, and it did say any time next week, so I booked a car to bring me over. Then I realised I hadn't confirmed it with you first. So silly of me, but I was excited, you see.'

'Do you not drive?'

'Yes, but I'm recovering from an operation and not up to driving there and back in one day.'

'Oh, I see. When did you book the car for?'

'Monday morning.'

'Oh dear. I've just put the phone down and one of the other applicants has booked Monday morning.'

'I see. I wasn't thinking very clearly, was I? It's just that I need to move out of this house by the end of next week, so if I got one of the houses, I wanted to see if I could move in immediately. I'm so sorry. I can change my booking for another time, I'm sure. Would Monday afternoon or Tuesday morning be all right instead?'

Nell took a sudden decision. She'd had to move out of her Australian house very quickly to get a lucrative sale and she knew how every day counted. 'Why don't we leave the booking as is? If you get one of the places, you'll want to meet the other applicants and see if you get on with them.'

'Are you sure?'

For some reason she felt quite certain it would be all right. 'Yes. I'd say if it wasn't. But how about you arrive around eleven? The other woman is arriving at ten. We want to have a private chat with each of you, but we can talk to you on your own after she leaves.'

'I'll do that. Thank you so much. I'm deeply grateful to you.'

'I'll look forward to meeting you. Oh, and could you please bring the two paintings you sent photos of and another one? However good the photos, there is something better about a painting in the flesh as it were.'

'Yes, I can do that.' She had no need to change her car booking. The timing was exactly right. What luck!

★ ★ ★

Now she'd spoken to the first two applicants they wanted to interview and made the necessary arrangements, Nell was free to work on the houses or catch up with her housework.

Both of them had sounded as friendly as their

240

letters and . . . well, warm-natured. Could you tell such a thing over the phone?

She couldn't wait to tell Angus. She debated going down to the lane to see him, but since the fitters were just finishing the kitchens in Numbers Two and Three, so would be able to keep an eye on the houses, she had said she'd stay near the landline at the house today and he could join her for a proper lunch.

If he didn't forget.

But for once, he didn't. He arrived just after noon, smiling and ready to discuss the news about the interviews.

After they'd eaten, he took her down to see the kitchens, which were looking great now that the units, surfaces and glass splashbacks had been installed.

Best of all, the guy in charge thought they'd be able to finish that night if they put in an extra hour or two's work.

He cocked one eye at her. 'Any chance of a bite to eat, Mrs Denning, so we don't have to go out for food? We don't need anything fancy, just something to fill our stomachs.'

Knowing that would make them more eager to finish that day Nell promised sandwiches and cake. She didn't correct his assumption that she and Angus were married.

She would be able to give the kitchens a thorough cleaning tomorrow and sort out her shopping list for food. It was all falling into place nicely.

Part Four

20

In the middle of that night the alarm system from Saffron Lane sounded in Angus and Nell's bedroom. When he rushed to look at the monitor attached to the security camera there, he could just make out two dark figures at the front door of the first house, which was on the outer edge of the surveillance system. One was crouching and seemed to be picking the lock.

He rang for police attendance then picked up a rounders bat. 'I'm not waiting for the police. Who knows how long they'll take to get here?'

'I'll grab my rolling pin as we go through the kitchen.'

'I don't want you involved in the fighting, Nell.' He opened the back door, but she came out to join him carrying her makeshift weapon. He sighed in resignation and switched on the big house's security system, then set off at a rapid pace through the dark gardens.

'I didn't do a self-defence course to play the helpless female now,' she panted, finding it hard to keep up with his longer legs.

'Just don't take any risks, right?'

'No more than you will.'

That shut him up.

* * *

The burglar found it harder than he'd expected to pick the big old lock on the front door of the first house in the row.

'How the hell can this damned lock be so difficult to open?' he complained to his friend. 'It doesn't *look* any different from others like it that I've dealt with. I can usually open one of these old-fashioned clunkers in a minute at most.'

He gave the door a thump, shaking it good and hard, but he still couldn't get the lock to do what he expected and open.

'We'll go in by the window,' his companion decided and got a small steel bar out of his backpack to smash it. It took several blows to do that and clear the glass away. 'What the hell is this made of? Old-fashioned glass isn't usually this strong.'

'There's something weird about this place. You don't suppose they've got a hidden security system or cameras, do you?' He looked round uneasily.

'No sign of any and I'm usually good at spotting them. That rich sod isn't getting any work done on this house so there won't be any tools stored inside. Why should they bother to put security in here apart from locking it up? That's why we were told to set this one on fire. Come on. Let's get in and do the job quickly.'

'Yeah. The sooner we're away from here, the happier I'll be.'

The other man clambered in, yelping as glass sliced into his hand. He cursed. 'I could have sworn I cleared out all the glass from the frame.'

'Well you must have missed a piece. Move out

of the way and I'll go over the frame again before I join you.' He ran his metal bar to and fro across the bottom of the window frame, satisfied from the tinkling sound of some more glass falling to the floor that he'd cleared it completely. Yet he too received a nasty cut to the leg as he swung his body through it, which ruined his new trousers into the bargain.

'Look at that tear! I paid a fortune for these trousers.'

'Never mind. Let's get on with it.' The other took out the combustion materials from his backpack. 'Where shall we start the fire?'

'Let's try the kitchen. If there are wooden cupboards, they'll catch fire quickly.'

There was a faint sound from the kitchen and they felt a sudden breeze from there, then the front door started rattling.

'What the hell's that?'

'It's just the wind. Don't be so jumpy. The back door probably doesn't fit very well. This won't take long.' He played his torch around the kitchen. 'Perfect. Old-fashioned wooden cup-boards.'

He pulled out the accelerant and tried to spray the nearest cupboard, but the nozzle must have been blocked and nothing came out.

'I thought you'd checked this, you stupid sod,' he grumbled.

'I did. And it worked perfectly.'

'Well it isn't working now. Aieeee!'

The small pile of soaked material he was holding glowed briefly and burst into flames. With a yell he flung it from him and it landed on the other man's shoulder. It ought to have fallen straight off again but tonight's bad luck was striking them again and it balanced there as if glued.

Another yell joined his curses and the second man danced around, beating at the flaming mass on his shoulder and finding it hard to dislodge it. When it did fall to the floor, the flames perversely went out just as suddenly as they'd flared up.

That was when they heard footsteps outside the house and both froze for a few seconds.

'What the hell?'

'They must have had hidden security cameras, damn them. I'm out of here.'

But when he turned towards the back door, it slammed open so hard it bounced on its hinges and he found himself facing a very angry man.

He turned the other way and saw a grim-faced woman at the other side of the kitchen, hefting a rolling pin.

He instinctively chose to attack her but quickly realised his mistake. She stepped slightly to one side as gracefully as a dancer and flipped him over in a practised hip throw. Before he knew it she had walloped him with her rolling pin to knock him down on the floor. As he lay half-stunned, she got one knee on his back and twisted his arm so painfully behind him he couldn't move it without dislocating it.

He lay watching in helpless anger as his companion managed to fight his way out of the back door, feinted as if about to throw a punch, ducked instead and tore off swiftly across the grounds.

* * *

'Dammit. I lost him!' Angus complained. Shutting the back door, he strode across the room to stand beside Nell and her captive. 'You're good at self-defence, my love.'

'I was a woman on my own for a good many years. It was worth the hours of training to feel safe. And I've always kept reasonably fit.' She jerked on the arm she was holding with both hands as the man wriggled.

They both looked grimly satisfied when he roared in pain.

'I know how to break your arm in a few seconds if you give me any more trouble,' she said in a cheerful voice.

He lay still again.

Angus had his phone out and was dialling the local police station. 'We've captured a burglar in Saffron Lane. Oh good. Tell them where we are. It's the first house.' He shut down the phone and said to Nell, 'They're already on their way. Want me to take over?'

'No. This hold is easy to maintain once you've got a firm grip on someone. He'll just dislocate his shoulder if he struggles.' She winked at Angus. 'I wish he'd try. I'd love to hear him scream.'

Her captive gulped audibly.

Angus paced up and down, his expression growing tighter as he saw the materials which

249

could have set the old house on fire. 'They weren't burglars; they came prepared for arson, damn them.' He stopped next to the captive. 'Just give me half a chance to punch you.'

The man stiffened but kept absolutely still.

'Who sent you?'

When the man didn't reply, Angus nudged him with one foot, then drew it back as if to kick him.

'How the hell should I know? We were offered a job anonymously. Easy money, it seemed, so we took it.'

'Not such easy money then, eh?'

'His hand's bleeding,' Nell said. 'It isn't serious, though.'

'Pity.'

There was a siren outside and Angus went to throw open the front door.

A burly policeman took over, complimenting them on their capture.

'Not mine,' Angus said. 'My guy got away. It was my partner who captured this one.'

The female officer gave Nell a thumbs up and peered down at her captive. 'Jock Crighton. How nice to see you again. Where's your brother?'

He glared at her but said nothing.

In a falsely sympathetic tone, she added, 'Aw, he's bleeding. Poor man. How did that happen?'

'That woman slashed me,' the prisoner said at once.

'With what? My only weapon was a rolling pin.' Nell jerked her head towards where it lay on the floor. She let the male officer take over and jerk the man on the floor to his feet, then turned to the woman. 'I demand that you search me immediately. I don't want any doubt about whether I'm carrying a knife.'

The female officer obliged. 'You're good. No knife.'

'She threw it away,' the man said.

'How? I was holding you.'

The male officer gave him a shake. 'Let's have the truth, eh, Jock? It'll make things easier than if you muck us around. You haven't been out of jail for long this time, have you? You couldn't even walk straight down a narrow corridor. Let's have the truth, now.'

After a moment's hesitation, the captive said, 'I cut my hand on that damned window getting in. You can check it. It got both of us even though I'd swear we cleared away all the shards of glass.'

'Serves you right. We'll get your brother's DNA from it.'

'But I thought Tam wiped the blood away.' He broke off, realising he'd given his brother away.

'Doesn't look like you managed to do much damage in here. You two make better burglars than arsonists, and that's not saying much considering the number of times we've had to arrest you. What exactly happened tonight?'

'The damned accelerant spray clogged up and the wad suddenly burst into flames on its own. How that happened, I'll never understand.' Jock looked round, scowling. 'This is a bad luck place. You'd have to drag me back here by my hair.'

Angus and Nell exchanged glances and he

251

knew she too must be wondering if they'd had some help from his ancestors in foiling the arson attempt. No, that wasn't possible . . . Was it?

'Seems a nice enough place to me,' the officer said. 'Are you going to be letting the houses out when they're finished?' But she looked round in a puzzled way. 'Did you hear something?'

'Sort of.' Angus explained quickly about the village.

'What a great idea! I love looking round places like that. Oh well, we'd better take this fellow away and charge him properly. We'll send someone to pick up his brother. It'll be easy to get some samples of blood from that window and prove who the other man was. There are a few big splashes. Don't touch anything till the crime scene team have checked the place over.'

When they'd left, Angus looked at Nell.

'Could my ancestors have intervened?'

'What other explanation is there?'

'Hmm. We're not going to tell anyone else about them, are we?'

'What's the point? They'd not believe us. But that female officer did hear the laughter, so she must be sensitive to such things.'

'I'm still not mentioning it. I'd better get a glazier in as soon as places open. We don't want our applicants finding the place trashed. I'm going to stay here till daylight, just in case. I'll walk part-way back with you first, though, and watch you to the door of the big house.'

She didn't try to stop him. Why attempt the impossible? Her Angus would always try to protect the ones he loved.

As they parted, he said, 'Well done tonight. I didn't realise I'd married a martial arts whiz.'

'Hardly that. Fighting's not my hobby and I detest people who solve problems by violence. But I prefer to be able to defend myself, if needed.'

'You did well. Now, put some lights on once you get into the house. I'll stay here till I see them and know you're safe.'

He shook his head admiringly as he watched her stride up the drive and veer off left to get round to the kitchen door, not hesitating or showing any signs of nervousness.

He didn't move till lights came on in the house, then he went back and waited for dawn, sitting on the floor with his back against the wall.

He smiled once or twice as he thought about Nell. What a woman! 'Indomitable' was the right word to describe her.

21

Janey's mother came round the next evening to visit her. Their relationship was still uneasy, but she knew how much her mother needed the reconciliation, so she was trying to forgive the past neglect.

Thank goodness for little Millie, who only knew a few words so far, but who could manage 'Nan-Nan' and always grew excited when her grandmother came round to see them.

Thank goodness, too, for Winifred, her landlady and honorary aunt, who sometimes joined them on these evening visits and who seemed easily able to oil the wheels of conversation when it faltered.

'Did you hear about the break-in at Dennings?'

Janey looked at her mother in surprise. 'No. What happened? You always seem to hear about such things first.'

'That's because the police are in and out of the shelter and the flats, keeping an eye on us. I never thought police officers could be so *kind*.' She lost her way as she stared into space for a moment or two.

'Go on, Mum. Tell us what happened.'

'Apparently someone broke into the first house on Saffron Lane — you told me your friends are doing up the houses there, didn't you, so I thought you'd be interested?'

'Yes, I am. But they weren't working on the first house. It's an architectural treasure or something. Angus hasn't said what sort of treasure because the heritage people want to keep it under wraps for the moment. Who tried to set it on fire?'

'Two young men. They're known to the police for thieving, but this time they went there on purpose to set a fire. The police reckon someone must have paid them to do it, but they're not saying who it was. They set off the alarms and the security cameras, so Angus and Nell went to investigate.'

'They were taking a risk.'

'Yes, well, maybe not so much. Your friend Nell caught one of them all by herself, it seems, and sat on him till the police arrived. I wish I had the strength to do that sort of thing. Judy, one of the police officers, was delighted that it was a woman who caught the fellow. She's promised to teach us some self-defence moves, if we want. Do you think I could learn to do it, Janey?'

'I'm sure you could.' She spoke bracingly because her mother was still very timid and lacking in self-confidence.

'You really do think so?'

'Yes. Anyone can learn some of the tricks, but not everyone can manage them all. Still, some would help, wouldn't they? You'd feel safer. They taught me a few tricks at *Just Girls* after I'd had Millie.'

'I might give it a try, then. Anyway, these men didn't manage to set anything on fire or steal anything.'

'I'm glad. Angus and Nell have been working hard on that little street. You'd hardly have known it was there before, everything was so overgrown. It'll be fascinating when it's an Arts and Crafts Village, won't it? We could go and look at what they're selling, couldn't we?'

'Oh, yes. I'd love to do that.'

'I wonder — ' Janey broke off and looked at her mother, who was now tickling Millie and making her laugh. That sight did her heart good. Every child deserves grandparents.

Her mother looked up. 'What do you wonder?'

'Would you mind looking after Millie for half an hour or so? I'd like to nip round to see Angus and Nell to get the full story. Winifred and her friend Dan are in the other room if you need any help.'

Tears started rolling down her mother's face.

'What's wrong?'

'Nothing's wrong.' She scrubbed at her cheeks. 'It's just, that's the first time you've trusted Millie with me on my own.'

'You didn't know her before and now you're both well acquainted. What time is your lift coming for you?'

'When I phone them. They don't mind if it's late. They like us to get out and about, if we can. So you could stay for a while if you liked. I'd love to put Millie to bed . . . if you don't mind.'

'All right. Thanks.' It was like treading on eggs sometimes, chatting to her mother. Would they ever be easy together again?

'Be careful, Janey.'

'Yes, of course. It's only a few houses away.'

Down a driveway about a hundred yards long, but she wasn't going to let herself be afraid of the world like her poor mother was.

She walked briskly along to the big house, enjoying the occasional crackle of the frosty edges of puddles beneath her feet and the brightness of the stars. They looked like glitter that had been spray-painted across the darkness of the sky.

If Nell and Angus were busy she'd just say she was out for a breath of fresh air. But it'd be nice to stay for half an hour or so. However much you loved your little daughter, you needed time for yourself occasionally. Maybe she could go out with some of the others from her technical college classes occasionally and leave Millie with her mother if this worked tonight.

★ ★ ★

'Who can that be?' Nell wondered as the doorbell rang.

'I'll get it.'

Angus was off to do so before she could say anything else.

There was the sound of voices then he came back with Janey. 'Look who's called to see us.'

'How nice. Are you on your own, Janey?'

'Yes.'

'You should be careful coming here after dark.'

She laughed. 'I carried a chunk of wood as a protector. I left it on your doorstep ready for the return journey. It's such a short distance, though, I could run to safety in two minutes. But

257

there was no one around. I don't know why I always feel safe when I come into your grounds, Angus, but I do.'

'You might not have been safe last night.'

'No, that's what I came about. I heard someone had broken into one of your houses. Are you all right? What happened?'

'How about a glass of mulled cider while we tell you? I was just making some. Have you time to stay for a while? Who's watching Millie?'

'My mother.'

'That's nice.'

'It's the first time I've left her in charge, but Winifred and Dan are there, so if anything goes wrong, Millie will be all right. And I'd love a glass of cider.'

When Angus had served them all with his special recipe and they'd sipped appreciatively, they told her about the intruders and the strange coincidences that had stopped the two men causing any real damage, apart from the broken window.

'Spooky,' was all their visitor said.

Janey didn't stay for longer than it took to drink her cider, then got ready to go home. She wasn't worried about Millie, well not exactly, but this first time of leaving her daughter she felt reluctant to stay away for too long.

Angus insisted on seeing her to the end of the drive.

'It's not necessary. We're only at Number Five.'

'Nonetheless, I'll feel better to know you're back safely.'

'You'd better let Sir Galahad have his way,' said Nell. 'He's very stubborn. I'm going to stay here by the fire. I'm feeling lazy tonight.'

★   ★   ★

Janey waved goodbye to Angus from the gate and walked into the house. Dan's car was no longer there, so he must have gone home. All was peaceful inside. Her mother wasn't in the sitting room, but was on a chair by Millie's cot, quiet as a ghost in the faint moonlight that shone through the window.

'Everything all right?' Janey whispered from the doorway.

Her mother came out of the bedroom to join her. 'Everything's wonderful. I was just enjoying the sight of her looking so peaceful. Doesn't she sleep soundly once she's given in to her tiredness?'

As they went back into the sitting room, she said, 'Thank you for trusting me with her, Janey. I don't deserve it but I won't let you down ever again, I promise.'

'Everyone deserves a second chance, Mum.'

After her mother had been picked up by one of the volunteers from the women's refuge, Janey gave herself the luxury of reading in bed. The technical college hadn't opened for the spring term yet and she'd managed over an hour of studying while Millie had her nap this afternoon, so she felt she deserved it.

As she closed her book and settled down for the night, she felt good. She had a home here with Winifred and enough money to manage on if she was careful.

Best of all, she had her daughter in the next room, the wonderful result of an evil man's attack.

It had been a lovely evening. This time last year she'd felt so alone in the world. Now she had good friends and a lot to look forward to. Even a small family, if you counted her mother.

She envied the people at college who had bigger families and talked about cousins, brothers and sisters, aunts and uncles. She'd never had that. But there you were, you couldn't have everything.

22

As she'd been asked to bring another piece of work to the interview, Stacy put a montage she'd just finished into the car. It was a miniature set of steam punk machinery, which had to be carefully linked together, then it could be set in motion to deliver a ping-pong ball from one end to the other by means of various wheels and cogs which spun round easily when she wound up the clockwork mechanism, which was the only thing she'd had to buy.

The ball zipped along tubes, travelled along tiny moving tracks till it dropped on to one bar of a vertical conveyor belt, which moved it upwards to plop into the metal mesh bowl she'd set at the other end.

She hoped she wasn't fooling herself, but she thought 'The Way To Go' was one of her very best pieces.

This had been created in the tranquillity of her room in the industrial centre. It had been fun to work on and Jim had loved it. He sometimes came in to see what she was doing in the room he sublet to her and seemed to treat his industrial unit as a second home. He was often pottering about there, whatever time of day she went there.

She hummed as she drove to Sexton Bassett and easily found her way up Peppercorn Street and into the drive at the top, then down to

Saffron Lane on the left at the rear of the grounds. The renovations were clearly works in progress, but Numbers Two and Three seemed more finished than the others. She liked the solidity of the houses, which looked as if they were there to stay.

She stopped outside Number 2, as instructed, and a woman came to the door to wait for her to get out of the car. When she went to unload her montage, the woman hurried forward to lend a hand with the pieces, holding the other end of the biggest one.

'You must be Stacy. I'm Nell.'

'Pleased to meet you.'

'Angus will be with us shortly. He's just finishing off a little job at Number Four. We'll take this through to the back, if that's all right with you, and put it in the kitchen. Go straight across the shop and through that door at the rear.'

Stacy backed along, holding her end of the central piece carefully, and found herself in a large, bright room.

'We could put it on the breakfast bar.'

They set down the piece and Stacy turned to go back out. 'There are two more parts.'

'Need more help?'

'If you don't mind.'

When she'd put the three pieces together she stepped back without another word.

Nell was studying it with a smile on her face. 'Does it work? It looks as if it does.'

'Oh, yes. I call it 'The Way To Go'.' Stacy produced the ping-pong ball, put it on the

262

starting dish and wound up the mechanism. Then she pressed the little lever that sent the ball on its trip round the system.

Nell chuckled. 'It's delightful. Steam punk, isn't it, that style?'

'Yes.'

'You're younger than I'd expected.' It was out before she could stop herself.

'Does that matter?'

'Oh, no. Age isn't important. It's talent we're looking for and a friendly personality to deal with people visiting the village. If your other creations are as delightfully quirky as this one, and the photo of the little animal you sent certainly was, you've got a lot to share with the world. Ah, here's Angus. Watch this, darling.'

When she gestured, Stacy set it going again and Angus watched in patent delight, asking for it to be run again.

After that the three of them chatted for a while and Stacy told them something about herself, breaking off when she heard the sound of a car outside.

Nell stood up. 'I'll get the door. I forgot to tell you because we started playing with your piece that the next person overlaps your visit a bit. I hope you don't mind, Stacy. Only she has to move house and if she's going to come here, she needs to know quickly.'

'I don't mind sharing time with her. Why should I? It's always nice to meet another artist.' As Nell went to let the newcomer in, Stacy turned to smile at Angus, who was setting off her steam punk machine again.

He looked at her guiltily. 'I'm a child at heart. I couldn't resist it. How much do you want for it? I have to have it.'

She was so surprised she couldn't speak for a moment or two. 'I, um, haven't even thought of a price. I've only just finished it, you see.'

'Well, when you've decided, give me first refusal.'

'Oh, right. Would two hundred pounds be too much?'

He rolled his eyes. 'Too little, I should think. Look at all the work that's gone into it. If it's all right with you, I'll get a friend who has a gallery to value it and we'll go by his judgement. I guarantee it'll be more than two hundred pounds.'

Which left her totally speechless, able only to nod.

⋆   ⋆   ⋆

The driver helped Elise out of the front seat of the car. It had seemed unfriendly to sit alone in the back when they were chatting so animatedly and they'd stopped after a few miles so that she could move into the front passenger seat.

'I'll carry your painting inside, Elise.'

'Thanks, Amy. It's quite heavy, but it's one of my favourites.' Victor had left her the bluebells painting in his will, to her great delight. And she wasn't going to sell it to anyone else unless she was starving and desperate to buy food and paints. Though if anyone loved it as much as she did, she'd be torn about whether to let them

264

have it. She greatly enjoyed giving people pleasure.

Amy knocked on the door and they heard footsteps approaching. A woman with a wonderfully friendly smile appeared.

'You must be Elise. I'm Nell.'

'Lovely to meet you. And this is Amy, my driver.'

She nodded a greeting. 'Is this your other item? Do bring it inside.'

Amy set it down where she pointed then turned to Elise. 'I'll go and feed my face in town now. Give me a ring when you're ready to be picked up.'

'All right. Thanks.' She turned back to see her hostess glancing down at the painting.

At that moment a breeze blew the covering piece of material aside and Nell looked shocked at what she saw. 'That's our path, surely? Yes, it is! It's the one through the little wood at the other side of the property.'

Elise was puzzled. 'If there's a resemblance, it's purely coincidental. I made up the scene. Well, I dreamt about it one night, which amounts to the same thing.'

Nell lifted the cover off without asking and let out a soft whistle. 'Then you dreamt of a real place, Elise. This is definitely our wood. Why, even the details of the tree branches are accurate.' She heard faint, tinkling laughter in the distance and saw Elise and Stacy both staring in the direction of the wood, as if they'd heard something too.

Angus shook his head slightly as if to tell her

to let the matter drop, so she didn't pursue it. But as she introduced the two women, her eyes kept going back to the painting. It seemed like a sign that the older woman belonged here and she really liked Stacy as well. She realised Elise was still waiting for an answer and said quickly, 'It's beautiful, Elise, exactly what our bluebells look like in spring. They seem like a blue-lilac mist under the trees from a distance.'

There was silence for a moment or two, then Nell grew brisk again. 'Shall we go round the upstairs of this house, then next door? These two houses are just about ready. Let's see if they catch your fancy as possible places to create and sell your work.'

Both visitors approved of the upstairs amenities.

As they walked along to the next house, Stacy asked hesitantly, 'Um, how much rent are you charging? You didn't say. But I'll be using my savings to come here so I have to be careful.'

'It's rent-free for six months to give you a start, but we'd have to charge you twenty-five per cent of anything you sell through our café-cum-gallery, once it opens,' Angus told them. 'An agent would charge at least thirty, so it's a good bargain.'

'You'd pay for your own electricity, though,' Nell put in.

'What if we don't sell anything?' Stacy asked. 'I'm only just starting up, you see.'

'Well, you've sold something today, haven't you, Stacy?' He looked at Nell ruefully. 'I've just bought her steam punk montage. I fell in love with it. She doesn't know what price to charge, but we'll ask Matt Tolson what would be fair, eh?'

Nell burst out laughing. 'And I've fallen in love with the bluebell wood. I was going to offer to buy that from Elise. Fine pair of business people we are!'

They carried on along the row, then walked back to the second house where Nell had set out some biscuits and brought the tea-making things.

Angus didn't even need to ask Nell's opinion. 'When can you two move in?'

The two visitors stared at him as if he were crazy.

'Is that it?' Stacy asked. 'I mean, can it possibly happen so quickly and easily?'

He shrugged. 'Why not? It's my property, after all, and the village was Nell's idea, so if we're in agreement, that's it.'

Elise got out her handkerchief and blew her nose hard. 'I thought you'd say I was too old.'

'You're never too old to be creative,' Stacy told her gently. 'At least, that's what one of my art teachers always told me. And *he* was still working at ninety.'

'Thanks. I've a bit of a way to go still to reach ninety!' She turned to Nell and Angus. 'I accept. I'd love to come and live here. I prefer Number Three, if that's all right with you, Stacy. Otherwise we'll have to toss for it.'

'I'd be happy in either house. It'd be wonderful to be living and working in the same place. I'll be able to potter about any time I want.'

'Well, let's sign you up and arrange your moving-in dates.'

⋆ ⋆ ⋆

When the two women had signed the necessary papers and left, Nell and Angus went back to the big house.

She filed the paperwork in the office, then sat on the sofa and cuddled up to him. 'Your family ghosts said Number 2 would be 'Stacy's house', didn't they?'

'Yes.'

'You don't sound happy about that, Angus.'

'I still can't come to terms with the idea of ghosts, and I never quite know what is really happening and whether we're seeing their influence where it doesn't exist.'

'Who cares? They always sound friendly and they were right about a Stacy coming here, weren't they? Her creations are delightful.'

'It may not be businesslike to do things this way, Nell, but I have a feeling she and Elise will go far and give our artists' village a head start. If they do, we'll more than get our money back.'

'I agree. I wonder what the other artists will be like.'

'I bet they're just as nice, but we can't get all the houses ready at once, and it'd be prudent to see how this goes before we put in anyone else. And the two biggest houses seem too big for one person. I still haven't worked out exactly what to do with them.'

'It'll come to you. You're good at getting ideas.'

'We'll have to be careful, though. I started this because I wanted to increase my regular income. Instead I've spent a lot of my contingency fund modernising the houses and now we've arranged for those two to live there rent-free.'

'Don't forget, you've also bought that steam punk gadget. I wonder what Matt will value it at.'

'At least double what she was asking, I should think. It'll be interesting to find out.'

'We'll manage somehow,' she said.

'That's what I'm telling myself.'

'Fate seems to be nudging us along in this. I wonder what will happen next?'

They both fell silent, looking thoughtful, then he shrugged. 'What will be, will be. I just hope we don't get any more intruders.'

'Or pushy developers. Do you think Dorling will try something else, Angus?'

'Bound to.'

'Yes, that's what I think, too. Damn the man!'

23

Darren Cooke had tried everything he could think of to find his ex-wife. Stacy wasn't going to get away with refusing to take him back. He'd taught her a lesson or two when they were together and she'd learnt to do what he wanted.

Unlike the woman he'd left her for. *She* had run away one day while he was at work. But she wasn't worth fetching back. She was far less capable in the house than Stacy had been, not even a good cook. He'd been wrong to break up his marriage, but he was going to put it all together again.

He'd be sweetness and light at first, because women were suckers for that approach, but if he had to teach Stacy a few new lessons to bring her into line later on, he would. Apart from anything else, he'd got drunk one night and boasted to his friends that he'd get her back, that he wasn't going to let her make a fool of him.

He shouldn't have boasted, because it made it even more important to prove he could get control of her again.

He found out quite easily where her parents had moved to, but he knew better than to approach them directly. It was partly their fault his marriage had broken up. They'd never made him feel like part of the family, had always undermined him.

None of their neighbours had seen Stacy

visiting them, either, he found from seemingly casual chats. And though he kept watch on the Walshes' house a couple of weekends, he saw no sign of her or of them going to visit her.

Then he was shocked rigid to be sacked from his job. Because of poor attendance and lack of productivity, they said. Well, to hell with them. He'd soon find another job. He always did. But that was the final straw. It was *her* fault, making him careless because he was worrying. Things would fall into place again once he got her back.

He had to think his plans through more carefully before he did anything else from now on. He was pretty sure Stacy wouldn't have moved too far away. He'd bet anything you liked that she'd still be within driving distance of her parents.

He was pretty sure she would have gone back to working on that rubbishy art of hers, too. She was obsessed by it. As if anyone could make a living from welding bits of scrap metal together! So he started searching online for articles on art or events where she might be selling things.

It was by sheer chance that he found the article about the Arts and Crafts Village that was opening up in Wiltshire. That was close enough to her parents' new home to be worth a try.

He doubted she'd win one of the tenancies, but she might very likely apply. She was always far too optimistic about her skills. He'd hack into the computer of the people offering the tenancies and see if she'd applied. Most people were very lax about computer security.

Only he didn't manage to break through their

security system. Someone who really knew what they were doing had set up a well-defended website, he had to grant them that.

OK then. He might have to go down there and see what was going on. He could pretend to be searching for her, think up some sob story about a lost love.

Or just go and visit this art village place a couple of times and say he was thinking of applying. He'd see who turned up there. Even if she didn't win a tenancy there, he'd bet she'd visit it. She was always wanting to go to art galleries and boring places like that.

Since he'd lost his job he had plenty of free time so he'd go this very weekend. No, during the week would be better. Then he got another temporary job as a barista. Never thought he'd be doing that again, having to smile at idiots spending a fortune on fancy coffees. Still, it paid the rent, and he could take leftover food home. There was no rush to go looking for Stacy tomorrow, after all.

When he was offered the barista job permanently, he postponed his little jaunt once again. Money was always useful and he didn't want to break into what he'd got from selling the house. He and Stacy would need it as the deposit on their new house.

He'd go down to Wiltshire in a week or two. Once she'd found a place to live, she would stay there, he was sure. She was a real homemaker and she did it well, he had to grant her that. She'd put her heart into that little house they'd bought. He'd thought that foolish but then her improvements brought them a higher price. So he'd find her, one way or the other.

24

Adam didn't like to leave the phone untended so he stayed in the flat and sent Gemma, who was twitching at the inaction, out to walk round town on her own. He gave her some personal money in case she wanted to make any purchases and asked her to bring back some food.

'You've got the information about buses, haven't you?'

She rolled her eyes as if he was stupid. How he hated it when she did that!

'Yes, Dad. I already told you I had. Anyway, I can look them up on my smartphone if necessary.'

'Right then. Well, off you go.'

As she walked out of the house she began smiling and he watched her run across the car park of the block of flats, as if she was afraid he'd call her back. He smiled to see her looking young and carefree again.

Best of all, they were getting on quite well now. And thank goodness for that.

The phone didn't ring, so he amused himself online, grew tired of that, then fidgeted around the flat, reading for half an hour, watching TV.

When the phone rang he wondered who it was.

'Adam?' The voice was breathless.

'Hope. How nice to hear from you again.'

'My counsellor said I should ring you back as

274

soon as I could face it. She was pleased to hear about . . . you know, what happened with the letter. I was pleased too.'

'I've never backed away from a responsibility in my life.'

'No. I should have trusted you. I panicked. And Lionel pretended to be kind. He just wanted a domestic slave, I think. He wasn't a loving man.'

'So you could face meeting me then?'

'Yes, I found I could. I *am* getting stronger. And I never was afraid of you.'

'Glad to hear that.'

After a pause she asked, 'Was your marriage happy, Adam?'

'At first. But a few years ago she met someone else and we separated and divorced. I'd been working hard and she felt neglected, apparently. But we'd not been getting on all that well for a while and, frankly, it was a relief to work away from home. I'd never have thought she'd die so young, though.'

'That's sad for your daughter.'

'Yes. Gemma and Judith got on really well.' He paused and when Hope didn't fill the silence, he asked, 'Can you tell me something about Janey?'

'I — ' She burst into tears.

'What have I said? Whatever it is, I'm sorry. Don't end the call. *Please!*'

He heard her gulping and trying not to cry, and waited for her to calm down.

'I was a terrible mother,' she blurted out. 'I let Lionel bully Janey as well as me. I can't believe she's even speaking to me.'

'She must care about you.'

'Not . . . a lot. I do love her, though. And my father was a wonderful grandfather to her, right until he died. After that things went from bad to worse with Lionel. I c-can't talk about the details yet. But Janey has a baby and he — it wasn't her fault, she was forced. But Millie is gorgeous, anyway, and she calls me 'Nan-Nan' and — look, I'm not ready to tell her about you, yet, but I will. I'll get back to you later, Adam. I can't do any more today. Sorry.'

The line went dead.

He stared at it for ages before he shut the phone down, his mind in a turmoil. What the hell sort of a life had poor Dorothy and her daughter had? He mentally corrected himself. Hope! He must remember not to call her Dorothy now. It must have been appalling to make her take refuge in a women's shelter. What could he do to make up to Janey for all the trouble? Would she even want to meet him?

Good heavens! He was a grandfather!

He stared at himself in the mirror, but he didn't look any older.

He flung himself down on the hard little couch — whoever considered this adequate seating for a grown man deserved to sit on it for a week as a punishment — then he stood up again, pacing round the flat. If Gemma hadn't been due back soon, he'd have gone for a long walk to clear his head.

Only he doubted whether anything would clear his head of the thoughts roiling round it until he'd come to terms with the news.

What had happened to Hope wasn't his fault exactly, but he still felt partly responsible.

Then the lift pinged and he heard footsteps coming towards the flat.

His daughter was back — his *younger* daughter! Thank goodness.

She'd need time to get used to the news as well.

★ ★ ★

Gemma walked into the flat, dumped the shopping bags in the kitchen and filled the kettle. 'I'm parched. Want a cup of coffee?'

'Yes, please. I'll put the food away, shall I?'

'We both can.' She looked at him. 'Uh-oh! What's happened now?'

'Hope rang again.'

'That's good, surely?'

'Her counsellor said to phone as soon as she could, and she decided she wasn't afraid to call me.'

'Afraid of you? No woman could ever be.'

He really valued that compliment.

Gemma opened a packet of biscuits and bit off half of one, talking through the mouthful. 'Go on.'

'We'll wait till we've got our coffee. And I wouldn't mind a biscuit too.'

When they were sitting in the so-called living room, which was more like an alcove off the kitchen, containing only the sofa, a small table and two rather hard chairs, he sipped his coffee and put the mug down.

'Hope told me a little about her daughter. Janey's about a year older than you and, um, she has a one-year-old daughter.'

Gemma choked on the mouthful of coffee and it was a moment before she caught her breath.

'She started early, didn't she?'

'Not voluntarily, from the sound of it.'

'She was *raped*?'

'Hope didn't use that word, she said 'forced' but what else could it mean?'

Silence, then, 'Poor thing.'

More silence, followed by a gurgle of laughter, the last thing he'd expected.

'That means you're a grandfather, Dad.'

'And you're an aunt.'

They looked at one another.

'My goodness! So I am.' She giggled. 'Auntie Gemma. That's good, though. I like babies.'

'Do you?'

'Yes. I want a large family one day.'

'You never said.'

She shrugged. 'You never asked. When can we meet her, this half-sister of mine?'

'I don't know. Hope got that far then started crying. She said she'd phone again.'

'She does a lot of crying, doesn't she? Was she always such a watering pot?'

'No. I think life and a very brutal man have done this to her.'

'Well, I hope she rings soon. I want to meet my half-sister, see what she's like.'

He too wished Hope would ring soon. He was eager to meet his other daughter — and his

278

granddaughter. 'The baby's called Millie, by the way.'

'Aw, that's a lovely name.'

'Tell me about your walk.'

25

Just before lunch on the day after the meeting with Stacy and Elise, Angus picked up the mail from the hall.

'Oh, damn!' It was another letter from the council. He tore it open and scanned the page quickly. They weren't giving up on visiting Saffron Lane, then ... as a precursor to a compulsory purchase, no doubt. Well, they'd only get hold of those houses over his dead body!

He rang the lawyer's office and explained to the head clerk what had happened, then he scanned the letter from the council and emailed it to Russell Alexander.

Five minutes later, his phone rang. 'Ah, Mr Denning. I have Mr Alexander on the line.'

There was a brief silence, then the lawyer came on. He didn't waste time. 'It'd be best for me to be there with you and also a structural engineer with no affiliation to the council.'

'I had the place surveyed by one before I started work and have the report. I'm quite sure the houses are sound.'

'Good. But get a different engineer along this time, then you'll have two opinions and he'll be there to counter their comments, if necessary. Never hurts. Fortunately, I can make the time they specified for the visit, so I've pencilled it in. Let my secretary know when you've confirmed it.'

Angus put the phone down and immediately rang Hedley Preece who had surveyed the Saffron Lane houses before, and explained what was going on. Hedley was angry at this waste of time and public money, as well as the slur on his abilities. 'I'll be taking a legal interest if they impugn my skills, believe me.'

He gave Angus the name of another structural engineer, and luckily this guy could make the appointment time as well. But Angus sighed as he put down his phone. The charges for both a lawyer and an engineer's time would no doubt be steep. Money was pouring out of his bank account at the moment, and on things other than the ongoing renovations to the big house.

And he still hadn't heard from the heritage people. Well, they would have to wait until he'd sorted this out, even if they did want something.

He went to find Nell and bring her up to date, then rang Hobkins to agree to the time.

'Um . . . we'll be bringing a structural engineer with us, Mr Denning.'

'You'd better clear that with my lawyer first.'

'We don't need to clear it. We have the right to make sure your houses are safe.'

'I see. Well, don't bring Dorling with you. I'm not having him on the premises.'

'He wasn't coming anyway. This is council business.'

'As if.' He heard Hobkins sputter indignantly and cut the connection on him and his lies. Then he let the lawyer's secretary know that there would definitely be a structural engineer there from the council.

When he discussed what was going on with Nell, she was even angrier than he was. 'How do they get away with it?'

'Who knows? Business the world over seems full of cheats and liars. It must be endemic in our species.'

'Well, it's still disgusting. I don't know how they think they'll get away with it.'

'They won't, if I can help it,' he said grimly.

'Oh, no! I've just thought of something.'

'What?'

'Elise is due to move into Number 3 as soon as she can organise it. What shall I do? I can't put her off because she's got to move out of her present house.'

'Don't, then. She can move in and if they win and she gets chucked out, she can stay at the big house till she finds somewhere else.'

'Stacy too?'

'We'll suggest she postpones the move.'

But when Nell rang Stacy, she found that the metal artist had given notice on both the house and her current job, and organised a removal.

'Is it certain that we'll be thrown out?' Stacy asked.

'No. We'll fight it tooth and nail, I promise you.'

'Then I'd get a few months there, whatever?'

'Yes.'

'I'd rather come for a while than not at all.' She hesitated. 'Could I move in tomorrow, do you think? Or would that be too soon?'

'Are you sure about this?'

'Yes. I've had a bit of a disagreement with the guy I've been working for. He's not easy to get on with, however clever he is, and he might be able to manage on a few hours' sleep but I can't. I rang up the people storing my luggage to check and they can either fit me in to move tomorrow afternoon, or not for another week.'

So Nell agreed that Stacy could take up her occupancy of Number 2 immediately.

It was all coming together. But would it stay together?

'Don't give in,' a voice whispered in her ear. 'Whatever they say or do.'

Now what did that mean? What lay ahead? Nell wondered. But she wasn't a quitter so the warning wasn't necessary to make her keep fighting.

* * *

She rang Elise to explain the situation and was greeted with dead silence for a moment or two. Then the feisty older woman said, 'How about I move in tomorrow as well and we present these sneaky rats with a fait accompli? After all, they won't be able to throw me out immediately, will they? And I have to get out of this house asap.'

'Can you arrange to move? Isn't it a bit short notice?'

'I was so eager I already checked and as it happens, yes, they can move me tomorrow. I was going to ring and ask you if that was all right.'

'Then do it. The council people aren't coming

283

till the day after tomorrow. I shall enjoy seeing their faces when they realise that two of the houses are occupied.'

When she put the phone down she smiled. The more she had to do with Elise, the more she liked her.

★ ★ ★

When she ended her call with Nell, Elise confirmed her booking with the remover who'd said he could move her and her things the following day as long as she was ready by seven in the morning. She hoped he was as nice as he sounded.

When she put the phone down, she looked round. Was she sad to be leaving? No. This house had a lot of happy memories but it wasn't the sort of place to live in on your own. She'd be ready to move at midnight if she had to be. The better her hip grew, the more eager she was to start her new life and get down to some painting.

What a good thing it was that she'd employed Harriet to help her clear things out!

She got on the phone again and persuaded her niece Mary to come home from work that afternoon and help her get ready.

That was the trouble with growing really old. You still wanted to do all sorts of things, even have adventures, but you needed more help doing them.

But she wouldn't need help with her painting. Oh, no. Images were welling in her mind. She kept taking notes, hunting out a photo she'd taken and put in her file of potential subjects, and moving it to her current file for early use.

She was longing to start work again.

★   ★   ★

She had her art things packed by the time Mary arrived. When she opened the door, she burst out laughing at the sight of her niece's worried expression.

'Stop expecting things to go wrong, Mary! They're going wonderfully.'

'I must say, you've done well to get a place in this village thingy. How many places were there on offer?'

'Two.'

Mary gaped. 'My goodness. That's brilliant.'

Elise didn't spoil it by telling Mary about the possibility of Angus and Nell's struggle against the council to retain the cottages.

Bless her, Mary worked like a Trojan and they had everything ready to go by midnight.

'I'm coming to see you in your new place soon, Auntie,' Mary said very firmly. 'I intend to check that you're all right.'

'You'll always be welcome, dear. Bring Harriet if she can get home for the weekend. I'd like to show it to you both. It's the most gorgeous place to live, set in the grounds of a minor stately home.'

'That does sound nice.'

★   ★   ★

Just before seven o'clock the following morning, the removers arrived. Phil, the older of the two men, suggested she find a chair and sit somewhere out of their way.

'I've already done that.'

'Show me where you'll be sitting?' He followed her to the kitchen.

'I thought I'd be out of your way here.'

'Yes, that's fine. How are you getting there today?'

'I'm driving.'

'I couldn't help noticing that you're limping slightly.'

She shrugged. 'I broke my hip a few months ago. I get achy days. I'm all right to drive again but I did a bit too much packing yesterday, that's all.' She changed the subject firmly, pointing to the items on the draining board. 'I've set aside the tea-making things and kettle. If you tell me whenever you're ready for a cuppa, I'll make it for you both.'

'Thanks. We always appreciate that.'

The two men worked solidly, but it took till mid-morning to pack everything into the garishly painted removal van.

As the last things were stowed away, Elise stood watching, not feeling in the least sad but definitely feeling tired.

The older man came round to stand beside her. 'You look weary.'

'I am. Anno Domini, I'm afraid. Still, I can take it easy on the journey. I never was a fast driver anyway, and I don't suppose you'll be speeding.'

'If you like, I could drive you there and my assistant will drive the furniture van. I'm a safe driver and I'm fully insured to drive other people's vehicles. Have to be, in my line of business.'

She'd taken a liking to him and trusted him instinctively. 'Would you mind?'

'Not at all. This means he and I won't quarrel about what music to play. Besides, I live to serve.' He took off his cap and flourished it in a mock bow.

She laughed, held out her hand and they shook on the bargain.

After locking the front door, she left the house keys in the estate agent's special security box on the side wall of the house and got into the car. It was all falling into place as if it was meant to be.

She sighed happily. Life didn't stop at seventy — and she hoped it wouldn't stop at eighty, either. She was so enjoying her painting.

★   ★   ★

They stopped once, early in their journey, to buy lunch, which Elise insisted on paying for. It was the least she could do when they'd been so obliging. Not many people would have realised she was still finding the thought of long drives rather challenging, let alone volunteered to drive her there.

When they got there Phil whistled softly. 'I can see why you want to move here. There's something about that row of houses. They have a welcoming air.'

'I feel like that too.' She studied Number 3 with a proprietary air. There were still men working on the houses beyond hers, but Number 3 looked ready for an occupant. She'd buy a couple of pots of flowers for either side of the front door.

Nell came out of the house and waved. 'Welcome to your new home, Elise! Anything I can do to help?'

'Thank you, but no. Phil and his mate have been wonderful, and I've worked out exactly where all the furniture will go. I shall simply sit on a chair and direct traffic.'

'Here are the keys, then, front and back doors, two of each. I hope you'll be very happy here.'

When Elise went inside she found a vase of flowers on the kitchen windowsill and a cheerful greeting card saying 'Welcome to your new home.'

She felt delighted to be here and with Phil having done the driving, she still had enough energy to finish today's removal. She spun round in a slow circle out of sheer joy.

Then the two men came clumping inside carrying her dining table. 'Where to, Elise?' Phil called cheerfully.

And so it began.

⋆ ⋆ ⋆

Stacy felt exhausted and drove more slowly than usual as she left the unit for the last time, giving Jim a hug and a warm invitation to come and visit.

'You mean it, don't you?' He sounded faintly surprised.

'I wouldn't have said it otherwise.'

'I will do, then. I like looking at those funny little animals of yours, and that mechanical thing was great.'

The men came and put her things into the removal van, then set off.

As she got into her car, Jim stood at the door of his unit, waving goodbye, looking rather old and lonely.

She suppressed a yawn and told herself to concentrate on her driving. She'd been up for most of the night, packing both at her industrial unit and at the flat, though the latter had been much easier to deal with since most of the furniture belonged to the owner.

But she was still running on excitement when she arrived. She waved to Elise and greeted her own removers as they pulled up behind her car soon afterwards. She could crash later, when the furniture and her art equipment were all inside. For the moment there was still a lot to do.

When someone knocked on the door, she went to answer it and found Nell with a bouquet of flowers and the keys.

'I just wanted to wish you happiness here and tell you that if there's anything you need, you mustn't hesitate to ask. We'll come and do an assessment of what's needed for your studio once we've got rid of these council idiots.'

'I think what I'll need most when the removers have gone is an early night. I didn't get much

289

sleep last night. I was still packing at two o'clock in the morning.'

'And your boss didn't ask you to stay on?'

'Oh, he sort of apologised and asked, but I said no. I did agree to do some contract work for him from here, though. It'll be good to have some money coming in. But I refused to work full-time even on that.'

'I'm pleased for you.' She thrust the bouquet of flowers into Stacy's hands.

'Thanks. I love flowers.'

'I wanted you to feel welcome.'

'Oh, I do. There's something about this place that wraps round you like a hug, don't you think?'

'I always feel like that about the big house.'

By the time the two men had gone, Stacy was running on automatic, finding it hard to keep her eyes open. When she peeped next door, she saw that the other removal van had left too. But there was no sign of Elise.

She didn't attempt to say hi to her neighbour, just grabbed a quick sandwich and went up to bed, not even taking the time to get undressed till she woke in the middle of the night. She didn't feel disoriented, just happy to be there.

After contemplating the shadows cast by the moonlight for a few moments, she went to the bathroom, changed into her night gear and was asleep again within a minute of putting her head back on the pillow.

* * *

Soon after she arrived, Elise noticed a car arrive at Number 2. She kept an eye on the other house as her things were brought inside and shortly afterwards another removal van arrived and parked close by.

Stacy came to the door, waved to her, then turned to speak to the two removers. She didn't come out again.

Later, as Elise got ready for bed she looked out of her bedroom window and saw the bedroom light from the upper storey next door shining down on the front pathway that ran along the whole row.

It was a relief not to be living on her own here. That prospect of being so vulnerable, since the phone hadn't been installed yet, had been worrying her more than a little. She'd tried not to let it show because this was such a good opportunity for her, and anyway, she had nowhere else to go. But still, a neighbour was a good thing to have.

'Goodnight, Stacy,' she murmured. 'Sleep well.'

26

Hope rang her counsellor and explained what was going on with Adam. Nina suggested that she should tell her daughter at once about the sudden arrival of the father Janey had only found out about last year and had never met.

'It wouldn't be good for her to find out he's here from someone else. Or even for him just to turn up on her doorstep. Don't you agree?'

'I suppose so. It'll be a big shock, however she finds out.' But telling Janey about Adam meant Hope had to risk upsetting her daughter and that possibility worried her too.

She was facing one difficult task after another as she built her new life and she was coming to the conclusion that it was better to get them over and done with than to mope around for days worrying about what might happen if she changed something. After some more thought, she decided to tell her daughter about Adam that very evening.

She rang Janey and asked if she could come round after tea. 'There's something I need to tell you, um, about your birth father.'

'Oh. Right. Of course you can drop round.'

As usual when something was very important the people at the refuge arranged a lift for Hope to and from Janey's, because it grew dark early at this time of year and she still felt terrified when she had to go out after dark on her own.

After that had been sorted out there was no going back and she spent the rest of the day alternating between fear of how Janey would react and relief that the secret she'd been holding inside herself with difficulty would be coming out into the open.

★ ★ ★

She had to gather all her courage together, though, when it came time to walk out to the car that was taking her to Peppercorn Street.

The woman driving it was a stranger, but she had a kind face and she gave the correct password.

'Want to talk about whatever it is?' she asked. 'I'm a good listener.'

'Thank you, but I don't think so. I've already spoken to my counsellor.'

'That's all right, then.'

They spent the rest of the drive in silence.

As they pulled up outside Number 5, the woman gave Hope a card. 'Phone me when you need picking up. I'm going to visit a friend a couple of streets away, so it'll only take me five minutes to get here.'

'Right. Thank you for doing this.'

'People helped me when I was in your shoes.'

Hope stared at her in astonishment.

'Don't look so surprised. If you've come so far along the path to recovery that they've given you one of the flats, then like I did, you can go further. It really is possible to get your life back to normal again if you keep trying, and there are a lot of people available to help you work through your problems.'

'Thank you for telling me.'

'I'll tell you one more thing. It helps me if I remind myself that no one in the world is problem-free and most people manage to muddle through life quite happily.'

That thought made Hope feel a bit better as she walked along the path to the front door. She didn't doubt that her driver had been telling the truth about having been in her place once. There had been such gentle understanding in her eyes.

★   ★   ★

Janey heard the car stop outside and peeped out to check that it was her mother. Yes, no mistaking Hope scurrying down the path towards the front door — her mother always rushed to get inside after dark.

After opening the front door, Janey locked it behind them. 'Millie's in bed, I'm afraid. She was really tired today and fell asleep on my knee.'

'Could I just peep at her? I won't wake her up.'

'Of course. You know the way. Cup of tea?'

'Yes, please.'

'And a piece of Winifred's cake?'

'Not till we've had our chat, if you don't mind.'

Janey shook her head sadly as she went to make the tea. Her mother looked even more nervous than usual tonight. What could have happened to throw her into one of her tizzies?

She'd been looking forward to a quiet evening finishing off her library book, but saying no to her mother, who didn't ask her for much, always felt like kicking a puppy. Not that she'd ever kicked a puppy, but she could imagine the same look of uncomprehending pain in a small creature's eyes as her mother had sometimes got when they lived with her husband, who had been the worst pretence of a father Janey had ever heard of.

When Hope joined her in the sitting room, she nodded thanks for the mug of tea and sat clasping it in her hands for so long that Janey wondered if she was having second thoughts about whatever it was she intended to reveal tonight.

Then Hope put down the mug and said abruptly, 'Your father contacted me recently.'

'Lionel?'

'No. *He* wouldn't know how to contact me, even if he cared about me, and I wouldn't give him the time of day if he did. No, it was your birth father, Adam Torrington, who contacted me. He's in England.'

'He never contacted you before. What does he want now?' Janey couldn't help speaking sharply.

'To meet you. It turns out someone intercepted the letter I sent him telling him I was pregnant, and he never got it.' She explained how Adam had found out about Janey's existence.

'And you believe this?'

'Yes. Unless he's changed beyond recognition,

Adam isn't the sort to tell lies, especially about important things like this.' She smiled, but it was clearly an effort. 'It made me feel better to know Adam didn't refuse to help me back then.'

'And his wife is dead, you say?'

'Yes. It's sad for their daughter, isn't it, to lose her mother so abruptly? Gemma is only seventeen. He says she's very clever and was a full year ahead at school.'

It was out before Janey could stop herself. 'Unlike me, struggling to catch up and win a place at university or at least on a technical college course. He won't think much of me being an unmarried mother, either, will he? He might leave rather than meet me and Millie when he finds out.'

Her mother came and sat beside her, putting an arm round her shoulders, for once offering instead of needing comfort. 'I told him you were forced and Millie's the result of that.'

'You did? And he believed you?'

'Yes. And if it's all right with you, I'd like to bring him and your sister to meet you.'

It came out as a whisper. 'A sister. I can't believe I have a sister.' She looked at her mother's face, so close to her own. 'It must be upsetting for you, the thought of meeting him again.'

Hope frowned, head on one side, then shook her head. 'Not now that I know he didn't deliberately abandon us. I've talked about it with my counsellor and it made me feel . . . better. I can't find words for why I felt so much better. Not rejected, perhaps that's it.'

She reached out and brushed away a tear from Janey's face with her fingertips. 'Don't cry. I won't bring him unless I'm sure it's the right thing to do, and of course, unless you want it.'

'*He* won't want to meet me.'

'He and Gemma have come all this way *especially* to meet us both. Remember that. Travelling ten thousand miles isn't a casual act.'

'I can't believe I — '

Janey couldn't help weeping a little in her mother's arms.

And afterwards, once her mother had left, she wept again. She wasn't ashamed of Millie, but it wasn't a good look to meet your father for the first time holding your fatherless child in your arms. It didn't make you feel confident of being accepted. He was more likely to pity her and she didn't want that either.

Her last thought as she was falling asleep was that she had a sister, well, a half-sister. That idea felt so strange.

There would be another layer to the meeting because of that and she didn't know what to expect. She'd always wished she had relatives, and now that two had turned up out of the blue, let's face it, she was utterly terrified of meeting them.

Terrified of being scorned.

For the first time she truly understood her mother's fear of anyone and everyone, and vowed to be kinder to her in future.

★   ★   ★

When she got home, Hope hesitated. Should she ring Adam now? Would he be in bed?

But the meeting with Janey had gone better than she'd expected and she suddenly felt she could face phoning him.

He answered the phone almost immediately.

'Adam?'

'Hope. I'm so glad you rang. Is everything all right?'

'Yes. I just, um, came back from telling Janey about you.'

'Good. How did she react?'

'She was afraid.'

He didn't answer straight away and when he did his voice was harsh. 'Of me? How could she be? She's never met me.'

'Afraid of you scorning her, because of Millie.'

'I wouldn't do that.'

'I told her so.'

'You did?'

Hope nodded, then realised he couldn't see her. 'Yes. You never were the sort of person to scorn others and you don't sound to have changed.'

'Thank you for that.'

'Can I meet you tomorrow, Adam? I have some photos of Janey and Millie and we should talk.'

'That would be wonderful.'

She hesitated. 'I've changed. I'm going grey and I've turned into a mousy sort of person.'

His voice grew gentler. 'I won't scorn you, either, Hope.'

Silence hung between them and she couldn't

think how to answer, was glad when he spoke.

'Shall I pick you up somewhere? I've hired a car.'

'We could meet at the Riviera Café in Sexton Bassett. I can walk there quite easily. Just you and me this time, don't you think? Not our daughters.'

'Fine by me. What time?'

'Ten o'clock?'

'Excellent.'

She switched off the phone and put it down carefully, staring at it for a long time.

She'd done it now.

And though she was afraid — well who wouldn't be in her situation? — she didn't feel as bad as she'd expected about meeting him. Maybe her driver tonight had been right. Maybe she was now on her way to a normal life, one painful step at a time.

She'd be careful, though, check him out carefully before she introduced him to Janey and Millie.

She didn't sleep well, but she didn't mind, for once. She felt to be living up to her new name and finding hope in the world again.

27

In the morning Nell and Angus got ready to meet the people from the council. Their own engineer arrived at the big house first, so that they could fill him in on the background. Sam Thompson was an older man, with a thin, intelligent face.

He snorted when they finished their explanation. 'If Hedley Preece says the houses are safe, they are. He's a stickler for the truth. Not that I won't check things out for myself. But I don't expect to find any problems.'

Russell Alexander arrived soon afterwards and they introduced him to Thompson. He stopped to study the row of houses. 'They don't look tumbledown to me.' He looked questioningly at the engineer.

'You can't tell for certain until you've done some checks, but my first impressions are good. You're a lucky guy, Denning, to own all this property.'

'I know. But it's a big responsibility and has all sorts of problems, not just structural.'

'I know: developers and greedy councils. Seen it all before. People always wanting to dip their fingers into other people's pockets.'

'Or take the whole pocket away,' Nell said grimly.

They showed the two men the first house and the hidden room.

'Should we reveal this, to show them how important this house is?'

'If they don't need to know something, don't offer the information at all,' the lawyer said. 'They aren't the sort of men to be impressed by history.'

'I'm glad you said that. We're afraid Dorling might send someone to destroy this room in the hope of making the house worthless.'

'He won't get a chance if you don't tell the guy from the council,' Thompson said. 'What a treasure this is! I'm coming back again when they open it up to the public.'

'So am I,' Russell said softly.

★   ★   ★

As they were leaving Number 1, a large silver car drew up. Hobkins and another man got out and stood looking at the houses, muttering to one another and not even attempting to exchange greetings with the proprietor.

'Hobkins' manners used to be better than this,' Thompson said with a frown. 'What's got into him?'

'Arrogance, I should think,' Nell said. 'He thinks he holds all the winning cards.'

'Don't go across to them,' the lawyer murmured. 'Let them come to you.'

It was a few minutes before the newcomers moved across and Hobkins looked at them sourly as he at last introduced his companion. 'This is John Grantby, a structural engineer who advises the council sometimes.'

The other man nodded, not cracking even a hint of a smile.

Angus frowned. 'Just a minute. Are you not employed by the council?'

Hobkins answered for him. 'Mr Grantby is a consultant we bring in sometimes.'

Thompson stepped forward. 'Haven't seen you for a while, Grantby. Who are you working for now?'

'I run my own consultancy.'

'You were with Dorling and Cavendish last time I heard.'

'Well, I'm not now.'

Hobkins had been scowling at the lawyer. 'There is no need for a lawyer to be here. You're wasting his time and your money.'

'I'm not letting you into the houses without him being present.'

Grantby looked at his watch. 'Nothing a lawyer says will change the state of the houses. Can we just get on? I have another appointment to go to.'

Angus resolved to check that Grantby really had left Dorling and Cavendish, then reluctantly showed them inside Number 1. Thompson and the lawyer followed, saying nothing.

He didn't open the secret door and was surprised when Grantby didn't even think of asking to see the rest of the attic. Indeed, the fellow seemed to be giving the house a very cursory examination.

'Needs a lot of work. Hardly worth it,' was all he said.

When they came out, Hobkins would have

walked straight into Number 2, but Nell moved to bar the way.

'We'll need to knock. This house and Number 3 are occupied.'

'What?' Hobkins glared at them. 'You haven't been given permission to rent them out.'

'He doesn't need it,' the lawyer said quietly. 'These are not council houses.'

'He surely told you that we considered them unsafe?'

'He has a structural engineer's advice that they are perfectly safe, and Mr Thompson is here to give a second opinion on that.'

Angus noticed Grantby shoot the lawyer a quick frown at that, so added pointedly, 'I shall have two expert opinions on my side after today and that should settle the matter.'

'You're assuming a lot,' Hobkins snapped.

Grantby's frown deepened but he didn't comment.

The front door opened and Stacy stood there. 'I couldn't help overhearing what you were saying because the window is open. I can't see how these houses could possibly be unsafe. They're in better condition than any of the rentals I've lived in recently.'

'That's none of your business, madam, and faults don't always show to amateurs,' Hobkins snapped. 'We need to come inside to check the structural safety, so kindly move out of the way.'

She didn't budge, looking questioningly at Angus.

'We have to show them round, but if this time is inconvenient, we can come back later.'

Hobkins opened his mouth and Nell said savagely, 'Be quiet please, Mr Hobkins. We prefer to deal politely with our tenants, and with everyone else we encounter.'

The lawyer had opened his mouth to speak, but with a faint smile he shut it again.

Stacy's eyes danced as Hobkins turned dark red and glared at them. She addressed Nell. 'It's in a mess, I'm afraid, because I've not finished unpacking yet, so be careful where you tread.'

'I'll show them round, if that's all right.' Angus turned to see that Thompson had already moved across to the hall table where the little animal was standing on a small table.

'That's an attractive ornament. Is it one of yours?'

'Yes.'

'I must bring my wife. She loves things like that.'

'Will you please stop delaying this?' Hobkins said loudly. 'I have work to get through today, even if you don't.'

He said nothing further as they went round the house and Grantby measured or took photos on his phone.

Angus got out his own phone and took shots of whatever Grantby photographed, which had Hobkins glaring at him even more viciously.

Thompson smiled slightly as he watched them. He already had his phone out but was taking his own photos, not copying the others' choices.

If it hadn't been so important it'd have made a

good comedy scene, Angus thought.

But it was important. Very.

⋆ ⋆ ⋆

When Grantby said he'd seen enough, Angus thanked Stacy and took his group round to Number Three.

Hobkins stood tapping his foot impatiently as it took a while for Elise to answer the door.

She was leaning on a stick, looking tired.

'Is it all right for us to look round?' Angus asked.

'Of course. But I'd like to know who these people are first.' She got a notebook out of her pocket.

Russell smiled at her. 'Here's my card. I'm Mr Denning's lawyer.'

'Thank you.'

'Why do *you* need to know, madam?' Hobkins looked aggressive. 'You're only a very temporary tenant. You'll be moving out as soon as the houses are demolished.'

Angus was recording the conversation, so didn't comment on a decision to destroy his property being assumed before it had even been examined.

The lawyer was looking more and more angry.

Thompson looked at Hobkins in surprise. 'Why are you saying that? Not only have you only seen two houses, but as far as I could see, those houses were well built and have been recently modernised to a high standard.'

'Mind your own damned business.'

305

'This *is* my business. I've been employed to survey the houses and that's what I'm doing. Though as far as I can see, this is all completely unnecessary and if a suspiciously unrealistic report is put in, I shall be taking it up professionally.' He stared pointedly at his fellow surveyor and Grantby flushed slightly.

'I too am a little concerned by your attitude,' the lawyer added quietly.

When they'd finished, Angus again apologised to Elise for disturbing her and turned round to see Hobkins already getting into the car.

'Probably one of the rudest officials I've ever had to deal with,' Thompson said mildly.

The lawyer watched the car drive away. 'He wasn't like that before. I wonder what's changed him? There's definitely something fishy going on.'

'I agree. And we'll no doubt find out soon enough.'

'They won't have a legal leg to stand on, I'm sure.'

'Unless they pull some other tricks. I wouldn't put anything past them. I think I'm going to sleep in one of the empty houses for the next few nights.'

'Sadly, I think that would be a wise precaution,' the lawyer said. 'There have been rumours in the past about sudden, unexpected problems to property that had been checked and declared sound structurally. Better safe than sorry.'

'I'll just take another set of photos of the row and dictate my findings, while things are fresh in my mind,' Thompson said.

'Come and have a cup of coffee at the big house before you go.'

'I can't, I'm afraid. I have wall-to-wall appointments today. I'll send you a summary of my findings this evening. I think you should definitely keep a good watch over the houses.'

'I too have to go,' the lawyer said. 'I'm glad I was here to see for myself how you were treated.'

Angus strode back up to the big house, feeling more worried than ever about what Hobkins would try to do next. Today he'd acted arrogantly, as if sure he'd get what he wanted. Why would he think that?

★ ★ ★

Just before teatime Angus and Nell took a stroll round the grounds and he called in on Elise and Stacy to let them know he'd be sleeping in Number 1. That seemed the most appropriate place to station himself because anyone wanting to get to the houses either had to climb over the perimeter wall or walk past the first house, and though the wall wasn't all that high, it was dangerously unsteady in parts.

He intended to place movement sensors outside the two houses at the far end and at the entrance to the street, to wake him if anyone passed by from either direction.

But was he doing enough? He felt sure he'd missed something.

★ ★ ★

After Hobkins had driven away from Saffron Lane he stopped and turned to the structural engineer. 'You know what to say at tonight's emergency council meeting?'

'It won't be believed. There is no sign of weakness.'

'There will be by tomorrow. And I believe Bryce Dorling has been assured of your co-operation.'

'Yes, damn him. Don't set off yet. I prefer to get out and walk, rather than ride with one of his toadies.'

'Pot calling the kettle black. Don't forget to email me your report summary.' Hobkins grinned as he added, 'We don't want those two women to live in dangerous buildings, do we? Their moving in gives me an excellent reason to call the meeting as an emergency.'

'You've got the report already. Dammit, you're the one who wrote it.'

'But we need it to be seen to come from you, so please make sure you email it to me as soon as possible.'

Grantby walked away without another word.

★ ★ ★

Darren had been to check out the arts village a couple of times, watching people come and go, because he had a feeling this place would lead him to her. But there had been no sign of Stacy.

He got into conversation with one of the men working there, on the pretext that he was looking for somewhere to rent. 'Will these houses be rentals or for sale?'

'They'll be for renting, but only to artists.'

'Artists? What do you mean?'

'It's going to be an Arts and Crafts Village. I overheard the owners talking. They're hoping it'll become a tourist attraction. The first two tenants are moving in tomorrow. One's a woman who does welding and makes ornaments out of scrap metal. Seems a funny thing for a woman to do. And who'd want a pile of scrap metal sitting on the mantelpiece?'

'Not me.' Darren hoped he'd hidden his elation. 'What about the other artist who's moving in at the same time? What does he do?'

'It's an old woman and she's a painter, but I don't know anything about her because the owners moved out of my hearing just then.'

'Well, I'd better carry on looking elsewhere for somewhere to rent. Thanks for telling me about the artists. It's saved me wasting my time here.'

He smiled as he drove away. *Gotcha, Stacy!*

28

Hope stared at herself in the mirror and sighed. These days she tried very hard not to fool herself about anything, and though she was wearing her best clothes and had washed and blow-dried her hair, she still looked shabby, faded and older than her forty-one years. She felt older too.

Well, there was nothing she could do about that. It was Janey who mattered now, and Millie, of course. But she had to make sure Janey wasn't going to be hurt by this new turn of events.

She arrived at the café five minutes early, but Adam was there already, sitting fiddling with a smartphone and frowning at it. She'd have recognised him anywhere, even though she'd not seen him for nearly twenty years. Unlike her, he didn't look anything like his age and his hair was still mainly dark, only lightly frosted with silver at the temples.

When she stopped by the table he looked up and pushed his chair back, taking her hand before she'd realised what he was doing.

'Dorothy? Is that really you?'

'I'm Hope now,' she corrected.

'Sorry — Hope. Do sit down. What can I get you?'

'Coffee, flat white. I can pay for it myself.'

'Let me. I'll just turn this off and put it away.' He fiddled with the phone and shoved it carelessly in his pocket, by which time she'd sat

310

down opposite him.

She watched him signal to the server then turn his attention fully on her. She couldn't work out what to say or do next so waited for him to speak.

'It's been a long time. I'm so sorry Judith stopped me knowing you and I had a child.'

'Are you really?'

'Yes. She could be . . . possessive. When she said she wanted us to split up, Gemma stayed with her and she deliberately drove a wedge between us. That upset me. I couldn't understand why my daughter suddenly didn't want to spend time with me.'

'And are things better between you now?'

'Much better. Gemma was there when I found quite a lot of other things besides your letter, you see, things that exonerated me of what her mother had accused me of. Even so, it's not easy going but we are starting to build bridges. As I hope to build connections between myself, you and Janey.'

The server brought her coffee across and Hope fiddled around, putting some sugar in from one of the long, thin little packets. She sat stirring it for longer than was necessary till she realised what she was doing and put down the spoon.

Adam broke the silence. 'How did Janey take the news? Did she agree to meet me?'

'Yes. But she's afraid you'll think the worse of her because she has a child.' Hope smiled involuntarily. 'As if anyone couldn't love an adorable little darling like Millie.'

'You said Janey was raped, so it wasn't her fault, let alone the child's. Why should I scorn either of them? Was the man caught?'

'Eventually. That's a story for another day. Janey's a really good mother, young as she is, and we all love the child. The woman she rents rooms from is like an honorary aunt and dotes on Millie, as you'll see for yourself.'

'It's good that she has people who care.'

Hope looked at him and found herself smiling involuntarily as something occurred to her. He looked too young to have a grandchild. 'How does it feel to become a grandfather so unexpectedly?'

'Great, actually. I like children. I'd have had more, but Judith refused.' And had then had her tubes tied without telling him to make sure there weren't any accidents.

'Well, now you've got two daughters. How did your Gemma take the news?'

'She's still trying to come to terms with the idea that she has a sister, but she's not too upset by it. And she loves children, so she's dying to meet her niece. Look, let's speak frankly: I presume you're here to suss me out before you let me near Janey?'

'Yes. But you don't seem to have changed much. You always were kind.' She took a deep breath and committed herself. 'Janey will be at technical college today. She's making up for lost time so that she can qualify to go to uni. Why don't I take you to meet her this evening?'

And then she took the greatest risk of all. 'I don't have a car so if you can pick me up just before seven that would be helpful.'

'Can Gemma come too?'

'If you think she'll be kind to Janey.'

'Of course she will. Slightly wary, as is only natural, but she's a nice kid.'

Hope finished her coffee, suddenly alarmed at how much she'd told him. She needed to get away from him and stay on her guard more when she next saw him. 'I'll leave you to get on with your day now.'

He opened his mouth as if to protest then shook his head slightly and said, 'Can I drop you somewhere?'

'No. I've got shopping to do and I need to contact Janey. We made a provisional arrangement for tonight and I have to let her know. Here's my address. Please don't give it to anyone else without my permission. It's a block of flats, all of them sheltered housing for women recovering from abuse.'

'Was it very bad, what happened to you?'

'Yes.'

'I'm sorry.'

'I don't want to discuss it, Adam. Not now, not ever. I'm moving on. See you at quarter to seven.'

* * *

Hope hurried out of the café, letting out a near groan of relief to have got this difficult meeting over. She'd acquitted herself pretty well, considering.

How good-looking Adam still was! If only her

life had been different.

She turned down a side alley then let herself break into a run. But when she stopped at the top corner of it to look back, there was no sign of him pursuing her. Of course there wasn't. He wasn't like that.

The fear of being pursued was inside her every time she went out, but it wasn't as bad as it had been and she'd be informed when they let her husband out of jail. Only he'd not be her husband by then.

Would he accept that? She didn't know.

In the meantime she had things to get on with. She thought she'd done the right thing in arranging to take Adam to meet Janey, hoped she had.

And she was going to book into a daytime class about using computers. She must be the only person her age who'd never been near them. Never been allowed to go near them.

What a fool she'd been! She should have got help much sooner.

⋆   ⋆   ⋆

Adam sat on in the café, signalling that he wanted a refill then going over the conversation in his mind.

How old Hope looked! She could almost have been his mother and the signs of a hard life were written all too clearly on her face. He had to warn Gemma not to stare at her. He had to warn his outspoken daughter to tread carefully with Janey, too, and not to blurt anything out which might hurt her sister.

He wished he could let Judith know how badly her meddling had impacted on poor Hope's life. And Janey's from the sound of it. That upset him.

But he doubted Judith would have cared about that. She'd grown very selfish as she grew older. He hoped to help Gemma grow up with a more compassionate attitude towards other human beings, especially those struggling with huge personal problems, as poor Hope was.

On that thought he got out his phone and called his daughter.

'How did it go, Dad?'

'Quite well, I think. We're going round to see Janey this evening, so Hope can't have hated the sight of me today. Is that all right with you?'

'Yes. Of course.'

'I'll be home in about an hour. I'm going to have a stroll round the town centre. I need to get some exercise and there are some interesting buildings here. They haven't knocked all the older ones down as they have in some places.'

He picked up a local paper to read while he finished his coffee then went outside and turned left up High Street. When he saw a street sign saying Peppercorn Street he stopped, wondering what had made them choose that name. On impulse he turned left again and strolled up it.

The first houses were mainly small blocks of flats, looking to be in quite good condition. Some were newbuilds and others conversions of large, nineteenth-century houses.

As he walked on up the slight slope, keeping to

the right side of the street, the houses were mostly semi-detached family dwellings. He stopped again at a small side street called Cinnamon Gardens, grimacing. Not in keeping with the rest of the street. Tiny box-like bungalows, the sort provided for older people. These were rather meanly built, in his opinion, but there you were. From what he'd seen, most modern buildings in the UK seemed smaller than those in Australia, especially those they called 'newbuilds'.

Nearer the top of the hill the houses were bigger, some quite grand, the sort that would once have needed a couple of maids to run them. They were pretty, too, with ornamental stonework around windows and doors.

The top end was a cul-de-sac, to his surprise, but there looked to be a narrow lane leading off it to the right. He had to step back quickly as a large silver car drove out of it, passing dangerously close without seeming to notice his presence because the two men inside it were arguing. He ventured along the lane, hoping he wasn't trespassing.

A man striding up from the rear of the property towards a lovely old manor house changed course to come across to him just as he reached a sign saying *Private Property* that was half-hidden by foliage.

'Can I help you?'

'I didn't see the sign when I entered the lane and I realise I'm trespassing. Sorry. I was just wandering round the town, exploring.'

'Is that an Australian accent I detect?'

'Yes. Though I come from this area originally. Not Sexton Bassett, but down the road in Swindon.'

'My partner's Australian, too. She's from Perth.'

'So am I.' He took a step backwards. 'Anyway, I won't trespass further. Looks like you have a lovely old house here.'

A woman came out of it as they spoke and strolled across to join them, so he stayed to say hello to a fellow Aussie.

'One of your compatriots, Nell, exploring the town,' the man said.

She frowned slightly at Adam. 'Actually, I think I've met you, or at least passed you regularly in the street. I used to work for a firm of lawyers in Subiaco.'

'I used to have an office there till I went to work for the university.'

'Small world.' She looked at Angus questioningly and at his nod, she said, 'Why don't you come and have a coffee? You may enjoy our house. It's very old, quite an architectural gem.'

'If you're sure you don't mind, I'd love that.'

'When I came back to England last year after emigrating as a child, I loved looking at historic houses. Now I live in one. I'm Nell and this is Angus Denning, by the way.'

'Adam Torrington.' He turned to walk with them, glad of a distraction to fill the waiting time today.

Angus shared a coffee break, then said, 'Sorry. I'll have to leave you to show our visitor round, Nell.' He added for Adam's sake, 'I need to

317

design a temporary security system for some houses I'm renovating at the rear of my land. 'I've a feeling someone is targeting them for vandalism, hoping to persuade me to sell the land for redevelopment.'

Because he was missing his work, Adam said impulsively, 'Could I help you in any way with that?'

His host looked at him in surprise.

As he explained that his job was lecturing in IT, with a specialisation in its uses for security, Angus beamed at him. 'How lucky is this! You're exactly the sort of person I need to bounce some ideas off. If you have time, that is.'

Nell watched indulgently as they exchanged remarks in computer-speak, presumably to explain their areas of interest. She hardly understood a word but they seemed quite happy about whatever they were discussing.

'Glad to have you on board,' Angus said as the spate of information died down.

'I can spare a few hours and I'll enjoy a challenge. I'll just have to phone my daughter so that she won't worry about me. She's at the flat we've rented and is expecting me back around now, only I got tempted into going for a walk. And before I do anything, I'd better go and pick up my car, which is still parked in town.'

'Why don't you ask your daughter to join us?' Nell said. 'She could get a taxi here.'

'Are you sure?'

'Yes, of course. I know what it's like to be a stranger in England and know no one. And a girl of that age must get rather bored waiting around for you.'

'She does. Once my business is concluded I've promised to take her sightseeing to other parts of England, but until then she's at a bit of a loose end.'

'Phone her. Tell her the address is Dennings, Number 1 Peppercorn Street. The taxi driver will know where we are.'

Angus stood up. 'In the meantime, I'll run you into town to pick up your car so that I can grab some electrical stuff, then when we come back I'll go over what I'm thinking of setting up with you. If you have any suggestions for improvement, I'd welcome them, though I have to make do with the parts I've got on hand here because I don't have the time to go into Swindon for anything out of the ordinary. The new system needs to be up and working by tonight because our tenants have moved in and I don't want them to be vulnerable.'

He smiled ruefully at Nell, knowing she'd understand the pleasure he always got from talking to a fellow IT specialist, not to mention the importance of keeping Saffron Lane safe.

⋆　⋆　⋆

When Angus dropped him near his car, Adam nipped into the supermarket to buy a few basic groceries and some fruit, as well as some flowers for Janey and a little toy for Millie. Then he went back up Peppercorn Street.

He was nervous about tonight, more nervous

than he'd expected. Well, who wouldn't be nervous in his situation?

How was Janey feeling? The same, probably.

As he drew up in front of the lovely old house, he saw Gemma getting out of a taxi and she turned to wait for him as it drove away.

'Is this guy someone you know from work, Dad?'

'No, someone I've just met. You know what it's like when you make contact with other IT people.'

'Other geeks. Yes, I've listened to you talking IT-speak and I don't usually understand a word, apart from 'and' and 'but', even though you've assured me it's English.'

He chuckled. 'Sorry. I forget there are other people around sometimes. I think Nell was feeling the same, as she got a glassy-eyed look while Angus and I were chatting.'

She linked her arm in his. 'Doesn't matter, Dad. Chat away if that's your thing. This is a great house, isn't it? We don't get ones like this in Australia; we aren't old enough as a country.'

The front door opened and Nell appeared.

Gemma let go of his arm to be introduced, but it had made Adam happy for her to touch him so casually. When he'd told her about this evening's meeting, she hadn't seemed worried, so maybe things would go smoothly between her and her half-sister. But who knew with teenage girls? They could take umbrage at nothing sometimes.

Anyway, this chance encounter would give Gemma and him something to do for a few hours. What nice people the Dennings were.

He'd be happy working with Angus to set up an electronic security system.

Was it really so urgent?

29

Gemma enjoyed exploring the beautiful old house and helping Nell do various small jobs around the place. What a lot of work an old house made for its occupants!

When she and her father left Dennings, they stopped to buy some fish and chips on the way home, eating them quickly because they were cutting it fine for picking up Hope, then rushing out again.

Adam parked the car under the big overhead light in the visitors' section of the parking area and got out to wait for Hope so that she could see him clearly and, he hoped, not be afraid.

Gemma joined him, leaning against the car, their breath making misty patches in the chilly, moonlit world. They turned as they heard footsteps coming down the metal stairs in the middle of the two-storey block of flats.

'She looks even more nervous than you do,' Gemma whispered.

'Shh.' Adam moved forward. 'Hi, Hope. This is my daughter, Gemma.'

'Pleased to meet you.' She studied the young woman openly. 'You look a lot like my Janey. They've both got your dark hair, Adam.'

When Gemma just made a soft sound, as if she didn't quite know what to say to that, Adam covered for her with an innocuous remark and suggested they all get into the car.

'Where to?' he asked.

'She lives at the upper end of Peppercorn Street,' Hope said. 'Do you know where that is?'

'We ought to. We spent several hours there today.'

'Really?'

'Yes. I was exploring the town and bumped into Angus Denning. We got talking, found we had a lot in common, and I stayed to help him put in a better security system. He's setting up a sort of artists' village in a group of houses he owns. The street's called Saffron Lane.'

'Yes. There was an article on it in the local newspaper. Everyone's wondering what sort of people the artists will be. You can see the gardens of the big house from the back of where Janey lives and there's a gate there to get into them. Miss Parfitt, who owns the house, is quite friendly with Angus and his wife, and Janey says they keep an eye on her because she's quite elderly. She's wonderful for her age, though.'

Another sign of what a small world it could be, Adam decided. What did they call it: seven degrees of separation? No, it was *six* degrees, he amended mentally. He liked the thought that you were only five acquaintances away from anyone on the planet, though he wasn't quite sure whether that could really apply to everyone in the world.

He drove carefully through the centre of town, where some shops were still brightly lit, and turned into Peppercorn Street.

When they got near the top, Hope pointed. 'That's it, the three-storey house with the light on over the front door.'

So they parked the car and as they got out, he admitted to himself that he was still extremely nervous about the coming meeting. He wasn't usually a worrier, but he wanted so much to make a good impression on his other daughter.

'We'd better let you go in first, Hope,' he said after he'd locked the car.

As they walked along the path to the front door, Gemma squeezed his hand and whispered, 'It'll be all right, Dad. Stop worrying.'

Her touch was comforting but he couldn't relax, just couldn't.

⋆   ⋆   ⋆

Janey had been peering out of the front room window without putting the light on, hoping she couldn't be seen by the visitors. She wanted to catch a glimpse of her biological father before he came inside because she didn't even have a photo of him.

As the visitors walked down the path the man turned to the young woman walking beside him, smiling as he said something. Wow! Her birth father was really good-looking. Janey felt surprised. Somehow she hadn't expected that. Lovely warm smile too, she decided.

Would he ever smile at her like that?

'They're here!' she called, hurrying into the hall as the doorbell sounded.

Winifred came out from the kitchen to give her a quick hug. 'Chin up, dear. You wanted to find your real father and now you have.'

But did he truly want another daughter? Janey wondered as she went to open the front door. She wished Auntie Winifred was staying with her for this important meeting, but she'd refused, saying it wouldn't be right for a stranger to intrude.

Janey's mother was standing at the front of the trio. Next to her father was a young woman who had dark, slightly wavy hair very like her own. She was even wearing it in a similar style too, long and tied back.

'Janey, these are Adam and Gemma,' her mother said in a voice that wobbled slightly.

'Nice to meet you. Oh, thank you! The flowers are lovely. Um, come in and let me take your coats. I've got a nice fire in my sitting room.' She didn't let herself babble on, but waited in silence to hang their coats on the hallstand then led the way into the nearby room. They didn't say anything, either.

Millie was sitting in the playpen, fiddling with her plastic bricks. She was rosy from her bath and ready for bed, wearing her teddy bear pyjamas.

Janey's mother picked up the child and that immediately put a loving smile on her face instead of the nervous look that sat there so often and seemed to take all the character from her.

'Adam, this is your granddaughter, Millie. *Our* granddaughter, I mean.'

He flashed a quick smile at Janey and moved towards the child, speaking in a soothing tone and holding out a little soft toy.

As Millie smiled at him and took the toy, Janey turned to study her sister and found herself being given a thorough scrutiny at the same time. Naturally. Who wouldn't be curious about an unexpected sibling?

Gemma spoke first. 'Amazing, isn't it, to have a sister you've never met?'

Janey relaxed a little because that wasn't a hostile tone. 'I've been wondering if we look at all alike. See?' She pointed as she turned to study their reflections in the mirror over the fireplace. 'What do you think?'

'I think we look quite a bit alike, but you're taller than me.' Gemma looked across at her father, who was tickling his granddaughter and making her chuckle. 'Can I hold Millie when those two have finished cooing over her?'

'Of course. She's a very friendly child. Oh!'

Adam was holding his hands out to Millie, inviting her to come to him. The little girl stared at him from the safety of her grandmother's arms, right thumb in her mouth, then suddenly she pulled out her thumb and dropped the toy, holding out both arms to Adam, waggling them impatiently. He took her gently from Hope.

It wasn't like Millie to go so quickly to a complete stranger. That was a good sign, surely, Janey thought.

'She's lovely,' Gemma whispered. 'I want lots of kids one day.' She turned to see her sister struggling not to cry. 'What's the matter? What have I said?'

'I've been worrying about tonight and how your — I mean *our* — father would react to an unmarried mother and her child. But look at him beaming at her and see how Millie's taken to him.' She swiped at her eyes. 'I'm being stupid.'

'That's not a crime.' Gemma put an arm round her and gave her a quick hug. 'Dad's all right. He gets on with everyone — well, he does with people who're nice, not ratbags, so you don't need to worry about him scorning you. I'll take Millie off him in a minute, then you can have a word with him on your own. Though goodness knows what you'll both say. This must be so awkward. How long have you known about Dad?'

'I found out last year that my mother's ex wasn't my real father. And thank goodness for that!'

'He sounds horrible.'

'He is. Mum told me my real father had gone to live in Australia, so I wasn't expecting to meet him. And then he contacted my mother.'

'If you don't mind me saying so, your mother looks very worn and weary.'

'She is. I'm glad they put her ex in prison. If I had my way, they'd never let him out again, because she's going to be terrified once he's released. He's the sort who always has to get his own back if he thinks someone's got the better of him.'

'I'm just beginning to realise how complicated life can be with families. Mine's been pretty straightforward so far, because there were only us three most of the time, though my parents divorced a few years ago and that made things a bit difficult. I didn't realise it, but my mother was keeping me away from Dad as much as she could and telling me lies about him not wanting to see me.'

'Difficult for you, torn between the two of them.'

'You've said it. Well, that's over and done with now so I'm trying to get over it.'

'Mum said you're doing well at school.'

Gemma shrugged. 'I've left school now and my results will come through soon.'

'How do you think you went?'

'Pretty good. My main worry is what I'm going to do next year. Maybe take a gap year before I go to uni, because Mum was encouraging me to study business and it's not a deep interest of mine.'

'I envy you that freedom of choice.'

'It's Dad's suggestion that I find something I really want to do. And I'd better stop babbling on about myself or I'll bore you to tears. You're easier to talk to than I'd expected.'

'So are you.'

'Big relief?'

'Yeah.'

They grinned at one another.

Adam turned towards them at that moment and smiled. Janey's anxiety ratcheted down still further. She hadn't been mistaken: he did have a really lovely smile.

Gemma moved forward towards him, arms outstretched. 'My turn to hold my niece. You're not hogging all the cuddles, Dad.' She turned to Hope. 'You'll have to show me how best to hold her.'

Hope nodded as if she understood that this was an attempt to give Janey and her father time together.

⋆ ⋆ ⋆

Adam moved to join Janey and asked in a low voice, 'Is there anywhere we can go to talk more privately?'

In spite of getting on well with Gemma, she had been feeling as if they were doing this first meeting under a microscope and was relieved by his request. 'We could sit in my study upstairs. It's not as warm up there, though.'

'I don't mind the cold.'

'Just going upstairs to show Adam my study, Mum,' she called across the room.

Hope smiled and made a shooing gesture. Gemma was murmuring to Millie and as Janey watched, her sister planted a big kiss on the child's fat, rosy cheek.

It suddenly occurred to her that if anything happened to her, Millie would no longer be alone in the world. Oh, the relief! She hadn't realised the burden of that responsibility until now.

They didn't speak as they went upstairs, but as soon as she had closed the door of the study, Adam said in a voice thickened by emotion, 'I've been worrying all day about what to say to you, Janey. Could I start by giving you a hug, please? Would you mind? We have such a lot of time to make up for.'

It was the last thing she'd expected and she

felt tears well in her eyes. Her voice came out choked. 'I'd like that.' She walked into his outstretched arms, feeling as if everything around her had faded, as if for a few moments there were only the two of them in the whole universe.

They didn't speak, but he held her in the same way Millie held her beloved teddy bear, close, heads touching. No one had held her like that since her granddad died.

When her father moved back slightly, she didn't pull away but stood within his arms looking up at him. Not as far up as she'd expected. She was nearly as tall as him. To her surprise there were tears on his cheeks as well as hers. Without thinking she reached out to brush them away.

'Men aren't supposed to cry,' he said in a husky voice. 'But I have a lot of hugging to make up for. I never expected the joy of having another child.'

She gulped. *Joy!* he'd said. 'I never expected to have a real father.' She was shaking, couldn't stop, so he kept his arm round her and guided her to the old, lumpy sofa. As he sat down beside her, he took her hand.

'I want to be a real father from now on, Janey, if you'll let me. But I don't want to come between you and your mother. I think that will mean me spending some time in England.'

'Can you do that? Don't you have a job to go back to?'

'Yes, I can stay here if I want. I've taken a year off for starters, then we'll all work out what to do next. If I decide not to go back, I have dual nationality so I can stay and get a job. It'll partly depend on what Gemma decides to do. If she goes to university here, it'll be a no-brainer that I settle here for a few years at least.'

'I like her.'

'She's easy to love. But I haven't been able to spend as much time as I'd like with her during the past few years.'

'She said her mother didn't encourage much contact.'

'To put it mildly. I won't go into that, not now. As to my work, I didn't really fit into academic life anyway, though it was a prestigious job and I learnt a lot. I prefer *doing* things rather than writing about them or giving lectures. And trying to get articles published in professional journals is a real bore.'

'Has Gemma any idea what she wants to do?'

'We did wonder if she might get a place in Oxford, or some other good university in England. It'd be good for her to get away. She and I both need to build a new life.'

It was out before Janey could stop herself. 'I wish I had the choice of studying at university.'

'You will have now, I'll make sure of that.'

She looked at him in shock. 'It's too expensive, costs thousands of pounds each year.'

'I'm not rich, but I'm not short of money, either. And you'll more than pay me back by letting me spend time with you and your delightful daughter.'

'Can it be so easy?' she wondered aloud.

'Nothing ever runs perfectly smoothly, and

this won't either, so don't expect instant miracles. But if we all work at it, we can build close family ties, I'm sure.'

'A family!' It was little more than a whisper, but he heard what lay behind it and gave her another of his quick hugs, as if he understood how much that meant to her.

'I have some other relatives in England still, though I don't know them very well. We went over to see them and they were more welcoming than I deserve. I was only twenty when I went to Australia and I was selfish and self-centred in those days. I didn't even try to keep in touch. I got my degree part-time there while I was working in IT in its infancy. No, not infancy, childhood. It was well beyond start-up point by then.'

He paused and gave her a very level look. 'One day I hope you'll trust me enough to tell me more about your life, warts and all. But if you don't want to, that's all right. I will, of course, help your mother in any way I can and I won't try to separate you from her.'

'She and I aren't all that close, though we're working on it. She let *him* trample all over me while I was growing up, as well as her, you see, especially after my grandfather died. She'd given up fighting and become a . . . a doormat.'

'Ah. Well, I'll try not to tread on any toes.'

'I'm seeing her regularly, letting her get to know Millie. I think how it goes between us from now on will depend on how well *she* moves on from her past.'

'Poor Hope.'

'Has she changed a lot since you knew her?'

'Sadly, yes. Out of sight. I'd not even have recognised her. She looks much older than I'd expected.'

They sat quietly, then he said, 'We'd better join the others soon. Just let me ask one thing: are you all right for money?'

'Yes. I get social security and I'm a good manager.'

'Will you let me do something for you? After all, I paid hefty private school fees for Gemma for all those years.'

'If you like, but I can't think what, except for an occasional present for Millie.'

'Hmm. Do you have a car?'

She looked at him in puzzlement. 'No. Why?'

'It'd be my pleasure to buy you one, just a second-hand one, but a decent, safe vehicle. When you next have some free time you can help me choose. And I'll pay the annual running costs.'

It was a moment before she could recover from the shock. 'I can't let you do that!'

'Of course you can. I'm your father. The car will be a . . . a belated declaration of that.'

'Thank you.'

'We'd better join the others now, Janey. We'll talk together another time.'

She led the way out, knowing that what had been said on the surface was only a fraction of what had been offered behind those words. And oh, she was so hungry for a real family and for . . . well, love.

He stopped at the top of the stairs to say, 'You

seemed to be getting on well with Gemma. I'm glad about that. She's as moody as any teenager, but behind it, she's basically a happy soul. Some people seem to be born with a sunny nature.'

'I'm still a teenager . . . technically,' Janey said. 'For another few months.'

'You don't seem like one. I should think you were forced to grow up in a hurry when you got pregnant.'

And to her amazement she got another quick hug from him. She'd never met anyone like him for hugging. It felt strange, but wonderful too.

She couldn't believe how lucky she was to have a man like him as a father. Not for a minute did she doubt that what he'd said and offered were genuine. It was written in his face that he was a decent man, and kindness shone out of him.

She reached out to prevent him from opening the door of her sitting room for a minute. 'I'm glad you're my father.'

'I'm glad too. Perhaps you could call me 'Dad' from now on?'

'Dad. Yes, I'd like that very much.'

'I won't knowingly let you down, Janey. I can promise you that. But I'm no more perfect than the next person, so I'll make mistakes. Just don't let any of them come between us.'

'I won't . . . Dad. Same goes for me.'

30

Stacy was clearing up the kitchen after a late tea. She'd worked hard and the house was pretty well organised with regard to furniture. Well, she didn't have a lot, just enough for herself and an occasional guest. Best of all to her, the studio was partly operational and she kept walking into it, simply to stand and gloat.

Her next big task would be to sort out the pieces of scrap metal she'd scavenged over the past year or two. They were stored in tea chests, for lack of anything better, and heavy enough that it'd taken two men to lift each one. They were lined up at one side of her new studio and she'd start going through their contents tomorrow — bliss!

When she heard someone knocking on the front door, she thought it was Elise, who had accepted her invitation to come round for a coffee. She glanced at the clock. Her neighbour was a bit early, but never mind.

The minute she opened the door, she was shoved back inside so roughly she stumbled and fell — but instinctively she began shrieking for help at the top of her voice and trying to kick out at her assailant.

She'd recognised him at once, of course she had, and recognised that look on his face, too. He wanted to hurt someone, preferably her.

With the element of surprise on his side,

335

Darren managed to grab her, forced her to the ground, then sat astride her and she couldn't fight free of him.

She continued to scream but he must have come prepared, because when she opened her mouth, he stuffed something in it, then banged her head so hard against the floor she felt her senses spin.

★　★　★

Darren watched her carefully as she lay there limply, not struggling now. Had he hit her head too hard? She looked dizzy and unfocused. No, of course he hadn't. She'd be all right in a minute or two. Serve the bitch right if it hurt.

Her disorientation gave him time to haul her to her feet, holding one arm behind her back. He loved doing that to her. When she started to struggle feebly, he said, 'Stop that! I can dislocate your arm in seconds.'

He kicked the front door shut behind them as he began to jerk her towards the rear of the house.

In spite of his warning she did start to struggle, but stopped with a smothered whimper when he gave her a sample of shoulder pain.

'Do not make another sound and if you don't do as I tell you, I'll damage that shoulder big time. Now, we're going into the kitchen. Walk forward slowly.'

★　★　★

The pain in her shoulder had been so sharp, Stacy didn't try to escape again. She had no choice but to do as he said, and anyway, she still couldn't seem to think clearly.

Once there, he dumped her on a chair and she tried again to yank her arm away. But he seemed prepared for everything and put one arm round her throat to hold her still from behind while he clicked a pair of handcuffs quickly on to one wrist.

In spite of his threats, that made her struggle desperately again to prevent him attaching the handcuffs to anything else. But he was too strong for her and managed to click the other end of them onto the chair arm.

She managed to spit out the gag and as she gave another scream, he slapped the side of her head so hard she went dizzy again. Before her head cleared, he finished the job of tying her feet and cuffing her other arm to the chair. Then he fastened the gag back in place with duct tape.

After that she was helpless — and very afraid.

He disappeared into the front room and she heard the front door lock click. When he came back, he studied her with a gloating expression. He'd never looked that vicious before or hit her so hard. Did he intend to murder her? Fear made her belly lurch.

He leant forward till his face was right next to hers, holding her head still by her hair. 'I'm going to enjoy this. You're not. But first I'll draw the curtains. At certain times a man likes privacy.'

He tapped the front of his trousers sugges-
tively and she felt literally sick with fear and
disgust at the thought of him doing that to her.

But she couldn't see any way of stopping him.

★   ★   ★

As Janey's visitors were starting to put their coats
on, the doorbell rang and Winifred popped out
to see who it was.

Her friend Dan gently moved her back so that
he could get in. He brushed aside her
introductions to the visitors and asked urgently,
'Have you got Angus's phone number, Winnie,
love? I can't find it and I need to warn him
quickly.'

'Warn him? What on earth about?'

'My neighbour came to see me, because he
knows I'm friendly with the Dennings. The
council held an emergency meeting tonight. He
happened to be passing and saw the lights, so
wandered into the hall to see what was going on.
They have to be open to the public, but there
were only a couple of other spectators there.'

He looked angry. 'My neighbour was surprised
when a structural engineer gave evidence that
some of the houses in Saffron Lane were in a
dangerous state, especially the ones nearest the
rear entrance to the estate. They voted to take
preliminary steps to put a compulsory demolition order on the whole of the row, because new
tenants had been let in and they could be at risk.
Someone suggested the tenants might even be
able to sue the council for allowing it.'

'And the motion was passed? I know a couple of councillors who'd want more information than that before suggesting demolition.'

'Yes, it was passed, and with only one vote against. Only about half the councillors were there, though, probably because it was held at such short notice.'

'But the houses aren't in a dangerous state,' Adam protested. 'I was working on them today and they seemed very solidly built and well preserved to me. We were putting in a security system because Angus was worried those particular developers might try to damage the properties. He'd been told they have a reputation for using dirty tricks to get their way, and were even suspected of burning one place down.'

'That's what my neighbour said and why he came to me, though I had to promise to keep his name out of it. He doesn't want them coming after him and he knows I'm acquainted with the Dennings. He reckoned they were going to make sure some houses were in a dangerous state before the council reps come to inspect the street tomorrow, which is why he wanted me to contact the Dennings tonight as a matter of urgency.'

Adam, who was still facing the open front door, aghast at what he was hearing, saw two people striding up the hill and realised it was Angus and Nell, so he called out to them.

They stopped, looking happily relaxed. 'We've just come back from the pub. Great food and — '

'Never mind that — ' Adam began but just then Angus's phone made a strident sound.

He watched the other man snatch it out of his pocket.

'Hell fire! The security system's been breached at Saffron Lane. I didn't expect anyone to attack it so early in the evening because Elise and Stacy will still be up. I have to get down there.'

'You were expecting an attack?' Janey asked, surprised.

But she was talking to herself because he'd set off running towards the drive that led to his home.

Adam turned to his daughter. 'Can Gemma and Hope come in again and stay with you for a bit longer, Janey? Angus might need some help.' He turned to Gemma. 'Stay here till we make sure it's safe.'

'Dan will stay with us, won't you?'

'Happy to.'

'Thanks.' He got into his car and drove off.

The others stared at one another until Janey glanced towards the stairs and said, 'If I didn't have Millie to look after, I'd be going after them.'

Gemma clutched her sister's arm. 'Why don't you and I do that? I don't know about you, but I'd be no use in a fight. We could act as witnesses, though, if there was a dispute. What do you think?'

Hope surprised them by saying, 'Good idea. Do it! I can keep an eye on Millie for you, Janey, love.' That offer earned her an approving look from her daughter.

The two girls grabbed their outdoor clothes.

'I've got my mobile phone. I can take photos.' Gemma waved it as she raced out of the house.

The three older people left behind looked at one another rather anxiously.

'I hope they'll be all right,' Hope said.

'Well, they won't be alone. Put Millie to bed and come and join us in the kitchen,' Winifred said. 'I'll switch on the baby monitor so we'll hear her if she wakes.'

'They said they were just going to observe what happened,' Dan said.

'I hope they keep to that. You know how impulsive girls that age can be.' Hope went up to check on Millie then joined the others to wait anxiously for news.

★   ★   ★

Adam slowed the car alongside Angus and Nell. 'Hop in. We'll get down there more quickly in this and have a bit of protection inside it if necessary.'

They didn't hesitate to pile in and he set off before they'd even finished closing the car doors, talking at the same time to tell them about the council meeting. 'Dan said the developer was there and gave testimony that he considered the houses in Saffron Lane unsafe.'

'That's rubbish.'

'Shh now.' They all stopped talking as he slowed right down just before they got to Saffron Lane itself. He switched the engine off, letting the car roll forward soundlessly down the gentle slope till it came to a halt.

'I can't see any vehicles other than the two belonging to the tenants, either here or out on the main street,' Angus whispered. 'I wonder what tripped the alarms. Let's go the rest of the way on foot. If there is someone up to mischief, it'd be best to surprise whoever it is.'

'Just tell me what you want me to do. You know the terrain better than I do. Oh, and if you think we'd better arm ourselves, there are some car tools in the boot. A spanner would be better than nothing, don't you think?' Adam suggested.

'Good idea.' They armed themselves and turned to stare at the houses.

'It looks so quiet,' Nell said.

'We'll not take any risks, though. We'll check things out before we make ourselves known. Nell, let me go first,' Angus said. 'You can be our back-up, if needed.'

'You can go first, but I'm not going to be left out.' She turned to Adam. 'I've done a self-defence course and I know how to look after myself.'

Angus studied the houses carefully before he began to move. No sign of any intruder, yet someone had broken the external circuit at the perimeter wall, which meant they'd climbed over the wall because the plumbers had put a temporary wire mesh fence across the end garden to keep their equipment safe and that would have sounded a different alarm.

He couldn't see why any of the locals living nearby would come in over the wall and the two residents had been warned how dangerous the wall itself might be. It was about two metres high and gave a visual protection to the small street but it would be easy enough to climb over, hence the electrical circuit now running along it, which would only be turned on after dark.

He moved quietly along the street, knowing the warning had come from the section behind Numbers 2 and 3.

As he glanced ahead he saw that the front door of Number 3 was open and Elise was alternately beckoning to them and putting one finger to her lips to show that they should be quiet. She must have seen something, then.

They hurried to join her.

'A few minutes ago I heard Stacy scream and yell for help a couple of times and then there was silence. I didn't dare knock on her door, because I'm not strong enough to help anyone physically, and if someone hurt me, I could be crippled for life after that hip replacement.'

'It was wise of you to keep out of things.'

'I didn't completely keep out. I tiptoed along the back and peeped into the house. I saw a man shove Stacy into the kitchen area. She seemed dizzy, so perhaps he'd hit her. He's got her tied to a chair now. I didn't recognise him, but he seemed to be taunting her. I know she's got an abusive ex-husband she's hiding from, so I called the police.'

'How long ago was that?'

'Only a few minutes but unfortunately they couldn't tell me when they'd get here because it's been a busy night for 999 calls. I was just going to phone you directly, Angus, when you turned up. Did that alarm system of yours go off?'

Angus nodded and turned to Adam. 'Are you

game to go in with me and tackle whoever it is?'

'Yeah. Who knows when the police will get here if it's a busy time? I'm not bad at looking after myself in a fight. How about one of us goes in at the front and one at the back?'

'Sounds good.' Angus turned to Nell. 'You stay near the car, love. You'll see more from there than from inside Elise's house. Lock yourself in it and call the police again if you think it's necessary.'

She glared at him. 'Don't be daft. I'm coming to stand near the front door after you go inside. I can phone from there just as well as from here and I may be able to help.'

'Elise says there's only one man, so you won't be needed.'

She folded her arms and looked at him. At the sight of the determination on her face he gave up and turned to Elise again. 'You'd be safer if you locked yourself in your house.'

She nodded and they heard her door close as they walked quietly along the paved path to the next house.

He tried the front door and it was locked.

'Break a window?' Adam whispered.

'No need. I've got master keys.' He took them out of his pocket. 'I'll unlock this door then go round the back. Unless Stacy starts screaming again, count steadily to fifty then go in as quietly as you can. We want to take him by surprise.'

He too started counting to fifty as he walked. When he reached the rear of the house, he saw that the kitchen blinds and the curtains over the French windows were all drawn. That must be recent if Elise had seen inside a short time ago. Damn! It'd make it harder to know when was the best moment to surprise the intruder.

It worried him more than a little that the man wanted to hide what he was doing in a room looking out on to a blank wall.

He slid the key into the lock and as someone began speaking loudly inside turned it, hoping the voice would mask the sound of the key.

He waited till the count of fifty to fling open the back door, but what he saw had him freezing on the spot. The intruder had a knife at Stacy's throat and a trickle of blood was running down her neck.

There couldn't have been a worse time to break in and betray his presence.

'Stay back, you, or I'll really hurt her!' the man yelled, shouting the same command at Adam as he appeared in the hall doorway. He manoeuvred Stacy's chair till he was able to see both newcomers as well as hold her chair steady.

He looked wired with rage and still had the knife at her throat. Both Angus and Adam quickly did as ordered.

'Get over to the other side of the room, both of you, and put your hands on the wall above your heads.'

He laughed loudly as they did this. 'See, Stacy, even your would-be rescuers aren't as smart as I am and I'm going to teach them a lesson as well as you afterwards, oh yes, and then I shall — '

He didn't finish what he was saying because while his attention was on the two men and his back to the other door, Nell crept across to him and cracked a spanner down on his shoulder. She dragged Stacy's chair to one side away from the gleaming knife blade as he crumpled.

To Angus's relief the attacker had let go of the knife. He and Adam rushed to secure the fellow before he recovered enough to fight. He had a bit of wire in his pocket and used that as a temporary way of tying the man's hands behind him.

Nell unstuck the duct tape and took the gag from Stacy's mouth while Angus felt in the guy's pockets and passed her a small key. 'I think this'll unlock the handcuffs, then you can pass them to me.'

'Who is he?' Nell asked as she did that.

'My ex, Darren Cooke. We've been separated for nearly two years and divorced for over a year, but I heard from a friend that his new woman had also left him. I suppose that's why he decided to come after me again. He said he was going to train me to be a more obedient wife. As if I'd go back to him under any circumstances.' She glared across at him and added more loudly, 'I'd like to kick him where it hurts most.'

Darren winced visibly.

Nell grinned. 'Go ahead. I'll turn my back and guarantee not to hear anything.'

Stacy lowered her voice again. 'It's tempting but that'd bring me down to his level. Besides I can't bear to touch him. I hope they lock him away this time. They only put a restraining order on him before and a fat lot of good that did.'

'You poor thing.'

'I thought I'd given him the slip. I don't know how he found me.'

'I'll always find you again, you bitch, and next time you won't get off so easily,' Darren threatened just as a police officer appeared in the doorway.

The newcomer stared round and after he'd seen that Darren was securely held, he turned to Stacy, who was rubbing her wrists and on whose throat the trickle of blood bore witness to how she'd been treated. 'What happened here? I can guess but I want it in your own words.'

'These two captured me and beat me up!' Darren shouted.

'Pull my other leg, it's got bells on it,' the officer said contemptuously. 'I heard what you were threatening her with as I came in.' He went across to Stacy and lifted her chin gently to examine her throat with its puncture wound. 'I don't think this is very deep. Are you all right otherwise?'

'More or less. I'm still a bit dizzy because he hit me hard before he tied me up.'

He checked the side of her head, frowning. 'No double vision?'

'No.'

'Who is he? Do you know him?'

The other officer came in just as Stacy was explaining who Darren was and about the restraining order.

The newcomer turned to Adam, who was standing closest to Stacy. 'Do you want me to call an ambulance for your girlfriend?'

'Yes, I think we'd better call an ambulance,

but she isn't my girlfriend.'

'I don't want to go to hospital,' Stacy protested.

'It'll be better if a doctor can give evidence in court about your injuries,' the female officer said mildly. 'The bruises can show a lot about what he did to you. You don't want him getting away with this attack for want of evidence, after all.'

She sagged. 'Oh. Yes. I see. All right, then. But they're not keeping me in the hospital.'

'That's up to you and them.'

'No need for an ambulance. I can drive her there,' Adam offered. 'I've driven past it so I know where it is. Angus and Nell would be best staying here and keeping an eye on things. They're the owners.' He got out his phone. 'I'll just let my daughter know what's happened.'

'I'd better check up on Elise next door,' Nell said.

Angus stayed with the two officers, watching grimly as Darren was taken away, then he locked the house up and after Elise had gone back inside, he switched on the rear perimeter alarm system again.

'If anyone was coming to vandalise these houses tonight, I bet the sight of a police car will have driven them off,' he said to Nell, yawning.

'I hope so.'

As they left Saffron Lane and began to walk towards the big house, two figures came towards them, calling, 'It's only us.'

Angus let out a sigh of relief. 'What the hell are you doing out here, Janey and Gemma?'

'We thought witnesses might come in useful.

What exactly happened?'

'It was nothing to do with the houses. Stacy's ex had attacked her and tied her up. You can guess what he was planning to do.'

Both girls shuddered and glanced involuntarily over their shoulders.

'It's all right. The police have taken him away and your father's taken her to hospital to get checked out, Gemma. They only seem to be minor injuries, thank goodness.'

'So it wasn't the developer trying to damage the houses.' She sounded almost disappointed.

'Not this time, no.'

Nell moved forward. 'Come on. We'll walk you two along to Miss Parfitt's and you should stay there till your father gets back.'

When they got to the front of the next house Angus reiterated that warning. 'Do not try to interfere again. You could have got hurt or distracted us and caused us to be hurt. That man wasn't playing. He had a knife at Stacy's throat.'

After seeing them inside he and Nell walked back to the big house.

★   ★   ★

Angus fiddled around as she made them a cup of coffee, unable to settle, worrying about his houses and not liking the thought of Elise being all alone there. 'I think I'll go back and keep watch once I've drunk this. You stay here.'

'I suppose you'll kick up a fuss if I try to come too,' Nell said.

'A big fuss.'

'As long as you promise no heroics.'

'No. I'll leave that to the police. I can't understand what the developer thinks he can do, anyway. He can hardly bulldoze the houses before I've appealed any demolition orders.'

'It is a bit puzzling.'

Angus nodded agreement.

'Well, if any would-be intruders see lights on in the first three houses, that should deter them from breaking in,' Nell added.

'Yes, but I still feel . . . uneasy.'

'So do I. I can't put my finger on it, but that Dorling creep isn't likely to play by the rules, so what else has he got up his sleeve?'

'Even if he had all the houses knocked down, he could hardly force me to sell these houses to him, or the land.'

She didn't say anything, but she didn't need to. They'd both heard tales about Dorling getting his way before through dirty tricks. Maybe he was underestimating Angus's stubbornness about not selling. Or maybe he was prepared to take some big risks.

She didn't undress and lay down on the sofa, dozing only fitfully, her phone on the floor next to her, ready.

Angus decided not to leave a light on in Number 2. If intruders came, he wanted to surprise them.

He didn't sleep at all but as the night passed, no figures came creeping through the darkness and the alarm didn't sound, so he might as well have.

31

It was a busy night in the small emergency medical centre in Sexton Bassett. The nurse practitioner doing triage listened to Stacy's tale and said she'd have to wait to see the doctor, since her problem clearly wasn't urgent. 'We only deal with the minor cases here and there's been a lot of fighting in town tonight. There's a group of hoods causing mayhem, and some of them have been using knives on one another. Time the police dealt with them properly.'

As they sat on the hard wooden benches as far away as possible from the irritating programmes on a tinny-sounding television high up on the wall and also at the opposite side from the noisy youths, they watched the hands of a big, old-fashioned clock tick slowly round. They chatted now and then but mostly were silent, both of them tired.

After a while Stacy grew restless. 'This is a complete waste of your time, Adam. Why don't you go home? I'll be perfectly safe here because there are plenty of police around, and I can get a taxi back after the doctor's finished with me.'

'Definitely not. I intend to see you right into your house afterwards. Anyway, the crowd of battle-scarred youths seems to be thinning, so you should get in to see a doctor soon. Surely there won't be any more accidents or fights in the town at this time of night?'

However, thanks to a car accident, it was almost dawn before Stacy managed to see a tired-looking doctor. He listened gravely to her tale, checked her out and swabbed her neck again with disinfectant, as the nurse had done.

'Best left to heal in the open air, but be sure to keep it clean.' He made some rapid notes. 'You don't need to go for any check-ups at the hospital, because if you had concussion, it'd have shown by now. But the police are right: I can now become your expert witness, if I'm needed. Your attacker must have been rough with you, from the bruising.'

'That's why I divorced him.'

'One of those, eh?'

As they walked outside, she yawned and stretched her arms above her head. 'Well then, home, James, and don't spare the horses.'

He smiled. 'Yes, milady.'

'I think it'll be quickest to go up the street before Peppercorn. It'll get us to the rear entrance near Saffron Lane. If Angus is still around, we'd better let him know I'm OK.'

'Fine by me.'

'And Adam, I'm very grateful for your help tonight. If you hadn't — ' She stopped and shuddered.

'I was glad to be there for you. Come on, let's get you into my car.'

⋆   ⋆   ⋆

An hour or so before dawn, three youths wearing hoodies climbed over the wall of the parking area where the council vehicles were kept, laughing at the useless barbed wire on top of the surrounding wall as they covered it with an old quilt and got inside without a problem. All were wearing black and they took care not to expose their faces to the two old-fashioned CCTV cameras as they checked out the vehicles.

'I wonder why that guy suddenly wanted us to wait till this time to do the job?' Sevvy asked.

Raff led the way across to the trucks. 'How the hell should I know? Maybe he knew something we didn't. As long as he's paying so well, he can give me orders.'

'Something must have happened to make him change the time of our job, though, and he should have told us what it was. For all we know, the police may still be hanging around the town centre. We're both over 18 now and — '

'Aw, shut your face and let's get on with it. You *want* to attract the attention of the fuzz once we get out of here, remember. Drive your truck past a few CCTV cameras, the ones people bother to watch.' They sniggered because they both knew which ones were imitation cameras. 'Ditch the truck as soon as you're sure you've got them following you. Don't stay in it for too long.'

'Yeah, yeah. You've told me that three times already, Raff, and I know exactly where I can run it into a garden without a wall and get away quick-smart down the side of the house. Now let's get these trucks started.'

By then the third youth had undone the locks on the big gates. He pushed them open before running across to cover the CCTV cameras and

353

then join the others. 'There you are.'

'Yeah, yeah. I've got eyes.'

'Where's my money, then?'

Raff passed him two banknotes and he kissed them before running off.

Sevvy was still worrying. 'Hurry up and get those trucks started! It's gonna be light soon. I don't like doing this sort of job in daylight. You should have told him we'd do it tomorrow instead.'

'He's not the sort you tell. Anyway, he's paying us good money an' it won't take long now. No one will see you. People are still in bed, not on their way to work yet.'

They drove both the big trucks away but Raff parked his on the edge of an industrial area and waited, engine still running, but with the window open so that he could listen carefully. When he heard the sound of police sirens in the distance, he waited. Then his mobile phone rang just once. Raising his fists in a victory sign, he set off again. He was going to enjoy doing this little job. He really enjoyed smashing things up.

The job itself didn't make any sense but who the hell cared? The money promised was good and it'd be fun. What more could you ask?

★　★　★

Angus heard the sound of a truck approaching and ran upstairs, staring out of the back window of Number 2, from which he had the best view of the approaches to Saffron Lane from the nearby street.

To his dismay he saw a truck barrelling down the street towards the entrance. It came straight through it, tyres screeching a protest as the truck was swung to the right into a screeching semi-skid by a very skilful driver.

Angus groaned and thumped his fist on the windowsill, helpless to do anything but watch as the truck smashed into the rear wall of the first house.

The vehicle had barely come to a halt before a youth jumped down and ran off into the distance, shrill, hysterical-sounding laughter trailing behind him in the still night air.

He'd left the engine running but it was making rough coughing noises, and after a moment it stopped completely, steam and dust clouding the air.

Angus closed his eyes in anguish, knowing he couldn't catch the guy. In spite of all his care, he hadn't saved the first house. The only tiny consolation was that the truck hadn't pushed on through the wall to do more damage. Strange, that. He would have expected such a big truck to smash right through such a small house.

This must have been organised on purpose, and whoever had done it had unerringly hit a weak spot in their defences. But then, who would expect someone to ram an expensive truck into a row of houses? It must have been stolen. He peered at the logo on its side, crumpled but easily recognisable: a council truck.

A skinny youth had leapt down from it, not a grown man, so it must have been a joyrider, damn him!

He rang 999 as he ran down the stairs and out into the grey, predawn light. While reporting the incident, he suddenly smelled petrol and told the emergency services responder about that, which had the woman promising rapid attendance.

He went to stand some distance away in case of an explosion, praying the truck wouldn't catch fire and destroy the historical material inside.

It didn't burst into flames but something strange happened. The wheels at the outer side of the vehicle began to sink, as if the ground was giving way beneath them. The truck started tilting very slowly forward, like a majestic hippopotamus sinking into a lake.

What the hell was happening? Were the foundations of the house giving way?

No, it couldn't be that because the front corner of the truck sank down further than the others, quite a long way, and when it stopped, it was well below the level of any foundations he'd ever seen. And the houses didn't have cellars.

Had the crash caused a sinkhole? Could you cause one or did they just happen? Whatever it was, he could do nothing about it but wait for someone to arrive and make things safe.

The truck stopped, crazily tilted, with one rear corner right up in the air and the front corner diagonally opposite that way down in the ground. He got out his phone and took a photo. At least he had these houses insured.

He looked along the street and saw Elise looking out of the window and waved to her to stay there.

The silence seemed to throb around him and

he closed his eyes briefly for a moment, then he pulled himself together and phoned Nell.

'I heard the noise. I'm already on my way to join you. That sounded to be one hell of a crash.'

He told her what had happened and a few seconds later she came racing through the grounds to fling herself into his arms. Then they waited together for the police to arrive, not going near the truck. If there was any evidence in or near it, they didn't want to contaminate it and though it hadn't exploded into flames and the engine had cut out, thank goodness, the smell of petrol was still very strong.

Elise came out of Number 3 with mugs of coffee and the three of them stood waiting for the police to arrive.

'That truck looks like it belongs in a surreal painting,' Elise commented at one stage.

'I can't understand why that side of the house hasn't caved in completely,' he said a couple of times.

Mostly they were silent.

When they'd finished Elise took the mugs from them. 'I'll go and slip some clothes on and put these in the kitchen.'

Angus and Nell walked up and down the street, listening for help coming. The worst was that they couldn't do anything but watch the truck and pray it wouldn't explode.

If this was rapid attendance, it was taking a hell of a long time.

32

As Adam was driving Stacy back from the emergency centre, a youth running flat out round a corner nearly bumped into them and he had to brake hard.

The youth leapt aside with an athlete's grace. When this caused his hoodie to fall off, he yanked it quickly back to cover his face, but Adam had seen him clearly.

'Did you get a good look at him?' he asked Stacy.

'Yes. He looked wild-eyed.'

'On drugs, I should think. Or high on excitement. I wonder what he was running from.'

Adam set off again, approaching Saffron Lane from the rear of Dennings.

Once again he braked hard, swearing under his breath as he saw the obstruction. He sniffed. 'I can smell petrol.'

The truck looked grotesque, almost standing on end like that. Its metalwork was battered and its engine was still steaming with something hissing faintly.

A siren behind them made him get out of the way. He passed the truck by going along the grassy verge and stopped his car further up the drive. They got out and watched a police car pull up.

Two officers got out, and one waved to them to stay back, shouting, 'There's been a petrol spill. Don't come any closer, please. You're lucky you got your car past it safely.'

Angus and Nell were on the other side, and he shouted to the police.

'We're waiting for the fire and rescue services as well, because of the spilt petrol.'

'Stay well back. We can't do anything till that's been made safe.'

★ ★ ★

The other officer had been getting out a roll of blue and white police tape and the two of them fastened it to bar off the rest of Saffron Lane, then came to string it across the main drive just below where Adam had parked.

'Never seen anything like it,' the policewoman called cheerfully. 'There must be cellars under those houses for the truck to sink down like that.'

Adam remembered Angus saying the houses didn't have cellars, but what other reason could there be for the hole? He looked at Stacy as a thought came to him. 'You know what? I reckon that lad we nearly ran down might have been involved in this. I could identify him, I'm sure. He was right under a lamp post.'

Stacy nodded. 'I was wondering about that, too. Actually I could draw him. That might help them identify him.'

'I thought you were into metalwork.'

'I'm into art generally as well and I often sketch out my pieces before I put them together. I'm pretty good at faces. I'm sure I can do a recognisable sketch.'

'The police might appreciate that.' He gave her a wry look. 'I'd better ring Gemma and tell her about this latest event. It's been quite a day — and night, hasn't it?'

She shuddered eloquently, one hand going up to her throat.

Adam explained to his daughter about the truck, then waited for the police to secure the site and the fire and rescue service to make everything safe. He was as nosey as the next person when something strange happened.

Stacy took a small sketch pad and soft pencil out of her backpack and rested the pad on the car roof. 'I'll sketch him while his face is fresh in my memory.' She bent her head and began work.

What would happen next? Adam wondered as he alternately watched her and the figures busy at the accident scene.

* * *

The sergeant who'd now arrived to join the two officers and take charge of the site looked dubious when Stacy presented him with a sketch of the lad they'd seen running through town just after the incident.

'I don't mean to insult you, but how do we know your sketch is accurate?' he asked.

She glared at him. 'I'll do one of you as a test. See how accurate you think that one is.'

A few minutes later she marched across to him and thrust a piece of paper at him. 'There.'

As he stared down at it, the officer beside him

craned her neck to have a look and grinned. 'It's you to the life, Sarge. Not very flattering, though.'

'How about this one?' Stacy again produced the sketch she'd made of the youth who'd been running through town.

'Raff Smales,' the woman said at once. 'It's a good likeness too.'

'Do you know where he lives?'

She rolled her eyes. 'Officers have been to his home to question him or bring him in a dozen times at least. You've only just been transferred to Sexton Bassett, Sarge, but believe me, you'll soon get to know that one.'

'Why is he running loose if he's such a slippery customer?'

'Because the magistrate's a softie and Raff's been under age. But he turned eighteen a couple of months ago and he's been a bit more careful of what he does since then in case they send him to an adult prison.'

'Well, go and see if you can pick him up. We need to find out what he was doing out in the middle of the night.' He turned back to Stacy. 'Sorry for doubting your skill, ma'am, but we have to be careful.'

⋆ ⋆ ⋆

When the firefighters had cleared up the petrol spill they dragged the truck out of the hole. As soon as it was clear, one of them yelled, 'Hey, come and look at this!'

'I'm not being kept out of it,' Angus muttered

and introduced himself to the sergeant, who let him join the group staring down the hole. It was over two metres deep at least, but it wasn't just a hole. There seemed to be a passage leading sideways from where the weight of the truck had breached the tunnel that lay beneath the ground. The tunnel was partly blocked by fallen bricks but clearly went back a long way.

The sergeant turned to him. 'I presume there were cellars under your houses, sir?'

'No. None that I know of, anyway, and I've looked round all of them many times.'

'Then why is there a tunnel here?'

'I can guess.' He paused to work out what to say.

'And?' prompted the sergeant.

'I've been asked by the heritage people to keep quiet about certain matters. Perhaps I could have a private word?'

The two men walked aside and Angus explained about the heritage people wanting him to keep quiet about the small communications centre, because they were afraid of people damaging one of the most perfect examples of such centres they'd ever seen. 'They're going to be very excited about the tunnel, too, I'm sure. Even they didn't spot its entrance.'

One of the firemen had come over. 'Well, they're going to have to be quick about it. If it were up to me, I'd fill in that hole immediately. It's a public hazard and we're not leaving it like that. There'll be children swarming all over it, given half a chance.'

'I'll phone them straight away.'

By then offices would be open, so he got on his phone and his call was passed through three people, each assuring him that this could be important but that it must be dealt with at a higher level.

As he waited he watched the fire and rescue officer station a guard at the hole, and heard the sergeant muttering about 'damned bureaucracies'.

He'd second that curse, he thought as a fourth person came on the phone and made Angus repeat his explanation of why he was calling. But this one didn't pass him on and seemed very excited indeed about the tunnel.

'Don't let them touch it, and especially don't let them try to go along it. I'll have some of our special curators there within the hour.'

One by one the various officials left, except for the man left on duty at the hole. Stacy yawned. 'I need to lie down.'

'We should have got permission for you to go into your house sooner.'

She grinned at Adam. 'I couldn't have borne to leave the scene till the excitement was over. At least it doesn't seem to have touched my house.'

He looked at his watch. 'Well, you go and have a snooze and I'll pick Gemma up.'

'My main desire is to feed my face,' Angus said. 'I'm ravenous. Come on, Nell. There's a man on duty and they've put temporary barriers round it. When the heritage people arrive, they can phone me and we'll come back down to join them.'

As they walked back, he put his arm round

her. 'There's always something going on in Peppercorn Street, isn't there?'

'And in the town. We've still to deal with the council's involvement and attempts at demolition orders. I wonder what they'll say about this?'

'Whatever they say, I'll deal with them better on a full stomach.'

★   ★   ★

Two of the police officers went to Raff's home.

The woman who opened the door scowled the minute she saw them.

'Sorry to trouble you, Mrs Smales, but can we speak to your son, please?'

'What's Raff done this time?'

'We're not sure but he was seen running away from an incident, so we need to interview him.'

'Well, he's a legal adult now, so he can damned well deal with this on his own. I told him: if he gets into trouble again, he can go and find somewhere else to live. I don't want criminals living in my house and police knocking on the door at any hour of the day or night.' She turned and yelled, 'Raff! You're wanted.'

There was no reply.

She called again, with the same result, then shrugged. 'You can come through and check but I bet he's skipped out through the back.'

There was no sign of her son in the house but the back door was open.

As she saw them out, Mrs Smales said, 'If you do have a reason to arrest him, tell him he's not to come back here. I'll pack his clothes and he can pick them up from the shed.'

She closed the door, muttering, 'Never had such a thing happen in the family before. He's a bad egg, that one, and what I've done to deserve him, I do not know.'

They were both smiling as they got into the car.

'Wouldn't it be lovely if Raff is proved to be guilty?' she murmured.

'Brilliant. Let's drive around a bit and see if we can find him.'

⋆   ⋆   ⋆

Bryce Dorling went for a little drive early in the morning, eager to find out what had happened to the houses in Saffron Lane, because he wasn't paying those lads the rest of the money unless they'd done what he wanted.

As he queued for a morning coffee to take out at a kiosk near the station, he overheard conflicting rumours being exchanged of an accident, of police being involved and also, to his puzzlement, the fire and rescue service being brought in. What the hell had required that?

He drove slowly along the street that led to the lower end of Dennings. As usual he felt angry to think of all that land being wasted on a tumbledown old house. Damned heritage idiots should keep their nose out of things and stop listing properties that were no use to anyone. And as for the houses in Saffron Lane, they weren't listed properties at all. Didn't people

365

realise there was a housing shortage in the real world?

From a distance the end house looked to be still standing undamaged, its roof intact and most of its windows unbroken. But the truck was something to see and he was tempted to get out his phone and take a photo. No, better not be seen doing that.

There was police tape strung about still. He got out the binoculars and scanned the area. There was a bloody great hole around the half-buried front of the truck. There must have been a cellar and that idiot had driven the heavy vehicle right on to it instead of hitting the house smack on, as he'd ordered.

Well, he wasn't paying good money for that stuff-up. The idiot should have seen the cellar windows and aimed elsewhere. Strange, though. Now he came to think of it, Bryce hadn't noticed any cellars when he looked over the houses. They caused extra costs, houses with cellars did, when you were levelling a block. No one built modern houses with cellars these days. Too expensive and not needed, unless you were on a slope and built an underport garage.

Shaking his head and letting out a little growl of annoyance, he took a swig of coffee and set off again, driving past the entrance and back to his office. He wasn't doing anything till he heard from Hobkins exactly what had been discovered and how it was going to affect his plans.

He'd get his way in the end, though. Everyone had a price for selling a house or a piece of land, or could be threatened into doing it. It was just a question of finding out what the best way was to get what he wanted.

And if you had to cut a few corners en route, well, that was life and to the victor the spoils.

33

A man from the nearest heritage office arrived two hours after Angus's phone call and knocked on Stacy's door. She in turn phoned the big house to tell them Bill Lynch was there.

Now that it was daylight, the police officer had left, because people could clearly see the obstacle and the Keep Out notices, and there was another emergency needing attention.

Bill went to stand on the edge of the hole and peer down it and she felt obliged to go with him and make sure he didn't touch anything till Angus and Nell arrived.

'Amazing,' he kept saying. 'Abso-bloody-lutely amazing.'

He'd stared at her bruised face, but she didn't feel the need to explain that to him. The police had rung to inform her that Darren was being sent for psychiatric checks, because he was still behaving strangely and had attacked a doctor brought in to see him. He wouldn't be released until they'd decided he wasn't likely to hurt her again and they'd let her know before that happened.

She felt safe for the moment but wasn't sure what she'd do when they did let him go. She'd had a little cry about that problem because it seemed obvious that she couldn't stay here now. Just when things were going right, Darren had to ruin her life again, damn him!

When Angus and Nell arrived, Bill said, 'Aaah! Now we can get somewhere!'

Nell stopped beside Stacy to ask, 'Are you all right? Your face is very swollen.'

'No permanent damage, but I don't want anyone taking photos of me, that's for sure.'

They turned as Angus told Bill about the secret communications room, and then the two men went inside the house.

'Come on!' Nell said. 'I don't want to be left out if they discover something.'

It took a while to check everything and it was Stacy who noticed that the kitchen door wouldn't close properly. Angus went to touch the wood panelling in the hall nearby.

'Don't touch anything!' Bill called.

Nell had had enough aggravation. 'This is a very frustrating situation for us. You lot are acting as if you own this house. Well, it belongs to my partner and if he wants to touch it he can.'

'I won't cause any damage,' Angus said more mildly.

As he pressed his way round the edges of the panelling to see what was making it uneven, there was a click and one panel swung outwards, revealing a very narrow passageway. To one side, probably under the main stairs, was a sloping set of steep stairs leading upwards, almost like a ladder. Two yards or so in the other direction were more of the steep, narrow stairs, this time leading downwards.

'It must be the entrance to that tunnel out there,' Angus said. He turned to Bill. 'It's all

369

right. I'm not going down there. I don't have the right equipment and I'm not stupid enough to go into dark places that might collapse on me at any moment.'

★ ★ ★

Two other heritage officials arrived just then and were ecstatic about the tunnel and passage. One woman clambered down into the hole and shone a powerful torch along the tunnel.

'I can see where a narrow passage from the house leads into it. I wonder how they hid the other end upstairs? We've got equipment in the van to check things out but it'd be better with more people involved. Government cuts are playing havoc with our department. Thank heavens for volunteers!'

She paused for thought. 'I wonder . . . Do you think the local fire and rescue services would lend a hand? They sometimes do when there's a possibility of danger to the public, which there is here. And of course it gives them a cost-free exercise for their junior staff.'

'You can just imagine what mischief some lads might get up to if they found a way in at the other end,' her companion said. 'Worth a try.'

'We'd better set up a temporary barrier at this end, at least,' the woman said. 'Sorry, folks, but we won't be investigating the tunnel till we get help. At best it'll be tomorrow.'

'Who's going to keep watch tonight on the tunnel?' Angus asked. 'I was up all last night keeping watch on the house and I've no intention of spending another night trying to stay upright.'

The woman hesitated then looked at her companions. 'I'll volunteer if my partner can come and join me. He's not in an official position but he does a lot of volunteer work.'

The three heritage officials turned to look at Angus enquiringly.

He waved one hand. 'Be my guest. But there's no furniture in the house for you to sleep on.'

'We've got camping equipment. We can make do. And we can start work on securing the things in the inner room while we're waiting for help.'

So Nell and Angus left them to it and went back to get some sleep.

⋆　⋆　⋆

Late that afternoon, Dorling rang up Hobkins and had to spend a long time soothing him. 'No one will know about our little agreement,' he said several times.

When Hobkins put the phone down, the door to his office opened and he swung round. No one was allowed to come in unless they knocked and he called out, 'Enter'.

Except his boss.

He stood up. 'Charles. Nice to see you.'

Then a man in police uniform stepped out from behind his boss and Hobkins' heart began to thump.

'You're being investigated for conspiracy and fraud. Pack your things and go home. If you get in touch with Bryce Dorling again in any way, you will be charged with further offences.'

Numbly he began to put his personal possessions together.

He drove home to the house where he'd been living alone since his wife left him and got out a bottle of whisky.

Dorling could fend for himself. Hobkins would co-operate fully with anyone who wanted him to.

Then he'd leave town. He didn't know where he'd go or what he'd do.

Then a terrible thought occurred to him. They wouldn't put him in prison, would they?

★   ★   ★

Dorling went back after dark, leaving his car in the town centre and walking the rest of the way. He was dressed in black and had a torch and a backpack, as well as a camera. Surely there was some way he could get into the tunnel? It ought to be quite easy to make some more of it cave in and do it in such a way that the houses were damaged at the same time.

A small charge of explosive would make it more unstable, he was sure. The only thing that puzzled him was why the truck hadn't done more damage to the house.

When he got to the street behind Saffron Lane he spent some time standing quietly in the shadows, observing. He'd wait here as long as was necessary. He wasn't into taking risks that might land him in trouble without a lot of care.

There were no lights in the end house though

the next two had lights showing. How the hell was it possible that they hadn't been damaged by the truck? And why hadn't the tenants been evacuated?

After a good half-hour, he was satisfied that no police were patrolling the area on foot. The people in the houses seemed to have gone upstairs, to judge by the lights. Presumably they were going to bed.

He continued to wait till the upstairs lights had gone out, then he moved, making his way slowly from shadow to shadow.

Suddenly a figure jumped in front of him and he couldn't hold back a grunt of surprise.

'Where's our money?' Raff demanded. 'You weren't there, as agreed. Me and Sevvy did the job and we want paying.'

Another figure moved out of some shadows to stand near him on the other side. Sevvy.

'I was delayed. I knew you'd find me. Let's move out of sight and I'll pay you now.'

'There's no one around. Just do it.'

Both youths took another step closer.

He gave up the idea of not paying them the full amount and took out his wallet, counting out the money. 'There you are. Exactly as agreed.'

'I need more because your change of time buggered things up for us,' Raff said. 'The police are on to me, my mother's thrown me out and I have to get away from this dump of a town.'

'I'm paying what we agreed and no more,' Dorling said firmly.

As he started to put the wallet back into his

373

inner jacket pocket, Sevvy grinned and punched him on the jaw.

He cried out as he fell and struggled when Raff bent over him to wrest the wallet out of his hand.

Just as he succeeded in doing this, lights from a vehicle parked in the drive in front of a nearby house flooded the area, and two police officers stepped out of places of concealment in nearby gardens.

For a moment everyone froze, then Raff and Sevvy turned to run, but were caught and though they struggled desperately they were quickly handcuffed.

Dorling made no attempt to run and when the police had captured the two youths, he thanked them profusely for saving him from the muggers.

'We aren't muggers,' Raff said. 'We did a job for him and he wasn't going to pay us what we agreed. I'll tell you all about it if you'll take it into consideration.'

'He's lying!' Dorling exclaimed. 'You can't believe the word of a thief against mine.'

'Oh, but we do. We've been keeping watch on you for a while, Mr Dorling, and are already aware that you've been involved in certain dubious incidents. Good thing we were following you tonight, eh?'

'But I'm not involved in anything dubious!'

'Our various witnesses say differently, and the lads' evidence will be very helpful. We'll find out more about this at the station, shall we, sir? And since you came here on foot, allow us to give you a lift there.'

The following day around midday, after negotiations at senior levels had been concluded, the fire and rescue service sent a team to help the three heritage officers explore the tunnels.

Angus and Nell were allowed to watch from a safe distance and the word must have got out somehow, because a few other spectators turned up.

'Oh, hang it,' Angus exclaimed. 'Let's invite Adam and as many of the others as are free to come and watch.'

It wasn't the most riveting show, because there was a lot of peering into the tunnel and slow arrangements of apparatus. But at last, when the tunnel had been deemed safe, the heritage officers were allowed into it.

They came out beaming and Angus hurried across to them before anyone could stop him. 'Well? Don't keep us in suspense.'

'The passage forks into two. One branch goes through to the biggest house at the inner end of Saffron Lane. Most ingenious to have two escape routes. The other part of the tunnel has caved in at one stage, but it won't cost a lot to shore it up and make it safe, then we'll find out where it leads — my guess is that little park just along the street, the one where there's an electrical substation. I've seen communication centres linked into places like that before.'

He beamed at them. 'We're bound to get funding for that, because it won't cost much and it's quite an important find.'

'Good heavens. And all this was unknown till we discovered that room?'

'Absolutely. Places are still coming to light here and there across the country, even all these years after the end of the war. There were groups of people who thought ahead during the war, especially in the early years, when they were expecting Germany to invade at any moment. They wanted to be ready to go into resistance mode.'

'But surely someone knew about the places?'

'It was an all-out war. Who knows what happened to their records? They may still be locked carefully away in some dusty drawer, or they may have been destroyed by bombing, or groups of local people may have been told to keep their mouths shut and did it all too well, right until they died.'

'I've seen things a bit like this discovered on that archaeology programme on TV,' Elise said. 'Fascinating stuff. I never expected such a place to be there on my doorstep.'

'What are you going to do about it now?' Angus asked. 'I'm still anxious to finish off these houses and find tenants.'

'There is funding being prepared to turn it into a miniature museum in memory of Jason Kinnaird's father.'

'Won't we have to rebuild that side of the house first?'

Bill grinned at them. 'Only some of the bricks from the outer shell of the house. They fortified the inside extremely well, in case there was fighting. They made it of reinforced concrete, so it's still pretty much all right. Amazing some of the quirks you run across in my job.'

★ ★ ★

As Angus and Nell walked into the house by the front door, he suddenly spun her round and knelt before her. 'Darling, I love you to pieces. Will you please marry me?'

'We've already said we were going to get married. What brought this on?'

'I wanted to propose properly.' He stayed on his knees, looking up at her, very serious for once.

'Then I'll answer properly too. I love you to pieces as well, Angus Denning, and I can think of nothing that would make me happier than to marry you.'

He stood up and pulled her into his arms, sealing the proposal with a kiss. Then he moved his head back a little and grinned. 'I think I did it rather well, don't you?'

She smiled back. 'Extremely well.'

'I'd been practising.'

She looked at him in surprise. 'Really?'

'Yes. It's a daunting thing for a guy to do, proposing. I tried it with fancy words, with a poem I found in a book, and in the end, I decided on straightforward and sincere.'

'That suits me very well, darling.' She pulled him closer and kissed him again. 'Of course, I'll want a *gigantic* diamond engagement ring.'

He knew her well enough to chuckle at her joke, but led her into his workroom and opened the safe. 'I knew you were mercenary so I got this ready.'

He pulled out a worn leather ring box and opened it. 'This belonged to my great-grandmother and I think it'll suit you.'

It was a single diamond surrounded by loops of gold. 'It's lovely. I shall be proud to wear it.'

It even fitted her perfectly — as Angus did.

Epilogue

Two months later, Nell and Angus got married in what had been intended to be a quiet wedding. And indeed, only a select group went along to the registry office with them.

But they returned home to find a crowd of people standing in the hall of the big house shouting, 'Surprise!' because their friends and relatives thought differently about celebrating their wedding in style.

A splendid party had been planned with all those attending bringing along a plate of something delicious for the buffet lunch, and a bottle of wine or something non-alcoholic but still special enough to use for the toasts.

Angus and Nell pretended to be vexed that their instructions had been ignored, then hugged one another again and settled down to enjoy themselves with friends old and new.

Adam and his daughters were there. He and Gemma had come and gone a few times from the small town, visiting other parts of England, as he'd promised her. But they'd spent more time than originally planned in Sexton Bassett getting to know Janey and to a lesser extent her mother, who was still very quiet and subdued.

Millie wore a frilly new party outfit donated by her proud grandfather and Janey drove her daughter, mother, Winifred and Dan down the hill with their various food and drink offerings in the car that had made her life so much easier since her father bought it for her.

Gemma was almost bouncing with joy for a different reason, because she'd heard the day before she would be given a place to study history at Oxford the following academic year because her results were exceptional.

Elise and Stacy strolled up to the big house from Saffron Lane.

They left behind at Number 1 the heritage officer who was now working on the practicalities of setting up the communications centre as a little walk-through museum. This would include a trip through the rebuilt tunnels for a small extra charge if you booked ahead. And below it, on the ground floor, would be a café.

As the party continued, Adam enjoyed a few private moments with Gemma. 'Glad we came to England now?'

'Very glad. I don't even want to go back to finish clearing the house.'

'That can't be avoided now that it's sold, unfortunately. But we're taking Janey and Millie with us for an Easter holiday, so I think we can fit in some enjoyable trips as well.'

They turned as a group nearby burst into laughter.

'Nell looks so happy,' he said softly. 'It was great that one of her sons could make it to the wedding. Did you see her face when he and his new wife turned up from Australia unexpectedly?'

'Yes. He looks like her, doesn't he? And I like his wife. Pity the other daughter-in-law was pregnant and they couldn't come over.'

'They'll come another time, I'm sure.'

Someone started banging on a glass and gradually people fell silent.

'I've been told that as the oldest person here it's my duty to propose a toast to the bride and groom,' Winifred said. 'I can't think of anything I'd like more than to ask you to raise your glasses to Nell and Angus. May they live long and happily together.'

'Nell and Angus.'

DESTINY'S PATH

THE WILTSHIRE GIRLS:
CHERRY TREE LANE
ELM TREE ROAD
YEW TREE GARDENS

THE TRADERS:
THE TRADER'S WIFE
THE TRADER'S SISTER
THE TRADER'S DREAM
THE TRADER'S GIFT
THE TRADER'S REWARD

GREYLADIES:
HEIR TO GREYLADIES
MISTRESS OF GREYLADIES
LEGACY OF GREYLADIES

PEPPERCORN STREET:
PEPPERCORN STREET
CINNAMON GARDENS

RIVENSHAW:
A TIME TO REMEMBER
A TIME FOR RENEWAL
A TIME TO REJOICE

HONEYFIELD:
THE HONEYFIELD BEQUEST
A STRANGER IN HONEYFIELD

We do hope that you have enjoyed reading this large print book.

Did you know that all of our titles are available for purchase?

We publish a wide range of high quality large print books including:

Romances, Mysteries, Classics
General Fiction
Non Fiction and Westerns

Special interest titles available in large print are:

The Little Oxford Dictionary
Music Book
Song Book
Hymn Book
Service Book

Also available from us courtesy of Oxford University Press:

Young Readers' Dictionary
(large print edition)
Young Readers' Thesaurus
(large print edition)

For further information or a free brochure, please contact us at:
Ulverscroft Large Print Books Ltd.,
The Green, Bradgate Road, Anstey,
Leicester, LE7 7FU, England.
Tel: (00 44) 0116 236 4325
Fax: (00 44) 0116 234 0205

Other titles published by Ulverscroft:

A STRANGER IN HONEYFIELD

Anna Jacobs

1916: Bella is working as a VAD, driving ambulances in England, when she gets engaged to Philip, on leave from fighting in France. His family strongly disapprove of her, but the two of them are happy together. When the worst happens, Bella must manage on her own, though there are shocks and dangers she did not foresee ahead. Thankfully, Philip's best friend, Tez, injured in France, steps in to offer assistance. Can he also help Bella build a new life? Meanwhile, Georgie, Philip's sister, is in trouble, having broken her engagement and fled from her bullying family. As she wonders who she can turn to for help when she needs it most, she finds herself at the gates of Honeyfield . . .

THE HONEYFIELD BEQUEST

Anna Jacobs

Wiltshire, 1901: Young Kathleen Keller is being forced by her cruel father into marriage with a man she despises. In an act of desperation, she runs away in a bid for a safer life, although one she might not otherwise have chosen. But when tragedy strikes, Kathleen is left vulnerable, and one man threatens the fragile peace she has made for herself . . . Meanwhile, Nathan Perry works for his father's accountancy firm but yearns for something more satisfying. He is brought in to help with the purchase of Honeyfield House, established by a charitable benefactor as a safe house for women in trouble, and there he encounters Kathleen. Their lives are set to intertwine, and neither will be the same again . . .

A TIME TO REJOICE

Anna Jacobs

After a stray bomb scored a direct hit on his childhood home in Hertfordshire, the only thing that has kept Francis Brady going while he works day and night salvaging what he can from the rubble is the thought that soon he'll be joining wartime friends Mayne, Daniel and Victor as an electrician in their new dream building firm in Lancashire. But things are not going to plan. Many marriages are breaking up in these times of change, and Francis is loath for his to be one of them — but how can he turn down the opportunity of a new life and career in Rivenshaw? Meanwhile, while clearing out Esherwood house in readiness for the rebuild, Mayne and Judith make a macabre discovery in the old Nissen hut — a body, buried in a shallow grave . . .

A TIME FOR RENEWAL

Anna Jacobs

In the aftermath of World War Two, there's a desperate shortage of housing and goods across the nation. Mayne Esher's only hope of preserving his family's war-damaged stately home of Esherwood is to turn it into flats. When he opens it up to his Army friends who will be starting a building business with him, it soon becomes clear that the house isn't the only thing that needs fixing . . . Victor is fighting his late wife's mother for custody of his daughter Betty; whilst Ros, a former Wren he meets, has been cheated out of her money and has nowhere else to go. Daniel, still unsettled after his wartime experiences, is waiting for his divorce to go through. And no one's heard from Francis at all . . .